The Seraphina Parrish Trilogy

SEEING
LIGHT

Michelle Warren

Editing by Pam Berehulke

Bulletproofing | *http://bulletproofing.blogspot.com*
email to: *bulletproofing@live.com*

Cover and book design by Michelle Preast at Indie Book Covers
https://www.facebook.com/IndieBookCovers
email to: *michellepreast@yahoo.com*

NOTE TO THE READER

This is book three in a trilogy. Though there is some recapping of the first two books, it is strongly recommended that you read them in order because this book does not stand alone.

To Mom:

*My main character is strong, independent,
and occasionally funny. I can only write those
characteristics convincingly because that's the woman
you taught me to be. Thank you for supporting every
creative endeavor that I've ever pursued. I love you.*

CONTENTS

"Man is his own worst enemy."
CICERO

№

1

THE PIT

NO ONE HAS EVER RETURNED FROM NOCTURNA. The thought chills me as I examine its entrance, an ugly gash in the earth before me that resembles an enormous square pit. Stone stairways slash its walls, forming crude zig-zags as they descend into the belly of the earth. When I lean slightly to peek over the edge, seeking the bottom and unable to discern it, a sickly tingle forms in my feet and shoots up my calves. An answering nervous flutter pools in my belly, leaving me ill and light-headed, so I step back a pace to compose myself.

"You don't have to do this, Sera," Bishop says, his British-accented voice plying me with tenderness as he tries to reason with me, but his efforts are wasted. Max Bishop—known to all simply as Bishop—is my Protector, an integral part of our three-person Wandering team. Samantha James is our Seer, and I, Seraphina Parrish, round out the team as its Wanderer.

"There's no other way." I frown and look over my shoulder. With our recent history, he's upset for many reasons, and my trip to Nocturna to find Terease, the now exiled former Harvester for the Academy of Wanderers, is just one of them.

"Stay with me." His brow furrows as he pleads with me, the familiar expression tugging at my heart. He makes it sound so simple, as if I could move forward in this life of Wandering without choosing who I love, who my family is, or even what I dream at night.

"If we could find Mum, we can talk to her." He looks away and clears his throat. "Maybe she can give you the answers you need." When he turns back to me, his eyes glisten in the darkness.

Bishop's parents, Mona and Joe, fled taking his little sister, Charlotte, probably fearing for their safety. In a cryptic phone call to Bishop, Mona claimed the Society knew she'd given me secret information about the Oaths' sacrifices and feared retaliation. She begged for Bishop to run away with them, but he refused. He claimed he needed to stay with me, to protect me.

"Even if we could find her, I won't involve her anymore,"

I say, my voice steely with resolve. "Who knows what the Society will do to her, to you, or to the rest of your family." I can barely live with the knowledge that Turner, Bishop's twin brother, died trying to protect me. Since that day a lurid shadow has been cast across my heart, leaving me nothing more than a shell. But no matter how I feel, I can't hurt their family any more than I already have. My eyes prick with dampness but I push the emotions away, shoving them deep into my soul where I lock them down with my guilt.

"I'll be back. I promise." A smile grazes my lips, but I don't know if I can really keep this promise. I reach back and grab Bishop's hand; his grasp is desperate and warm. It's the only time I've allowed him to touch me since that day in Turner's apartment, when I realized Turner knew he would sacrifice his life and role as my Protector to save me from my nemesis, Cece, head of the Underground. After I blew up at Bishop, I told him we needed to take a break from each other, but staying away from him has been one of the hardest things I've ever done.

Bishop gives my hand a strong tug and pulls me into an embrace, wrapping his firm arms securely around my waist. As he nuzzles his face into the curve of my neck, his feathery hair brushes my skin, and he breathes heavily. If I let him, he'd never release me.

Resisting the desperate urge to relax into his warmth, I sigh because I still want his love. Despite all his lies, I want every part of his generous soul swaddling me, my fingers tangled in his thick hair and my head resting on his chest, feeling his wild heart beating beneath my ear. I want to smell his aftershave, let the aroma of oiled leather and citrus consume me. I want to stretch up on tippy toes to kiss him the way I used to—before I learned the truth. But I can't.

Emotions surge into my chest, threatening another rush of tears. Instead of giving in to my feelings, I shut them down, then summon the anger that brought me to this point in the first place and focus on it, absorbing it, honing it to a dangerous weapon. I need to control myself and force everything within not to hug him back. So I arch my upper body away, still locked in his arms. When I look at his eyes, squinted in upside-down smiles, I can't deny my love for him; it twitches and flutters, lodged deep inside, irremovable from my Wandering heart. Our connection as team members, Protector and Wanderer, make us a perfect match, but I don't want to live in a world where I have no choice whom I love.

With nothing else to say, I drop my shoulders and heave another inward sigh, then tear my gaze away from Bishop to survey the distant glittering buildings of the secret Wandering city of Gibeon. It's night, very late, and the perfect time to sneak past the Nocturna guards. If we don't hurry, one may find us on their security rounds.

Samantha James, my Seer, stands in the distance, allowing us a moment alone. I give her a beckoning nod and she walks over, rejoining us.

"Here." She hands me a set of goggles and a backpack

tightly stuffed with a parachute. Sam's job as Seer is to use objects, or "relics," to help us transport, or "Wander," to distant places and times. Unfortunately, there are no relics that can take you to Nocturna. It may not even be possible because no one has ever returned with one. With guards patrolling the vicinity of the pit, I can't simply walk down the stairs, so breaching the perimeter in a surprise attack and parachuting into the pit is the only option.

"For someone who's afraid of heights, you sure are brave." She smirks at me, a signal of the new respect between us. A sisterly and patronizing one, but respect nonetheless.

"Thanks." I grasp the strap and swing the backpack over my shoulder before shrugging into the harness. After I've snapped myself in, Bishop stands in front of me, tugging on the buckles and checking them over.

What I'm about to do is crazy. Beyond crazy. There's a tightening in my chest at the thought of jumping into the pit, and a shiver of a nervous tremor crawls over my skin.

"Are you okay?" Bishop tips my chin back with his finger, seeking my eyes.

"Of course," I snap, but he knows better.

"You understand how to repack the parachute, right? You'll probably need it to return to Gibeon because chances are you won't be able to Wander back."

"Yes."

He tries to engage my eyes again as though he could talk me out of what I'm about to do with his handsome looks alone, but I avert my face, knowing full well that he could.

I turn to Sam. "So what else do I need to know about this place?"

"We know little of Nocturna through our mythology, so my information may or may not be credible. As you know, Nocturna is the mirror city of Gibeon, so it literally sits upside down beneath us. When you reach the bottom of the pit entering the other city, the world will flip upright for you," Sam explains.

"Nocturna is a historical graveyard for everything," she goes on. "When a building burns or wastes away in one of the cities of time, it reappears there until it crumbles and dies a final death. That's what keeps the city growing. To say it's huge would be a gross understatement. The inhabitants are few, mostly the Wanderers exiled there from the Society, and some other awful creatures." She doesn't elaborate on the "awful creatures."

"In Nocturna, all Wanderers' lives are set on fast-forward; they age incredibly fast. Being exiled to the city is a literal death sentence. It's only been two weeks, but if Terease is still alive, she won't be easy to track down. You must find her quickly, acquire the information you need, and escape before the city claims your soul as an inhabitant."

"How long do I have?"

"It's not exactly a matter of how long." Sam shifts uncomfortably and crosses her arms.

Bishop tenses next to me, his Protector nature obviously

ratcheting into high gear. "What does that even mean, Sam?"

Sam's eyes lock with mine, and her features shift for a microsecond before settling into an apologetic mask. "The Time Reaper will be looking for you from the moment you arrive. He'll smell your life essence the instant your feet hit the ground. If he finds you and sucks the soul from your body, it's too late. You'll never be able to leave."

"Great!" I bark out a tight laugh, not because it's funny, but because it sucks. Literally.

"Sera, let me go with you." Bishop grips my arm tightly, clearly communicating his growing alarm. "Sam might be able to use our telepathic connection to keep us up-to-the-minute with the Time Reaper's location. I could keep you safe."

Sam grimaces and mumbles, "If it works, which is highly unlikely since we can't connect in Gibeon."

"No, absolutely not." I set my jaw. After everything that Bishop's done, there's still a fierce need in my heart to protect him from danger. I could never intentionally put him in harm's way.

Sam reaches in and hugs me good-bye. I hesitate for a second, surprised by her uncharacteristic show of affection, then hug her back fiercely. After all, she's the closest thing I've ever had to a real sister.

"You there! Step away from the edge!" a guard yells.

Collectively we jerk our heads toward the sound. In the distance, a flashlight's beam cuts the darkness, bobbing up and down as the man carrying it rushes forward. A barking and snapping dog lopes just ahead of him, frantically tugging at its leash and urging him on.

Bishop, Sam, and I take off sprinting far away from the edge, back to the safety of a nearby line of trees. When I'm certain they are free from danger, hidden to my satisfaction by dense bushes, I give them one last lingering glance, knowing that this may be the last time I'll ever see them. I drop my goggles over my eyes to hide my rising tears, and without another word, I dash back toward the pit of Nocturna.

Floodlights snap on, illuminating every inch of the field, and then an alarm sounds, wailing and alerting the guards on duty. More and more silhouettes appear in my line of sight. If I didn't know better, I'd think I was in the middle of a jailbreak. But instead of breaking out, I'm attempting to break in.

The original guard and his dog zero in on me, which will allow for Bishop and Sam's escape, so I open up my stride, extending my legs. My arms swing madly as I dig deep, pumping them like pistons at my sides as I speed across the empty field.

Fifty feet.

Forty.

Thirty.

The guard races in at an angle, on a collision course with me. He reaches for the dog's collar and releases it from the chain.

Fifteen.

Ten.

Five.

The dog lunges the final feet and snaps at my leg. His teeth graze my calf, ripping the seam of my pants at the same moment my feet leave the earth and take one final push from the edge of the pit. I launch like a bird and dive into the endless pit of Nocturna below.

№

2

NOCTURNA

I N THIS MOMENT, WITH MY ARMS STRETCHED out wide and surrounded by complete and utter darkness, I'm terrified beyond words. And though I have almost nothing to lose anymore, my heart pounds in my chest, ramming against my ribcage. I turn my face away from the punishing wind that meets me, but it doesn't help. My skin, my lips, my cheeks all ripple fiercely, blasted by the force of the air current that pushes with tremendous force against my body, making my clothing snap and whip like a flag on a windy day.

With one hand, I reach in and fumble around my chest, searching for the ripcord. When I find it, I wrap my fingers around the pilot and tug hard. The parachute slips out of the backpack with a whoosh and snaps open, yanking me to a violent, suspended halt. The whiplash shocks me, but it gives my heart a moment of ease because I'm no longer in an uncontrolled free fall. I relax my shoulders, tilt my head back, and sigh with relief in the sudden quiet.

I did it.

As I glide to the bottom, the light above shrinks into the distance, swallowing me in the pit's darkness. How long will it take to reach the city? In this world, the answer could be anything: an hour, a day, a month. I should have researched that more. Sometimes it's impossible to think of all the scenarios. Luckily Mr. Tash, our mythology teacher, was a wealth of knowledge on Nocturna. Thank goodness he never questioned Sam's interest.

A hazy blue light appears in the distance below me. As I drift closer, its glow ripples as though I'm looking up from underneath the ocean in the dark, with moonbeams dancing on the surface.

A moment too late, I realize the light actually is water, and quickly take a huge gulp of air before I plunge into the oval pond. Water pressure engulfs and consumes my body. Twisting and turning with confusion, the parachute's lines tangle and bind my legs, making it impossible to kick each separately. But kick in what direction? Up? Down? I'm disoriented. Has Nocturna turned right side up yet?

In a panic, I let out a scream, allowing salty water to flood my lungs in painful stabs. As I choke and start to panic that I'm drowning, bubbles release from my mouth, floating upward. In a flash of insight I move with them, snapping my restrained legs and undulating my body like a mermaid, carving out a path with my strokes toward what I pray is the surface.

I erupt through the surface to fresh air, gasping and violently expelling thick water. Flailing about, my arms beat the water faster than hummingbird wings. There's a strange resistance to my movement, and the activity quickly exhausts me.

For relief, I float on my back. The salt-dense water allows me to lie here effortlessly, so I turn my head and cough, attempting to clear my lungs and expel the lingering briny taste from my mouth.

Several large waves lap over me and I roll forward, floating upright as I blink against the water blurring my eyes to see sparse lights twinkling in the dark distance. They dot a crumbling skyline of blue-tinged buildings on land that's maybe a quarter of a mile away.

Despite the lines that hamper me I begin to swim, eventually settling into a modified breaststroke to compensate for my bound legs. Since I'm tiring easily, I stop at intervals to float and rest, but the surf at the beach is the worst part. Foamy froth sticks to my face, its saltiness bringing tears to my eyes, making it hard to see. I tumble and roll relentlessly in the angry surf until I finally grip the sand with my fingers and awkwardly crawl to shore with only the strength of my biceps. I'm grateful to Miss Swift, my defense arts teacher, for forcing me to lift weights even when I protested. Without that training, I surely would have drowned.

Drained of energy, I collapse on the wet sand with the unforgiving waves crashing around me. Yes, I should be rushing to find Terease, but I need a moment to recover.

I roll over on my back, breathing heavily. The velvety midnight sky casts the same blue tone on everything, and four hazy halos surround an enormous moon. The three inside rings are white; the outside band, black. According to legend, the moon never concedes to the daylight. That's how Nocturna received its name.

I sit up and inspect the parachute that's washed up on shore with me. I'd hoped to use it in some way, but there's a large gaping rip in one of the seams. I remove a pocketknife from my boot and go to work, sawing at the tangled suspension lines still binding my legs. Even if I could use it to return to Gibeon, which I now realize that I can't, I fear the Time Reaper would find me before I could repair it, anyway.

Finally free, I stand and brush the gritty sand from my hands and face before surveying my surroundings. A small beach wraps the inlet. Skyscrapers, some barely standing, line the shore. Beyond the waves, I hear a wall crumble and turn toward the sound to see a series of splashes as chunks of concrete plummet into the ocean.

Heading in the direction of the city, I take off in an awkward jog, slipping and sinking in the dry sand as I make my way to an embankment of rocks. The uneven wall is high, maybe eight feet. I lean in to climb the rocks, reaching for a sturdy handhold, but pull back and stifle a scream when the cold, rough rock I expect to feel is instead smooth and neither warm nor cold. Staggering back a step, I take a closer look, realizing that what I mistook for rocks are really bones and skulls, thousands of them, stacked in heaps to form a wall that snakes its way around the beach. How many years of Wandering lives do these awful remains represent?

Though horrified, I fight to compose myself. I'm angry that my fear slows me because, according to Sam, the Time Reaper's already tracking me. So I grit my teeth and force myself to climb the hill of skulls, which is no easy task. They dislodge when I dig my foot into the crevices or grab for a sturdy grip, but somehow I reach the top. Loose bones clank and clatter, rolling with me as I slide down the opposite side. When my feet hit solid ground, I stand and take off running up an inclined cobblestone street that appears to lead to the heart of the city.

A dark maze of buildings engulfs me as I run. Enormous mutant rats scurry in the shadows. Several times a shadowy motion on the edge of my vision startles me but when I look, I see only decaying bodies crumpled in heaps. Some are dead, some barely alive, but it's the stench that's overwhelming. In my hurry, I accidentally kick a pile of bones. A skull dislodges and rolls back down the hill toward the wall at the sea. This puts me on edge so I run faster, pumping my arms as I lengthen my stride.

When I come to a corner, I round the bend at full speed and collide hard with a man. He clenches my arms with bony fingers, and I jump back, aghast at his eyes. They're glossed over with a blackness that appears infinite in its depth, and telegraph unmistakable despair. He stumbles and sways, collapsing against a wall. On impact, his brittle bones crack and crumple into a pile on the ground.

Under normal circumstances, I would run to his aid. But here in this twisted place of evil, I turn away and take off instead. Sickening guilt instantly consumes me even though I know nothing can be done because I've literally landed in Wandering hell.

The sounds of my ragged breathing and the squishing of my soaked boots slapping against the cobblestones are my only companions as I sprint another mile. When I turn another corner and enter a town square, an old concrete fountain stands at the center. Water trickles from the top, pooling into a circular basin. Caution demands that I slow down and take stock before blindly rushing into the open, so I duck my head down and slow to a walk, surreptitiously scanning the square.

Several people, old and broken, drift around; some moan, heads tilted back, mouths hanging low, toothless, and slack like zombies.

A woman near me with her head wrapped in a dark covering leans into the fountain and dips a bucket into the water. She draws it out and staggers under its weight, spilling most of the contents and soaking her clothes. She huffs with frustration and squats down.

"Here, I'll help you." I grab the bucket and help her stand, intent on pumping her for information about Terease. I hope that when I find her, she can finally give me answers to the questions that torture me: Why my mom was still alive when I believed she was dead, why she was part of the Underground, and why this information was kept from me. I always believed that Terease was just the Harvester and the administrator, enforcer of the rules at the Academy, but when she was arrested as a traitor to the Society of Wanderers, it shocked me. Obviously she had more layers than I knew.

"Oh, thank you." The woman pulls back her head covering.

"Mona?" I gasp with disbelief.

Her lips tremble as she reaches out blindly; her wide, soulless black eyes can't see. "Seraphina?" She places a hand on either side of my face. "What are you doing here?"

Before I can answer, another voice calls out. "Mummy, are you okay?"

My head whips around at the sound. Small Charlotte, just slightly older than she should be, stands in a nearby doorway. Her father, Joe, standing behind with one hand protectively on her shoulder, pulls her close. Each holds the door frame, feeling their way through their blindness.

"Go back inside and shut the door, Charlotte, quickly!" Mona commands. Joe pulls his daughter back into the darkness and slams the door.

"No, no, no! Why are you all here? What's happened?" My

heart seizes for a moment, despair washing over me at the realization that Bishop's family members aren't safe at all, but instead are trapped here in this hell.

"Sera, darling, listen very closely." The woman I'd once known and loved as my aunt releases my face, then grasps my hands and squeezes. "You must remain strong and leave this instant. I can feel the life in you; you still own your soul. You don't belong here." Her haggard face pinches as her brow furrows deeply, her words spilling out rapidly as she anxiously clutches my hands.

"Neither do you." Tears fill my eyes, spilling over to run in warm rivulets down my cheeks. "Come back with me, I can save all of you." I tug at her arms to leave, but she stands her ground.

Mona shakes her head sharply. "Without our souls, we're stuck. But there's still a chance for you. Please, I'm begging you!" She presses my face between her palms and kisses my forehead.

"Youth!" a woman cries out.

At the accusation, Mona and I turn our heads to the sound.

A woman with a body as crooked as an old tree sniffs the air in a peculiar way. "Youth," she shouts again, pointing in our direction.

At her words, the zombies of the plaza react and screech. There's instant chaos, and I look around the square, confused. For some reason, everyone scurries away like I carry the plague.

"Run!" Mona pushes me away with her palms. "Go home!" she screams and hits me again, swatting me like an unwanted animal.

Before I can argue any more, she drops to the ground, covers her ears, and shrieks, "No! They're already here."

I drop down beside her to help her if I can, but that's when I hear it, what everyone else must be hearing, why everyone else is freaking out. It's not me that causes their terror; it's the sound of a galloping horse.

Everyone in the plaza rushes into dark doorways, alleys, and shadows—everyone except a wrinkled man sitting on a nearby bench. In the bedlam, he remains calm, chanting like he is possessed. "When the briny wind blows upon a moonlit sky, the Time Reapers come to veil your eyes. Blackness, death, despair, no one can withstand their evil glare."

As if on cue, a menacing black apparition, a ghost of a human-like form with a single crooked horn protruding from his head, appears on the opposite side of the square. The beast he rides, a terrible horse-beast rippling with overdeveloped muscles, bucks and writhes beneath him.

The Time Reaper.

№

3

THE TIME REAPER

I DON'T THINK, I JUST GRAB MONA AND RUN
in the opposite direction, pulling her with me, but she
wriggles away and scampers back toward the monster. Again
I grab her, and she shouts, "Run and save yourself, I tell you!
Holy ground, it's the only safe place. Go!" Then she shoves
me.

It hits me suddenly that she's not crazy, she's trying to
protect me.

She turns and waves her arms like a maniac, doing anything she can to draw attention from me. I do what she says
and dart through the courtyard, noticing that the others who

can walk have hidden themselves. The zombie-like ones fall to the ground where they stand, shrilling when the horse-beast cries out in a horrific snarl.

When I glance over my shoulder, the beast and the Reaper launch forward in a frenzied gallop, hurtling across the court-yard. The sound rumbles and echoes, shaking the weathered buildings, causing stone structures to crumble and collapse around me. Just in time, I leap over a rolling boulder but my landing is unsteady, causing my feet to slip on small stones as they search to grip solid earth.

In the billowing waves of blackness surrounding the Reaper's hazy body, a scythe appears in his hand. The long curved blade, razor sharp and deadly, gleams wickedly in the moonlight.

As I sprint out of the courtyard, Mona cries out behind me. I imagine her arms still waving erratically, doing anything she can to distract him. Inside I wail with absolute heartbreak that I've left all of Bishop's family behind. I will never forgive myself now.

The gallops don't miss a beat, they continue forward, fol-lowing me unerringly as I sprint up the hill, weaving through an onslaught of falling rock and debris. I pump my arms, my legs, pushing faster, wishing for a Protector's speed. The air rushes in and out of my open mouth, matching my heaving chest.

Somewhere nearby a bell tolls and immediately I search the horizon, scanning the buildings for the silhouette of a bell tower, knowing it will lead me to a church. When I spot it, it's close. So very close—just a few hundred feet ahead, encircled by a low stone wall, a metal gate guarding the entrance.

The huge horse-beast grunts behind me, its weight pounding the ground heavily as it leaps over and then weaves around the detritus of fallen rock walls. Both rider and beast are relentless and I can almost feel their excitement and rising sense of triumph as they practically breathe down my back.

Run. Run. Run. I'm almost there.

"Open the doors! Help! Let me in!" I scream in the direction of the church, praying someone will hear me.

Behind me, the Reaper laughs. A sound so dark, so menacing that it penetrates my bones, causing them to buzz with pure anxiety. I pump harder, push farther, running so fast that I fear my chest may explode.

A pair of glossy obsidian eyes blink behind a hole in a shattered and broken stained glass window of the church. They widen with shock as I barrel forward.

"Help!" I cry as I reach out.

My body slams through the gate. One footstep past the churchyard's wall, the horse-beast shoves his muzzle firmly into my back and with a flick sends me flying through the air, crashing into the base of the church steps. I crack my head on a stone riser and warm blood oozes from the wound.

With my body twisted in a mangled and aching mess, I

struggle to lift my head and glance up at the now fuzzy Reaper. He's halted outside the gate and his horse-beast writhes, kicks, and paces back and forth as though they want to push forward but can't. The animal bares its fangs—long, pointed, and brilliantly white against his dark beast-face.

With a surge of relief, I realize they can't step into the churchyard. This ground is sacred, and if anything in this world is the devil, I'm looking at two prime candidates right now. Crawling slowly, I pull my body up the stairs, one step at a time, biting back grunts of pain. I need to seek shelter in the church. Somehow. It's my only chance of survival. And surviving is my only chance to go back and help Bishop's family.

The Reaper slides off the horse-beast. His shifting face finally hardens to a recognizable shape, but it's not completely human. Unable to look away, I gape at the sickening combination of dragon, snake, jackal, and hyena, all mixed in a grotesque mask of cracked skin, hovering just above his body of hot lava. His eyes burn with fire—simmering and menacing eyes that are so much scarier than Terease's. He opens his mouth and I shudder when I see flames release with his heavy breath and deep rumbling laugh. He knows I'm done. He has me now.

I drag myself to the top of the stairs and pound on the door with my palm, sobbing and crying out, "Please! Help!"

"No one escapes me," he roars. "And your soul," he pauses to sniff the air, "it smells divine." He opens his mouth hungrily and the split tongue of a serpent unrolls itself from it, then lifts in a slow and obscene motion to lick against what must be his lips.

I prop myself against the door and turn to face my death, watching as the Reaper slides a massive bow from his saddle, pulls an arrow from his quiver and breathes on its tip, setting it on fire. Then he loads it into the rest and pulls back on the bowstring effortlessly, aiming it directly at my racing heart. All while holding my gaze with his horrible blazing eyes.

If this is it, my final moment, then I will not be a coward, so I sit up straighter and refuse to look away.

At the moment the arrow releases, slicing the air in half, the door propping me up suddenly opens and I fall backward, my body dropping flat on the ground. Heat from the flaming arrow screams past, narrowly missing my fallen head.

Two strong hands grab my shoulders and heave me inside. My savior pushes me out of the way as another flaming arrow whizzes by, sinking its fiery point with a loud *thwock* deep into the back of a wooden pew. The person slams the door shut, shrugs out of their coat, and quickly throws the fabric on the flames, stifling them into a roiling cloud of smoke.

I breathe heavily in relief, certain that my life is about to end. "Thank you," I say but don't move. I'm in too much pain, too upset, and too tired from running.

The shadowy figure turns in the darkened vestibule and walks toward me. When moonlight hits their face, I blink several tears away to clear my vision, unable to believe that I'm really, truly seeing the person before me.

№

4

TEREASE

PERPETUA GRAY, MY FORMER CLASSMATE, stands with her hands on her hips looking down at me. Her eyes are no longer a crystalline blue but are now varnished with black ink. Wrinkles feather the skin at the corners of her eyes and her hair hangs limp, its youthful sheen washed away with expedited time. She's a grown woman now, aged twenty-five years since I last saw her, making her appear at least forty. I try to stifle my shock because it's only been two weeks since she left the Academy.

"Bet you thought you'd never see me again." She extends her hand, helping me from the ground. I ignore my protesting muscles, my broken heart, and stand to meet her gaze.

"I thought the Society sent you home. And you're—"

"Old?" She raises a graying eyebrow.

"Just older." It's so strange to see her image and beauty fast-forwarded into her future. Mona and Charlotte hadn't changed this much. Perhaps they just arrived. Then I realize with a jolt that they'll all be dead within a few weeks.

Perpetua ignores my expression, but I have the feeling she knows where my thoughts have led me. "Why are you here?" She lets out a little huff. "As it turns out, there's no leaving the Society. Not alive, anyway."

My eyes widen. "I had no idea." And all this time I believed that Perpetua and her team had been sent home to their families, as if expelled from an ordinary boarding school. More proof of the Society's twisted practices.

"The good news is that I'm not going to treat you like a sixteen-year-old mega-witch anymore. At least my brain has matured with this wrinkled bag I have to call a body." A grim smile touches her lips. "And I guess you could say being here has given me a new perspective."

Before I can respond, she says, "We should get you cleaned up." Then she grabs my arm and throws it over her shoulder. "Lean on me."

"What about the Reaper?" I glance back. The horse-beast circles the building. I catch glimpses of him and his rider through cracked windows and wonder if there's a way back into town to save Bishop's family.

"Eh, he's like an amnesiac cat with a new toy. He'll be there until the next new soul arrives and distracts him," she says. "Don't worry, you're safe for the moment."

We walk down the main aisle between the pews, then weave past the altar and enter a side room, perhaps an old office, dusty and overflowing with books and cobwebs. An elongated stained glass window rises on one wall, casting a design of rich colors on the wood floor. Perpetua lowers me into a large wingback chair.

Now that I've had two seconds to collect my thoughts, I remember why I'm here. "Have you seen Terease?"

She nods, opens a drawer, and pulls out a towel.

"Is she—"

"Dead? Ha!" She shakes her head. "That old cockroach would survive a nuclear attack." She pours water from a pitcher into a basin, dampens the towel, and then uses it to dab at my forehead where I'm bleeding.

"So you've seen her?"

"Yeah. Been waiting for you since she arrived."

"Waiting?"

"Apparently you two have something to discuss," she says with a quizzical expression. "I'm sure she's on her way. You've practically warned all of Nocturna that you're here. Didn't you notice the bands around the moon?"

I frown with confusion. "Does that mean something?"

"The black ring, it means there's a new soul that shouldn't be here, which means the Reaper wants you dead, not just your soul."

"Figures." With my luck, this doesn't surprise me. "What about the other rings?"

"Those are the number of souls taken today. Probably students who decided not to take the Oaths to the Society. Turns out, it's more like a stay-or-die proposition. If you're not one hundred percent committed, dedicating your life to the Society, then they don't want you. Or in my case, if you're not one hundred percent perfect." She stands up straight and tosses the bloody towel on the nearby table.

I look down at the floor. "Actually, I think it was Bishop's family—not students."

"Sorry." She huffs and shakes her head. "I didn't know." She grabs a jar from the drawer, unscrews the top, and dips her fingers into some thick ointment. She leans in close to rub the salve on the wound at my hairline.

"What about your team, Stu and Jess? Did they..." My words drift off as I realize I might not like the answer to my question.

Perpetua immediately stiffens and pulls away. "Stu's here." She swallows hard. "Jess—she, she didn't make it to shore." Her black eyes turn away from me to gaze uneasily around the room, then they glass over. Even if the Reaper has taken her soul, it's obvious he hasn't taken her emotions. But she pulls herself together quickly, adopting a stoic expression, and busies herself clearing her workspace, returning everything to its proper place.

"Sorry." For the first time ever, I want to give Perpetua

a genuine hug. Something I never dreamed that I would do considering how horrible she's been to me in the past, but as I stand, someone screams.

Two dark silhouettes battle outside the stained glass window. From what I can discern, one is the Reaper, mounted on his horse-beast. He slices the air with his scythe as the other person flips over the weapon, right before they crash through the church window. Colored glass implodes and Perpetua and I duck, shielding our faces. The woman rolls across the floor, pops up, and grabs us.

"Run!" she screams.

Two flaming arrows fly through the missing window's frame. One explodes on impact, the resulting concussion launching us into the air, and we collapse near a row of pews.

There's no time to recover, so I sit up and brush debris from my body, lean over, and retch from the suffocating smoke.

Before I can compose myself, Terease stands over me. "Took you long enough." She extends her hand. "With your, shall we say, insatiable curiosity, I would've thought you'd arrive much sooner." She pulls me to my feet.

"You could've saved me the trip by just telling me the truth when you had the chance." I brush bits of debris from my body and straighten my jacket.

"You weren't ready," she says in her thick accent. "But I can see that you are now." She looks me over but doesn't engage my eyes with her painful dark fire the way she used to.

Instead, she waves for Perpetua and me to follow her.

Behind the altar, between two icon statues, spiral stairs twist their way into the earth. We follow Terease as she descends into the silent darkness, away from the frustrated roar of the Reaper and the crackling and popping of the burning church.

Below, the air is musty and chilled. A spark flicks to life, igniting a blaze that burns at the end of a torch. Terease holds the light high, leading us through an ancient corridor. Niches line the walls; several lead to private rooms for worship, while some hold ancient statues and primitive altars. Other areas are catacombs, several empty and some filled with the dead.

When we reach the end, we enter a low room with a circular domed ceiling, beneath which an elongated stone box sits centered. Terease hands me the torch, and she and Perpetua squat down on either side of the tomb and grip the lid of the sarcophagus. With great difficulty and the gritting of teeth, they push the stone slab to one side. It screeches its resistance, rubbing stone against stone, and an opening appears.

"Come." Terease waves me forward. She climbs into the stone box, which I can see hides another set of stairs that descend deeper into the bowels of Nocturna.

№ 5
THE PROPHECY

TEREASE'S HAND REACHES UP AND I PASS HER the torch. With free hands, I lift myself onto the stone box, swing my legs over the ledge, and let my feet drop inside, settling them on a step. Inhaling deeply, I stand and descend the stairs.

Below, the cavern is unnatural, manmade, and cut into stone. Wood beams support the walls and ceiling much like a coal mine.

"Where are we going?"

"We have to travel deep underground so that the Reaper cannot sense us," Terease explains.

The cavern funnels into a smaller corridor where the land declines steeply, leading to more stairs. Water trickles down the rocky walls making the uneven floor slippery, and a few times I slip and grab on to Perpetua to right myself. The farther we travel, the more the temperature drops. A dewy layer of nervous sweat covers my skin.

Finally we enter what could only be described as a bunker, a cot-lined room filled with tables, maps, radar equipment, and a mishmash of gadgets for who knows what. It's a command center, looking very much like the inside of a World War II submarine. Many people are working, some are chatting and eating. Gauging the group, I realize that, like Terease, the Reaper has not taken most of these people's souls. I can tell by their eyes; they're bright and alive.

Terease leads us behind a curtain to a space that is simple, but as private as it will get in this cramped bunker.

"Sit," she commands and then drops herself into a deep-cushioned chair, waking a sleeping Animate cat that lays curled on the back. She reaches and grabs a canteen of water from a hook on the wall and offers it to me. Gladly I take it and unscrew the top before throwing my head back and chugging the liquid. When I'm done, I pass it to Perpetua.

"I just saw Bishop's family. Do you know why they're here?" My voice catches and I want to break down again at the thought of them weakened and soulless, but I remember Mona's plea to stay strong.

"They entered the city several hours ago. I tried to reach

them before the Reapers but failed. When I arrived, I found the three on the beach, but only after the Reapers had fed on their souls. For their safety, I put them up in the home of an ally." She relaxes in her seat, resting her pale hands on the chair's wide arms.

Terease glances at me and continues. "When I spoke to Mona, she said the Society was punishing her for sharing secrets with you and also for fleeing. Apparently, Charlotte showed signs of becoming a Wanderer. Not wanting this life for her youngest child, she fled to hide her away."

"So she's here because of me?" My lip trembles.

Terease shrugs. "Her defection with the child would have been enough in the Society's eyes."

I bite my lip, wanting to cry.

"I'm sorry," she says, appraising my demeanor. "Even though the Reapers have taken their souls, they will be safe for the moment." She leans closer and places a hand on my leg. "And there is a way to help them, to set them free, but we're getting ahead of ourselves. I know you came for other reasons."

"Set them free?" I allow myself to hope.

"Yes, but first, we have other business." She reclines in her chair and lifts a leg, anchoring it on a stool.

I nod, remembering why I originally came to this god-awful place. "What do you know about my mom, and why didn't you tell me she was alive?" Anxious for her answer, I scoot to the edge of my seat.

"Perpetua." Terease jerks her chin toward the exit.

She nods, not giving off the normal Perpetua attitude, and slips behind the curtain to give us some privacy. It drapes shut, and I look back to Terease.

"Your mom's been fighting against the Society since before you were born. When you were very young, she realized quickly that she couldn't keep you safe. If the Society knew she was alive, they'd always be looking for you, to use you as bait, to hurt you for her defiance. Faking her death and hiding within the Underground was the only way to secure your safety until you became a mature Wanderer. She hoped by that time her transgressions would be forgotten. Somehow, she knew it would work out."

I let it sink in, allowing my gaze to drift along the floor as I fall into thought. Even though I shouldn't be shocked at what she's revealing, I find that I am.

"Why did her loyalties change?" I lift my eyes to her.

"Like many of us, she saw the power the Society holds over their members and also the world." Terease looks away as she traces a pattern of circles over the chair's arm. "Having the power to manipulate time can sway every event, every election, and every war, corrupting the future, bending it in their favor, and it's not what our Makers meant for us when they brought us into this world." Her voice rises with passion as her gaze settles on me. "As the myths say, we were to use the gift of time travel to observe history as a way to improve ourselves, to learn from our mistakes, to reach for higher enlightenment and nothing more."

"But the Society always told us that the Underground manipulated time too. You told us that!"

She shakes her head of silky black hair back and forth, lips pressed into a line as if to agree but not agree. "At the time, I had to keep up appearances, feed the students a well-choreographed script, one approved by the Society. What I said is true, both sides are corrupt, but it was not always so." She leans into the conversation, elbows dropped on her knees. "The Underground started out as a movement against the Society and they were pure in their goal, dedicated to the doctrines of the Masters, wanting to return us to who we were before we were stripped of our wings and before Gibeon started moving through time, but something went wrong when Cece took over the Underground. With the invention of crystal dreamdrives, she was able to control all the members with their dreams and fears, turning them into something worse than the Society." The inflection in her voice rises with her passion.

Suddenly Terease halts her story and stares at me, her eyes narrowed. "Have you hidden the dreamdrives? Are they safe?" she asks in hushed tones.

"Yes, they are." I think back to the day we fought Cece in Gibeon. "But why did you offer Cece my dreamdrive?"

She leans back again and as she does, an Animate cat jumps into her lap, rubbing itself against her chest, purring. She looks down at the mechanical animal and strokes it from head to tail as she continues to explain. "It's no secret that Cece has had a special interest in you since your meeting in Rome last semester. I thought showing her your dreamdrive would help us bargain with her and stop the attacks on the Academy, but I never intended to hand it over. I would have died to protect it from her. It's too special." She looks at me meaningfully.

"Why? I'm nobody." I shove my hands between my closed knees, pulling my shoulders inward.

Terease shoos the cat away, and it leaps from her lap onto a nearby table, then she leans forward, looking serious. "Because there are a few of us that she doesn't control, and we are the ones who will set this world right. You are one of us."

"Me?" I sit up at the accusation, shocked that there is something I could do.

"Why do you think I have not been able to search your mind like the other Wanderers for all this time?" She looks to the ceiling and rolls her hand in the air at the question.

I shrug. It's impossible to know what revelations this life will hold.

"When your mother passed in Gibeon and the guards arrested me, pulling me away, I saw clearly that the transition was taking place. It was the first time I was able to see into your mind." She taps her head. "And that's when I knew you were ready to know everything."

Thinking back, I remember. That's when the darkness that always followed Terease disappeared.

"You, Sera, were able to block me from your thoughts because you're a Watcher, a potential Chosen. You may have sensed it for yourself, that you're different from other Wanderers. A very small number of Watchers are born to the Society. However, only a few Watchers ever developed fully into a Chosen."

Terease stands, crosses her arms, and paces the room in short rotations as she continues. "Your mother was one of them—a Chosen. Like some of the others before her, she took it upon herself to attempt to change our histories, make them right, and fulfill the prophecy of the Masters that has been passed down through the centuries—a prophecy to end the world of Wandering as we know it, set the inhabitants of Nocturna free, and return us to our state of purity. To right our wrongs."

"End us?" I gulp and turn in my seat to face her.

She nods and continues. "We only know that the outcome will return control of the earth and destiny to its original inhabitants—humans. There is much debate over what returning to purity means." She stops and regards me. "But there is one thing we can surmise, and it's that the Society's corruption will end."

"Maybe my brain's just different. That doesn't mean I'm one of them, one of the Watchers, or that I'll ever be a Chosen."

In response she walks to a broken sliver of a mirror hanging on a wall. She lifts her hands to her eyes and gently touches her cornea with her finger. She turns to me. One eye is violet and the other black. She's been wearing contacts all this time, hiding their true color.

"Violet, like mine and Mom's. Are you a Watcher too?" I stand to get a better look at her eyes. She allows me to venture close.

"Most like myself, Miss Swift, and many, many others will never completely develop our skills."

"Skills?" I cross my arms, mirroring her as we talk face-to-face.

"To be the Chosen, you will manifest all three qualities of a team: Wanderer, Protector, and Seer. A Watcher merely manifests a combination of two, but never all three at once." Terease circles me, strutting like a cat, looking me over from head to toe. "Sera, you're a fiercely independent Wanderer. Instinctively you're always resisting utilizing the abilities of your team, looking to solve problems on your own, even protecting them when necessary. These last several months, you've surpassed the abilities of your own Protector. Just now, from a high-rise, I watched you outrun the Time Reaper's beast, something only few are fast enough to do. Clearly you've awakened the Protector within you, and the only quality left to develop is your Seeing ability. In doing so, you will become more than just a Watcher." She pauses in front of me, pivoting quickly to snare me with her intense gaze. "Do you understand?"

I nod and look down.

"In the last fifty years, only your mother has completed the transition to Chosen." She lifts my chin so our eyes meet. "And before her death, she secretly confided in me that she has reason to believe that you will do what she couldn't and fulfill the prophecy."

My breath hitches in my throat and her hand falls away. The confusion that's plagued me this last year suddenly settles into focus. For so long I've been on a path of my own, a selfish one that often left out my team. A path I couldn't explain to anyone, couldn't share with anyone, or change even when I desperately tried to.

"How?" I avoid her eyes, scanning the room. This conversation is not going at all like I'd imagined, and I'm beginning to wonder if I'll like what she has to say next.

"You must take the Oaths, dedicating your life to the Masters, and be anointed in the Grand Lodge. After that, if our Makers choose you as the One, you'll complete the transition from Watcher to Chosen."

"Then what?"

"That's for you to decide. Will you follow your destiny and return earth to balance and set everyone in Nocturna free? Set Bishop's family free?" She places both hands on my shoulders. "Or will you live as one of the Society, corrupt, allowing them to control you and every other Wanderer?"

"I'll do anything to save Bishop's family and to set everyone free, but how?"

Her gaze drills into mine. "That is something I do not

know. Your mother did not share this information with me before she passed. But luckily, Mona informed me that your mother kept a journal." She steps away and paces again, her voice rising with what sounds like hope. "We believe it may help you understand what lies ahead."

A hand pulls back the curtain, startling me. Terease spins to face the interruption. It's Stu—older, a man now, dressed in fatigues. "The Reapers are looming. We must smuggle her out of here before they zero in on our location." He nods his head in my direction.

"There's more than one?"

"Three," he answers. "They're from one body, broken into three more, and fragmented from time. Really interesting story, actually—"

I hold up my palm, hoping it will halt a science lecture. "Stop. Please, I don't even want to know how that's possible." I'm too upset to hear any more after what Terease just dumped on me.

"Suit yourself." He shrugs.

Terease marches out of the room with authority, past the curtain and straight toward a large periscope secured from the ceiling of the bunker. She grabs the handles and leans into the eyepiece, looking through it to visually search the surface.

"I thought Terease said that going deeper underground would protect us?" I look to Stu, trying not to stare at his new, older face.

"You're not like the rest of us. You're not supposed to be here. Maybe their need to take your life gives them a stronger sense of your location." He looks me up and down, giving me the leering, confident once-over with drifting eyes the way he used to, but now it's even more uncomfortable than before.

"Blast!" Terease growls and steps away from the periscope.

A gadget nearby sets off an alarm. The piercing sound, reinforced with a group of red blinking lights, sends everyone running for their workstations. The chaos increases when the machine activates a needle on the seismometer. It jumps and scratches a thin black zigzagging line on a rolling paper drum. They're tracking the thundering hoofbeats of the horse-beast, recording them like an impending earthquake.

"Come!" Terease barks, racing out of the room. "We need to get you home!"

We rush back through the tunnel, away from the bunker, leading the Time Reapers away from the group. The corridor splits on several occasions but Terease never falters. Without her, I would never be able to navigate the tunnel.

"But Bishop's family, I can't leave them here!"

Terease stops and turns, getting in my face. "Sera, I promise you this, the only way to save them is to set Nocturna free and fulfill the prophecy of the Chosen."

"But—"

"The only way, Sera. They're already aging. The Reapers have taken their souls, setting their lives on fast-forward, and the sooner you return home, the sooner you can save them."

I nod, trying to stay strong. It's the only way I'll get through this. We take off again, but this time I have a new determination. My path is clear now. I must fulfill the prophecy to save them, to save me, to save all of us.

"So, I'm gonna guess that there's no Wandering home from here?" I ask, my breath heavy from running.

"Ha! We are not that lucky." She rushes on.

Finally Terease stops in a new chamber, faces me, and pulls a necklace from inside her black leather jacket. It's a key on a cord. She lifts it over her head and places it around my neck, tucking the length into my jacket.

"What's this?" I look down.

"The key to the Member Archives. I believe that's where your mom's journal will be. And this too." She removes a small white case from her pocket and holds it up. "Contacts. Begin wearing them as soon as you return to Gibeon."

"Why?" I ask as she pushes the case in my hand.

"Because only a few can see the true color of our eyes—other Watchers and sometimes our team. Everyone else sees blue. But recently the Society has developed tests to see past our genetic defenses."

Almost everyone I've ever known mistook my eye color for blue. I stopped correcting them a long time ago. I inspect the case for a moment, then tuck it into my jacket pocket.

She turns to the wall and grabs a large lever attached to a circular metal hatch. Gritting her teeth and using all her weight, she rotates the handle, opening the door with a screech. Hissing smoke rolls out and dirty water pours onto the ground, lapping over our feet and rushing against the far wall with a splash.

Terease laces her fingers together and holds them at thigh height. I step up on them, and she lifts me inside the pipe.

"This tunnel dumps out at Nocturna's coast. There you'll find a boat. Row out to Gibeon's rock, dive into the water, and swim to the dark hole in the ocean floor. That's where you entered."

"You're not coming with me?"

"I'm needed here to help protect the others. Find your mom's journal and research the prophecy, Sera. It will take courage to become who you are meant to be, but you will. Your destiny awaits."

Terease closes the hatch before I can say any more and the lever rotates, locking me on the other side.

No 6

AN ESCAPE

CROUCHED WITHIN THE TUNNEL, DARKNESS surrounds me. When I pivot away from the hatch, I see a distant pinpoint of blue light at least a hundred feet away.

The tunnel is too small to stand upright, so as I crouch to crawl forward shallow water sloshes around, soaking my clothes again. When I reach the end, I peek through a gridded metal gate. A beam of moonlight shines over the body of water that I swam through when I originally arrived. Carefully I scan as far as I can see, searching for the Reapers, listening for the destruction they bring. But there's nothing, only the sound of rolling waves. The boat Terease mentioned bobs gently past the surf line, tied to the end of a long dock.

I'll have to make a run for it. As quietly as I can, I push open the grate. I stiffen, waiting for the rusted thing to creak and moan, but surprisingly it swings open smoothly, and I shimmy out of the pipe and drop to the hill of skulls below. They are uneven and loose so I fall to my knees, but use this moment to scan the horizon. There's an eerie silence that I don't trust for one second, and I recall that the wind will carry the scent of my living soul, alerting the Reapers to my position.

Making a run for it, I stand and dart across the pass, slipping and sliding over the bones until I reach the pier. The aged wooden boards squeak each time my soaked boots slap against them, and I run for my life.

Like the flip of a light switch, the sound of the horse-beast's gallop appears, echoing through the city. When I glance over my shoulder, it's easy to spot the direction the Reapers travel from. Buildings shake and rattle, and weak structures collapse from the movement, crumbling to the ground. One after another they fall like dominoes. Just as I reach the boat, three Reapers appear on the edge of the city, perched atop their screaming horse-beasts. They gallop like a roll of thunder to the coastline and my heart rate accelerates. Nervously I yank loose the rope tied to a piling and leap into the old boat with an unsteady thump.

By the time I settle myself and grab the oars, the trio of Reapers rein in their beasts to a shuddering halt behind the wall of bones. Two whip their bows into their hands, load, and point their arrows at me. They release simultaneously and two flaming arrows arc across the midnight sky just as I push the boat away from the pier. Surprisingly they miss me, but the arrows sink their flaming points in the wooden hull. As I row away, the wood ignites and burns, scorching to black.

My heart racing, I row harder, pushing my biceps and my entire body to escape. At the same time, in a desperate attempt to quench the fire, I rock the boat with my weight, throwing the dinghy from side to side to douse the flames. Water rushes over the hull, and mercifully the blaze begins to sputter out.

Several more arrows fly past, cutting through the water with quick whooshes. The Reapers' aim worsens as I gain a lead, growing the distance between us, but the waves become larger, rocking the boat, and I adjust my pulls, rowing in longer sweeps to push against the force of the current.

I glance over my shoulder to ensure I'm headed in the correct direction. Gibeon's rock sits just a few hundred feet ahead. A smile broadens over my face—I'm beating them. I'm going to make it home.

When I look back to the shoreline to give them a victorious glare, the third Reaper slides off his horse-beast, expertly navigates the hill of skulls, and marches to the end of the pier. He stands, claws clenched at his sides and leans forward, blowing a powdery mist from his mouth. The thick silvery cloud whirls around and then, to my complete surprise, the Reaper jumps down onto the water's surface and runs. He continues blowing a gust of wind from his lips while he's running over the water, chasing me, but how?

Scared, I row harder and push farther to close in on my destination. I don't know how he's doing this but at his quickened, superhuman pace, he's gaining.

My eyes widen in horror when I finally comprehend what's happening. The ocean water clouds behind me and curling crystallized fingers wrap around the boat, slowing it down. The water stiffens and cracks, freezing into a solid block of ice. The boat halts, trapped atop a high, icy wave, and I scurry out of the vessel and slide down the side, struggling to stand and race atop the forming ice. If it reaches Gibeon's rock, I'll be trapped in Nocturna forever.

The rock is close; I'm almost there. At the last minute, I suck in an enormous breath of air and dive headfirst over the jagged edge of forming ice into the now-freezing water. Pressure surrounds me, pushing painfully against my eardrums, and I probably only have a few seconds to reach the bottom before it hardens too. I stroke my arms wide, kick and snap my legs, forcing myself deeper.

The entrance to Gibeon appears as a dark ellipse. I stretch one arm, reaching to save my life. My belly flops with nausea as the world flips back over, righting itself.

Finally my head pops through the water's surface and I gasp the warmer air at the bottom of the pit of Nocturna where I originally entered. But with each breath I'm hyper-ventilating, feeling my lungs contract, and the water slowly cementing around me. In a state of panic, I reach up for an outcropping of rock to drag myself out, but with no energy left, I think I'm done, stuck halfway between both worlds.

Sobbing, overcome with despair and berating myself for my abject failure, I'm yanked by my sleeve and hauled out of the hole at the exact moment the water cracks and freezes into a solid block of ice.

№
7
BISHOP

"SERA! ARE YOU ALL RIGHT?" BISHOP SHAKES ME, his eyes wild with concern.

But I can't answer. Overcome with hypothermia, my body shivers in waves of tremors, leaving me gasping for air. Air that my lungs don't seem to be able to push in and out of my aching body. Bishop's image fades to black as the lack of oxygen blurs my vision.

I'm in and out.

Freezing.

My clothes. He's tugging at them.

I'm cold.

Warmth.

When I come to, I'm stripped down to my wet bra and underwear. Bishop's body wraps around mine, his warmth transferring to me as we're cocooned within a wool blanket. My immediate reaction is to push him off but I'm too exhausted, and after a little thought, I understand he's only done this to save me, to raise my body temperature. My clothes, drenched with freezing water, only worsened my situation. They lie in a soaked pile on the rocky ground next to the frozen entrance to Nocturna.

"Thanks," I croak, teeth chattering. He wraps his arms tighter around my back, fingers splaying across my cold, damp skin riddled with goose flesh and squeezes, hugging every warming angle of his body to mine.

"You're welcome." He lowers his cheek to my drenched hair with a look of relief.

We lie like this for some time. No words; we just hold each other. And despite all that's happened, it feels good to be near him again, to feel safe, and to know that I share the burden of this strange life with someone else. He understands and loves me, even if he's done many wrong things in the past to show it.

"There's an abandoned lookout post just a few floors from here. We should relocate there, make camp for the night, and start a fire," Bishop says. "Are you feeling well enough to move?"

Reluctantly, I take a quick inventory of my condition.

My temperature has risen, the shudders have abated, and my breathing is not so ragged. I lift my limbs and wiggle my toes, then look up at him and nod. "Fire sounds good."

A wave of sadness fills my chest when he peels his body heat away, and we stand. My blanket falls to the floor, and he scoops it up and meets my eyes. Our gazes lock together as he takes his time to drape the fabric over my shoulders and close it tightly around my body. I want his love, even though I shouldn't. I want to press my lips to his, but I can't. To break the tension, I glance away, attempting to save my aching heart.

"Thanks," I mumble.

Bishop sighs before he leans down to repack his backpack. He grabs my drenched clothing and shoes from the ground and turns to climb the zigzagging stairs that line the walls of the pit.

In a haze, I follow, hugging the wall to stay far away from the stair's edge. Three flights up, there's a room carved into the side of the pit. I step inside, following a very quiet Bishop. He lights a lantern that sits on a three-legged table and the room comes into view under a warm glow. There's a fireplace against the far wall, two simple chairs sit at the desk, and a old dusty bed. When I look back to him after assessing the bed's small size, he's staring at me and I quickly glance away. It's not like we haven't shared a bed before.

"I'll sleep on the floor," he says.

"No, it's fine. We can share."

We could Wander back to the Academy from here with our Wandering compasses, but I'm not ready to go home. Staying here in Gibeon, hidden for a little while longer before facing my problems, seems more enticing. Safe.

"Looks like no one's been here for a while." Bishop waves a cobweb away. "I don't think the Nocturna guards come this far down into the pit. I snuck past their lowest post about midway down."

"Why did you come for me? It wasn't safe." A cold draft invades our sanctuary and I pull the blanket tighter, fighting a shiver.

"I think you know the answer to that." He stares at me intently, silently professing his love with his beautiful eyes like he has done many times before. "And you've been gone three days. I was starting to worry that I may never see you again, and I can only tell our teachers that you're ill for so long."

"Three days!" I gasp. "Only felt like a few hours."

"Maybe time speeds up for everyone on some level in Nocturna, not just the soulless."

My thoughts whirl and I frown at the thought of what I must tell him now; what he needs to know. Starting slowly, I ease my way into the worst news. "The Society sent Perpetua and her team there." I pause. "Jess didn't make it."

Bishop freezes and glances up from where he's crouched on the floor, gathering sticks from a wood box to start a fire. "What?"

"Perpetua said that if you don't take your Oaths to the

Society, if you choose not to be a Wanderer, the Society sends you to Nocturna. They lied. You don't really have a choice."

"That's—that's insanity!" The sticks drop from his hand and clatter to the floor. He sinks to his knees and his face darkens with disgust.

Against my better judgment, I step forward to comfort him. I know he's held on to the hope that the Society isn't as bad as I've been making them out to be. But they are; they're murderers, plain and simple. Kneeling down, I drop part of the blanket to extend my hand and grasp his shoulder.

"What's happening? I used to think being part of the Society was the most amazing honor. And finding Sam and then you..." His words weaken. "Then Mum tells me how they blackmailed her, that they would have killed either Turner or me just for being twins as some crazy sacrifice during the Oaths if she hadn't made a bargain with them to watch over you and pretend to be your aunt, and now this?" His voice trails off to a murmur.

"What we are," I explain, "it's unnatural in the Normal world. You can't have this ability without consequences, without those who will use it for evil." I prepare myself for the next thing I must tell him, and close my eyes, summoning courage. "Bishop, there's something else. Something that's not easy to say. It's Mona, Charlotte, and your father. They're, um—"

"Tell me, Sera. What?" He turns to me, eyes piercing.

"They're in Nocturna too. The Society sent them there

just a few hours before I arrived."

"What!"

He pulls away and jumps to his feet, snatches up a mason jar from the mantel, and throws it across the room. It explodes with a crash, sending shattered pieces skidding across the floor, and I flinch.

"Bishop, I can save them. There's a way I can make everything right. I can save us all from this life." Every reason why I shouldn't get too close to Bishop is shoved to the far reaches of my mind as I rush to his side and grab his shoulders, just as he sinks to the floor on his knees, crying.

My own grief churning inside me, I console him the best I can, kneeling next to him on the damp stone floor and rubbing his back. "I'll fix this, I promise," I whisper.

"How?" He looks up with puffy, reddened eyes, and my heart breaks further. If I were alone, taking this information in for myself, I'd be crying too, but I need to be strong for him.

For once, I tell him everything, starting with my arrival in Nocturna as I plunged into the salty water and fought my way upward and to shore. I tell him about the city and its inhabitants. He cringes at my descriptions of the people and their eyes, knowing full well what lies ahead for his family. When I reach the part about the Reaper chasing me on horseback, he stiffens, unable to contain his sense to protect me. The information from Terease interests him most. Of course he has a lot of questions about the prophecy, being a Watcher, and the

Chosen, but I only have enough information to make my next move—finding my mom's journal. That will lead us to more information.

Bishop relaxes somewhat; I feel the tension leaving his body and pray that he finds comfort in my words. When he turns his face to mine, his eyes are no longer anguished and angry, but tender and hopeful. A warmth steals over me as he assures me with just his eyes that he loves me and believes in me. I can practically see the cogs and wheels turning inside his head as he lifts a hand and touches my cheek with his fingertip, his eyes widening and his lips parting with what looks like awe. Watching him process all that I've told him, I realize that he believes that I can free Nocturna, save his family, and fulfill the prophecy. Though, at this moment, neither of us knows what that entails.

This is how much he trusts me, and that responsibility settles on my shoulders. Even though I act confident, I'm not completely sure of myself, even with all that I've done these last few months. Do I really have it in me? Can I second-guess myself? Insecurity breeds uncertainty and uncertainty is not an option. Failure is not an option. Instead of folding into my emotions the way I always did in the past, I put my arms around him, tug him close, and tell him what he needs to hear. "I promise, I'll bring them home."

"I know you will. I believe in you." His body relaxes further and he smiles for the first time in an hour. When he looks at me that way, I almost believe in myself too, and I smile back.

As he stands, I tug the warmth of the blanket back around my arms. He moves back into Protector mode and gathers the wood that's been scattered through the room, though I'm sure he's probably still thinking of his family. Kneeling before the fireplace, he makes a teepee of wood. After a few flicks from a lighter, the dried stack ignites, and Bishop leans down to blow on it and spread the flames. Soon the fireplace rages full and bright, crackling and radiating heat.

I shuffle closer and hold my palms to the blaze, soaking up the small pleasure, but one last chill from the hyperthermia causes me to shiver.

With just that small gesture, Bishop's at my side in a split second. "You need rest." Before I can respond, he lifts me, cradling me into his arms wrapped securely in the blanket, then walks across the room and gently places me on the bed. My body relaxes, and he sits on the edge, leaning over me for a moment. He tenderly wipes a strand of damp hair from my face, then glides a knuckle along the curve of my cheek. "Sleep for a little while, and then we'll go home. We have a lot of work to do."

I nod. Though it feels like just a few hours since I've left him for Nocturna, the longer I'm here in Gibeon, the longer it feels as though I've been awake. My eyelids droop, heavy, so heavy.

The bed creaks when his weight lifts from the mattress, and he walks away. My sleepy gaze follows him around the room. He drags both chairs near the fire, then bends over and grabs my wet clothes from the floor. He carefully wrings out the fabric and drapes the damp clothing over the back of the chair to dry, then he places my wet boots on the hearth. My hearts swells, watching him take care of me like this. I wonder how things would be if we weren't Wanderers and hard-wired to love each other. If we were human, with no extra interference, would we feel the same? Would we still love each other?

Fighting off my own exhaustion, I watch through half-lidded eyes as he lowers himself to the floor, positioning himself on his back near the fire. He stacks his hands behind his head and stares at the ceiling. The firelight flickers, casting a golden glow over his beautiful face, and as his eyelids sink shut, several tears escape.

Instantly, I feel I must be there for him, but cringe at what I'm about to do. "Bishop. Don't. Come lie next to me." I look down at him and reach out my arm, inviting him.

He regards me for a moment, then looks away.

"Please," I plead, maybe a little too much, but it's stupid for him to be uncomfortable because he's come a long way to find me, to save me, and now he's obviously so sad. We both are.

Bishop closes his eyes and sighs, but gives in and joins me in bed. I turn on my side, leaving a spot for him to spoon me. It's the only way we'll both fit comfortably on the narrow bed. He wraps his arm around my stomach and settles close. Heat radiates from him: his legs, his arms, his chest.

His breathing, which is at my neck, rushes over me like a hot shower, causing the energy between us to prick my skin.

I inhale deeply and close my eyes, trying to bury my feelings, camouflaging the confusion I feel inside. I shiver again, and he squeezes tighter. If only I could turn over to face him, to kiss him, just to release this tension inside of me. God, I don't want to want his love, but I do.

"Seraphina." He whispers my name like he did once before, letting the syllables draw out languorously. The vibrations of each syllable send ripples through my body, and I squeeze my muscles tighter to fight the spell he's casting over me.

"Mmm," I respond. Pretending to be asleep is my only defense against him—against my traitorous self.

"Never mind." He sighs. The release of air brushes over my neck. My eyes begin to prick and burn, releasing a single teardrop through my lashes, a silent protest at the incredible unfairness of what I'm going through. Love shouldn't be so hard. Our lives shouldn't be so complicated.

Bishop rolls me to face him, pressing his chest against mine. Our faces are so close to each other, but my eyes still look away from his. It would be so easy for me to give in to my feelings, just to live in the moment for a little bit of time, be happy, and forget everything else.

I glance up from under my lashes. His breathing becomes heavy and dries the moisture from my lips, so I lick them. His gaze falls there and he leans closer, so close our lips are an inch apart, our breaths commingling. I don't object because the truth is that I want them there. In fact, I want them closer, pressed against mine, then nibbling their way from my mouth, along my jawline...

At the uncontrolled thought, my breath hitches in my throat, and I stop breathing. He gives in first, pressing his lips gently against mine just as I'd wanted. Like the push of a button, my reaction is immediate. My tense muscles relax and I moan, letting my eyelids flutter down to close with relief. His warm lips feel better than I remember; he tastes better than I remember. My mind wipes clean, freeing itself from worry and grief and pain, and there's only the two of us— safe, warm, our bodies pressed against each other.

I look into his eyes, so hypnotic and mystical with their green depths, and together we suck in a breath, stealing the only thing holding us apart—air. Leaning forward, we're immediately on each other, kissing and touching frantically as though this is our last hour. Insanity overtakes me and I luxuriate in his kisses as they cover my neck, my shoulder, and then my heaving chest. Everything that we've been fighting about or for, all the hurt, all the emotions pour into this moment. Each kiss energizes me, leaving me breathless with relief to just give in, to relent and love him no matter what.

Together we roll onto my blanket. Bishop braces himself above me with his strong arms. Grasping at the back of his shirt, I pull him to me, and he dives in for a deeper kiss.

His hands slide behind my back and he aggressively lifts

me upright so I'm sitting, legs straddled and locked around his waist. His hard abs press against my stomach, and I pull him closer. His hands press firmly into my back as I'm cocooned in his warmth, in his love.

In a movement that makes my heart stop, he slides his hand lower and slips a finger into the top elastic of my panties and lightly strokes, tracing the skin just beneath the fabric along the small of my back. Flames of passion race across the trail, and I remember the last time I felt exactly the same.

Turner's heartbreakingly beautiful face flashes behind my closed lids, and I instantly freeze. Guilt rushes into me, pouring into every nerve of my body. What am I doing? What am I doing! My hands press against Bishop's chest, forcing him away, and I fall back onto the bed with a thump, detaching myself from him in every way.

Bishop tenses in that instant and lets out a moan. He sits up and roughly drags a hand across his unshaven face, his fingernails digging into his skin, and I feel a stab of guilt for the pain I'm causing him.

Shivering, I huddle back into my blanket, concealing my half-naked body, desperately wanting to shrink away into nothing for losing myself in Bishop again. After everything that's transpired over the last few weeks—and in just this past day! It only proves how strong our connection is; so strong that I'm clearly not even in command of my own body anymore. We can't control our lust even during the most heartbreaking times. My stomach lurches with nausea.

Bishop rakes his fingers through his hair and looks at the floor. "I'm sorry. I don't know what happened. I just—I know you don't want me anymore, we're broken up or on a break, or whatever. I'm sorry." He glances at me. "Everything inside of me needs to love you. It's not easy."

"I know." I'm trembling; I want so desperately to stand my ground. If he only knew how much I want him too. "It's my fault, we shouldn't—I can't," I stutter. My feelings are still raw with the confusion of loving two boys at once.

"This is hard to say," he says with a grimace, "but my brother would've wanted you to be happy, even if it was with me. And if the roles were switched, I would want the same for you and him. If being apart is what you want, then I'll try my best to comply."

Focusing anywhere but at him, I pick at the edge of the blanket as I try to choose my words carefully. Looking away, I murmur, "I'm just confused." I love Bishop, and even though Turner is dead, I still love him too. Despite this, I don't want to love either one of them because I have to or because our genetics force us to. I want the freedom to choose real love. "For now, I think it's best if I focus on the prophecy." My voice wavers because I know that as the words leave my mouth, they will scar him, but I just can't live like this. And he shouldn't want to, either.

"Right," he says, his tone emotionless. "And you should rest. We have a lot to do in a short amount of time." It seems so sad that he agrees without a fight as he often does, putting his heart aside to please me.

I nod and watch as he rolls out of bed to stand, noticing from within my own pain that each step he takes from me is slow, reluctant.

We start over, back where we started. Him on the floor, and me in bed with my arms wrapped tightly around my body to secure my own space—far away from Bishop. I roll away from him, angry with myself, angry at everything and everyone. By the time I corral my guilt, the sleep that I've delayed hits me. My eyelids sink shut, heavy with schalg, and I pray for a small measure of peace in slumber.

No 8

A GIFT

MY ARM EXTENDS AND LANDS IN A CLOUD OF
fluff. I roll over and snuggle my face into a soft, clean
pillow. Somewhere in my mind, I'm happy, peaceful even, in
a state of bliss. My muscles relax so deeply that they seem to
melt into the bed. I hold on to this paradise for as long as I can
before I allow my reality to consume me. But by the time I've
thought of it, the memories rush back: Nocturna, Perpetua,
Terease, being the Watcher, a possible Chosen, the prophecy,
the Reapers, Bishop and his family. My eyelids pop open to
darkness, and I realize I'm not in the pit of Nocturna anymore. This bed is my own, in my own bedroom, within the

apartment at the Washington Square Academy of Wanderers in Chicago that I share with my teammates, Sam and Bishop.

I sit up and yawn, stretching my arms wide. Each muscle trembles with tension. Bishop must have teleported me home with his Wandering compass while I slept. At least we avoided the awkwardness of facing each other after what happened between us last night.

I grab the down comforter, throw it off my body, and roll out of bed to find a small white box with a loopy pink bow sitting on my nightstand. An envelope rests upright against my contrapulator—the machine that students listen to at night to subliminally absorb classes in their sleep. But since I found out it has a dual function, not only to teach but also to steal hopes and dreams, recording them onto a crystal dreamdrive so that the Society can manipulate their owners, I stopped using it. And so have Sam and Bishop.

Hesitantly I pick up the envelope and flip it over, push my finger under the corner, and rip open the flap. There's a note on parchment inside that reads, "I'm sorry. This is the only possible way I can make things right." It's Bishop's handwriting. My heart hurts that he's sorry, knowing I'm just as much to blame, or maybe neither of us is to blame.

I place the note on the table and pick up the box. It's smaller than my hand. With one tug of the satin bow the box unfolds, revealing its contents. Inside is a miniature Animate, a mechanical bronze scorpion, the ancient symbol for a Protector.

A smile takes over my face as I raise the small machine to my eyes, admiring the craftsmanship: all its tiny bits, cranks, pieces, and its sparkling crystal body. It's an unusual gift, definitely unlike anything Bishop has ever given me.

With my finger, I poke at it. Tiny claws clamp and its intricate, segmented tail curls open and closed. Eight legs work in sync, lightly pricking my skin as the animal circles several times on my palm and then crawls to the tips of my fingers. At my prodding, a pillar of light shoots from the scorpion's flat crystal face like a flashlight beam, landing across the room.

I follow the light shaft with my eyes, but in that same instant, a click of a switch ignites the blazing bulb of a floor lamp near the far wall. A body sits on a chair beneath, its long, muscular limbs relaxed. A face inches forward into the light, revealing itself. Dark waves curl, framing his beautiful face and accentuating his sculptured features. His sensuous slate-colored eyes lazily scan my half-naked body. He picks up a bra I'd discarded nearby and spins it negligently in the air around his finger as the corners of his mouth twitch with amusement.

Turner.

Immediately I jump to my feet and stare, my heart pounding in my chest. He isn't real—only a hologram projected from the scorpion Animate. I know this, but still, I haven't been able to see Turner in hologram form since the real Turner died. The hologram training program hasn't worked properly since.

Bishop's gift to me isn't really the Animate; instead, he's giving me Turner—a small piece of him—what's left of him. A knot forms in my throat. I just want to stare, soaking in his presence. If only he were truly real.

"What's wrong, love?" Hologram Turner drops the lingerie and leans forward with concern. His gaze continues to drift along my bare limbs. Despite a zapping pop of electricity here and there, he's so real, alive with Turner's confidence, wit, and dangerous charm. And in this moment of understanding, I lose it, gasping a sob, and fall to my knees, dropping the Animate. The machine takes off skittering across the floor, only to project Hologram Turner at my side.

"Sera, please, tell me what's wrong." Hologram Turner pulls me close and brushes my hair from my face. I look up in his eyes and understand immediately. Hologram Turner doesn't know that his live counterpart is dead. He doesn't know that he fought Cece to protect me, and they rolled to their deaths into a crack in the earth created by the movement of Gibeon. My brows furrow from a pain that I can hardly bear and I leap into his lap, wrap my arms around his neck, and squeeze so tightly I may never let go. I cry against his chest with uncontrolled intensity, plunging my hands into his dark curls, threading them between my fingers. Lifting my face to his neck, I press closer, deeply inhaling the spicy, masculine scent of him. It's so real.

He shushes me, rocking me, consoling me.

Oh, how I've dreamed of the moment that I might hold

him again. I cry for his death, for the knowledge that this is the closest I will ever be to him again, and I cry for everything that never was and surely never will be between us.

"Just hold me," I whisper in his ear. His body immediately responds and his strong arms lock tight around my waist, constricting me. I tuck my head into his chest, and he rocks me from side to side while humming a soothing melody.

After some time, I pull myself away only to stare at him again. I want to thank him for what he did, everything he gave up for me—gave up for Bishop. I say it in my mind because I don't know how to say it out loud. Thank you. The simple words will never be enough.

"Now, tell me what's going on." He lifts my chin, leveling his simmering blue eyes with mine. "I know it's bad because you're practically naked in my arms and you haven't batted me away," he says with a chuckle. "What will Bishop think, hmm?"

Needing a moment, I wipe the tears from my wet face, but the truth is that I don't know what to say to him. How can I explain? My lips tremble as I stutter, "I-if only I could tell you."

Hologram Turner pulls me to my feet. We face each other and his gaze lands on my chest. He reaches out and wraps his fingers around the cord and key—the one that Terease gave me in Nocturna before I left. "Does it have anything to do with this?" He tugs the necklace, pulling me forward, testing the personal space between us, just the way he would when he was still alive.

"It's just a key to a storage space." Of course it's not the whole truth, but I really don't want to explain that right now. It's bad enough that I'll have to tell him that he has died, but I also have to figure out how to break the news about Mona, Charlotte, and his dad, and how they're serving a death sentence in Nocturna. If only for a moment, I want to enjoy being near him, even if it's just a mirage.

"The always elusive Seraphina, scheming every chance she gets." He smirks and grabs my robe from a hook on the wall, handing it to me. "You can tell me anything. You know that, right?" He holds up the robe, helping me slide my arms into the silk sleeves.

"Yes, it's just—" I tie the robe off at my waist and turn to find Hologram Turner is gone.

Before I can react to his disappearance, my bedroom door unexpectedly creaks open and a man I never expected to see here confidently walks into my room. "My personal physician is on the way," he says.

"Grand Master?" My voice squeaks from the shock that Grand Master Phineas Levi, the leader of the Society, has come to see me. I pull my robe tighter, covering myself, and look around for Hologram Turner, but the scorpion Animate has tucked itself away, hidden beneath a chest of drawers across the room. The machine must have sensed someone else's presence approaching and turned off the hologram.

"I understand that you've been locked in your room for days, fighting the flu." He boldly walks past, inspecting the room for what, I don't know.

"Yes." I nod at the lie. That's how Bishop explained my three-day absence to Nocturna.

Grand Master Levi drags a gloved fingertip over the windowsill and then pinches his fingers together, rubbing away the dust.

"Why are you here?" I ask. "You could have knocked. I was getting dressed." I haven't seen him since that day in Gibeon when we fought Cece, the Underground, and my mom and Turner died.

"When I heard about one of our brightest students missing school for days on end, I had to rush over." His voice trails off with a dramatic sigh. "Well, that's not completely true." He faces me and leans on his cane. Three silver skulls sit atop a slender column of twisted black wood. "It's only because it was you, Seraphina. And you—well, quite honestly, let's just say I have a vested interest in you."

"I'm not sure what you mean." I cock my head.

He clicks his tongue, cutting his eyes at me in a mischievous manner that makes me nervous. "Let's not play this game, shall we?" He paces, tugging at the wrists of his white gloves. "I believe—hope, really—that you're special."

I stand up a little straighter. Warning bells go off inside my brain, telling me to play dumb, to act as though he isn't alluding to the fact that I'm a Watcher, a possible Chosen. There's something about this man—his overconfidence, his hard-lined face, his importance—that puts me on edge. Or maybe it's just the fact that he could exile me to Nocturna quicker than a blink that makes me want to hide the fact that he scares me.

"I'm just like any other student," I say as I cross my arms. But I'm not, and we both know it. He's probably also referring to the fact that just a week ago, the now dead leader of the Underground, Cece, was willing to hold off attacks on the Society of Wanderers in exchange for my dreamdrive—the crystal hard drive from the contrapulator that stores all my dreams while I sleep at night, one of two that I have stashed at Mona's house in my old room.

The Grand Master taps his finger to his chin, sizing me up with his piercing gaze. With strange energy, he approaches, plunges his hand into his jacket pocket, and pulls out a pocket watch. "Wandering is like a fine watch, a luxurious time piece, Miss Parrish. Without all the cranks and gears working together in perfect harmony, time ceases to work. Much like this watch." He flips open a hidden compartment, revealing the mechanical inner workings, and presents it for me to see. "The Society and all its dedicated members contribute to time's functions. We are the gears and cranks, but there's a reason for each piece, just as there is a reason for you. And my newest, most thrilling agenda is to confirm what I now believe that is." He steps away and grabs the doorknob. "I can tell you're as excited as I am." He smiles, but the expression doesn't reach his eyes. Instead, they narrow with an emotion that looks to me like cold calculation.

When the Grand Master opens the bedroom door, there's

an older man standing in the living room, holding a doctor's bag. I'm guessing that he is the Grand Master's personal physician, but the look of him scares me. He appears overworked, untidy, and angry. All the things a doctor shouldn't be.

"I want a full physical examination, Dr. Shockey," Grand Master Levi commands. The doctor flicks a quick glance at me and then returns his attention to his employer, nodding his assent with a pleasure that seems out of place, and a chill rushes over me.

"Splendid," the Grand Master says with a broad smile. "Let's find out if our little Sera is"—he looks me up and down—"extraordinary." Without another word, he shrugs into his long black coat, skull cane in hand, and disappears as quickly as he arrived.

No 9

THE DOCTOR

A HOLLOW DREAD CREEPS INTO MY LIMBS AS the overzealous doctor steps into my room, followed by two Society soldiers. Who brings henchmen to a physical exam? They are the Grand Master's personal guards, overgrown meatheads with biceps the size of their thighs.

Across from me in the living room, Bishop appears. "Sera?" He tilts his head, taking in the scene. "What's going on?" Worry contorts his features and he steps forward to defend me, but Sam rushes to his side and tugs at his arm, then whispers in his ear. When his eyes widen at her words, one guard deliberately shuts the door, separating me from my team and my freedom.

If Grand Master Levi ever found out what I really am, he'd just send me back to Nocturna, and then I'd never be able to save Bishop's family or stop the Society's corruption.

"I'm feeling much better," I say brightly, though I'm certain I look pretty awful after crying my eyes out from Hologram Turner's visit.

The doctor ignores me, walks to the end of my bed, and holds up his briefcase, flat side up. He presses a button on the side and gives the box a quick mid-air bounce. Four retractable silver legs mechanically extend until they hit the floor, converting the briefcase into a table.

"We'll just make sure, won't we?" he says with a coldness that nearly makes me shiver. "Take a seat, Miss Parrish." He gestures to the bed, then looks up from behind his round, wire-rim glasses. I comply, sitting down, desperately attempting to control my anxiety. My gaze pings from the window to the door to the pair of Society guards, as my brain calculates an exit strategy.

The doctor pops open the latches on his briefcase and lifts the top. Hinges squeak before locking in the upright position, and two small workspaces slide out, one from each side. With precision, he drapes a white cloth across each, and one by one he removes several medical apparatuses, placing them methodically on the tabletops.

My jaw tightens when each new shiny and complicated contraption appears. These are terrifying tools of Wandering medicine that he will no doubt, poke, prod, and torture me with to decide if I'm a Watcher or even a Chosen.

He stops to inspect a gadget with several rotating lenses and numbered cranks. It reminds me of the machine at the eye doctor's office, but this one is different, smaller and more complex, with several spidery legs and colored lenses that extend in every direction.

Immediately, I register what it's used for and Terease's warning rushes back. Begin wearing them as soon as you return to Gibeon. I scan my bedroom, looking for the clothes I wore to Nocturna, hoping Bishop left them here. The contacts she gave me are still in the pocket of my jacket.

"Everything all right?" The doctor pins me with his stare, one brow arched in question. My facial expressions must have betrayed me because even the guards stiffen, analyzing my reaction.

"Fine." I stand. "I need to use the restroom."

"Go." He nods and continues polishing a lens.

I walk to the bathroom, picking up piles of clothes along the way.

The doctor steals a glance over his shoulder and glares at me.

"I'm a little embarrassed that my room's so messy, sorry." I pick up my clothes from Nocturna, nonchalantly bundling them with the rest, acting like I'm going to dump them in the laundry basket in my bathroom.

He eyes me suspiciously, causing the guard nearest to approach.

I smile, step into the bathroom, then shut the door as normally as possible and lock it. Now by myself, I frantically dump the clothes on the floor, drop to my knees, and begin digging through them, checking all the pockets. If I can't find the lens case, who knows what will happen? The doctor will use the eye machine on me and learn that my eyes are violet, then he'll know what I am. Will they send me back to Nocturna or just kill me?

My mind spins with the possibilities, which are many, and my options, which are limited. Even if I could find a way to escape, I don't have the option to do so. I need to have access to the Academy and its archives if I'm going to find my mom's journal and save everyone, so I need to keep myself in check and stay the course.

Just as I take a breath to calm myself, I find my jacket and dig into the pocket. "Thank God!" Relief washes over me as I grasp the little white container. I rush to the sink, pop open the box, and lean toward the mirror. I pause, not exactly sure how this works because I've never worn contacts before. So I do what I've seen on TV: with a lens balanced on the tip of my finger, I use my free hand to hold the eyelid open and then gently place the clear disk on my eye. It settles on the cornea uncomfortably, and I blink away several tears. Immediately the lens grows like it's alive, reaching across the surface and covering every part, then sealing itself shut at the edges. I shiver at the creepy sensation, but no one will even sense its presence now.

I dip my finger back into the box, searching for the matching lens, but nothing's there. Where is it? I lean close to the sink and glide my hand over the porcelain—and find nothing!

"Miss Parrish." The doctor knocks. The sound startles me and I accidentally drop the plastic case on the floor. It clanks as it bounces across the tile.

"Just a minute!" I call out.

When he knocks again, I panic and flush the toilet. At the sound he relents, and I turn on the sink faucet like I'm washing my hands to buy a few more seconds. Terrified for what might happen, I realize there's nothing more I can do.

Facing my fear, I open the door. It's better than making him think something's wrong. But when I stare at him, taking in his curious face, my lens-covered eye begins to twitch. The eyelid muscles jitter uncontrollably, and I reach up to rub it.

"Sorry it took so long." I shrug, trying desperately to act normal.

His eyes narrow.

The bridge of my nose itches like a rapidly spreading rash, and I scratch it, digging my fingernails into my skin as I push past the doctor. The irritation travels from the contact-covered eye, under the bridge of my nose, and spreads over my other eye. I rub both hands over my forehead, massaging the skin the way you would with a bad headache, until the uncomfortable tingling recedes, then I turn and sit down facing him.

"Let's begin, Miss Parrish." He picks up the eye contraption and sets it on the bed. "Now, let's have a look at those eyes." He leans in, exhaling the scent of stale coffee.

I expect the doctor to raise the eye machine to my face, but he doesn't. Instead the machine, a living Animate, walks like a spider across my hand, my thighs, and slowly journeys its way up my arms and shoulders until it settles itself on top of my head. Uneasy, I pinch my shoulders to my ears as each of its willowy metal legs clamps down, driving its defined points into my skull.

The cold metal contraption presses against my forehead and cheeks, leveling itself with my eyes so that I'm looking through round lenses. With no prompting from the doctor, the machine clicks and clanks, changing various lenses. Through blurry eyes, I can make a distinction of assorted colors and quick flipping movements, but I'm never asked "one or two" or "before or after." The machine does all the work, evaluating my sight.

Upon completion of the test, the doctor harrumphs loudly.

"Everything all right?" I feign worry with a creased brow. The contact has somehow worked. Apparently the single contact reached across my face and grew itself into the uncovered eye, saving me. Or perhaps there was only one to start, and this is how it was meant to work.

"Yes, yes, fine." The machine unclamps itself, slowly climbing down my head, shoulder, and arm. Ignoring the tedious pinches of each leg is not easy, but now that it's moved away from my face, I can see perfectly well.

The doctor picks up a new contraption—one that I can only describe as a short, clear light saber with pink lightning inside. "Please stand," he says.

Inside the wand, lightning whips back and forth, crackling with wicked electricity. Wild fingers of light sizzle around the edges.

"What's that for?"

"Hmph." He laughs. "This will show me your marks. If you have any, that is." He reaches inside his briefcase and pulls out a long strip of leather. Iridescent marks, designed like tattoos, stretch along its length.

I pinch my lips in disgust when I realize that the leather is dried skin from a Watcher, perhaps a Chosen. My mind leaps to another awful thought: Could it be from my mom, the only other recent fully developed Chosen who would most certainly have the marks they're looking for? My heart pinches with hatred, and the blood drains from my face as I sit back down, fighting the urge to vomit.

"So, you *are* ill." The doctor presses a hand to my clammy forehead.

When I look at him I want to finish him, take him down for being one of them, destroying my life as well as my mom's, Mona's, and little Charlotte's. The guards edge closer; I must not be hiding my feelings very well.

I let out a deep breath. It's not her, I tell myself; it's not her. Lying to myself is the only way I'll move past this as I urge some sense of self-preservation to kick in. "Let's get this over with," I snap.

"Fine," the doctor continues. "The machine works like this." The doctor waves the wand over the leather. Electricity shoots from the tip, creeping and crawling over the mark, causing it to burn with pink light. "And if this were your skin, you'd scream like a dying banshee." He snickers. "Now, it's your turn." He smiles, revealing a mouthful of uneven brown teeth.

I tremble with repulsion and step forward. "I promise, I don't have anything like that on my body." I try not to look at the leather, not wanting to recognize it.

"Ahhh," he says gently, barely able to contain his excitement. "But it may be below the upper epidermis, and if so, this extractor will draw it out, bringing it to the surface. Just stand perfectly still." He lifts the electrically charged wand to my skin and I cringe.

Nº 10

THE EXAM

I STRAIGHTEN INTO A PLANK, ARMS PINNED AT my sides, because there's nothing I can do but allow the doctor to examine me.

Pulsing pink strands of electricity extend from the rod of the machine, twining themselves around my arms. On contact there's an instant shock, twenty times worse than static electricity, but bearable. My muscles tense and I grind my teeth, desperately trying not to react with sound.

"Just relax. It'll be over faster if you don't fight it." The doctor moves closer.

There's a way I can fight it?

Dr. Shockey doesn't move the wand over me like I expect. Instead, the electric branches crawl, creep, and wrap the length of my arm, searching my skin for any hidden marks, demanding their extraction. Each surge seeps beneath my dermis, igniting every pore with an intense fire. The roiling energy snakes over my shoulder, heading toward my back and neck. The ribbons will systematically consume every inch of my body, and I find that the more area it covers, the more the pink oscillations feed the unbearable fire within.

Trapped, my body begs for a scream, some kind of release. I drop my chin to my chest to stare at the floor to hide my reaction. In a moment I'll lose it, and the doctor will know that it's affecting me.

When I think I can't contain the agony any longer, from the corner of my eye I see my scorpion Animate skitter across the floor. It disappears under my bed, but it's the guard who screams first. "Did you see that?" He points but the doctor ignores him, too wrapped up in the torture session.

The guards scramble, searching the floor, when Hologram Turner's hand reaches out from under the bed and tips over the good doctor's table. It tumbles over and all the delicate tools crash and fracture into a thousand little pieces that roll across the floor.

"What's going on here?" The doctor retreats, trips backward over the mess, and falls awkwardly. To my relief, the electrical wand slips from his grip, plummets to the floor and splits in two, releasing me. At the reprieve of pain, I let out the smallest breath of a moan. The sound is so small, it could be from anyone in the room, but the doctor's head whips to me with evaluating eyes, like he knows.

"There's nothing here." The guards stand and circle the debris. "Must have been a faulty table leg, sir," one says. The doctor shoos them away with an irritated wave of his hand and crawls to the damaged remains.

Now that I'm emancipated I relax on the edge of the bed, appearing indifferent, but the truth is that every part of my body burns. And when the doctor isn't looking, I rub my arm, attempting to soothe the skin.

"You did this," the doctor says, accusing me with his eyes. A limp, broken machine dangles as he cradles it his arms.

"Are you insane? Did you not notice the electric beam I was stuck in?" I throw my hands in the air. "And I don't even know why. You failed to explain that part!"

The doctor approaches and grabs my hand. Before I can pull it away, he pricks my finger with a needle, grabs a vial, and secures the blood sample within the glass tube.

I jump to my feet and glare at him. "What was that?"

"Just finishing my tests, Miss Parrish," he says with a self-satisfied sneer. "And if you are what I believe you are, you won't be able to fake the blood test."

My mouth hangs open with shock but under the circumstances, I respond the best that I can. "I don't know what you think I am, but whatever it is, I hope I can kick your butt!" I scream and push him. He stumbles and the guards leap to his defense, but the doctor only slides a hand over his head of wiry hair and laughs. I recognize that laugh; it's the sound of victory.

"I'll confirm it soon enough." Dr. Shockey backs away on his heels and exits the room, leaving the guards to fumble around, collecting the broken bits and pieces that lay scattered on the floor. Finally they stumble behind him, larger pieces of metal stacked in one's arms while the other carries the open briefcase, the smaller pieces thrown haphazardly inside.

As they exit, Bishop and Sam rush into my bedroom. But I can't stop staring out the door, jaw set, fists clenched at my sides, and ticked off for what I can't hide—the truth. Terease didn't prepare me for everything and that angers me.

"What was that about?" Bishop asks.

"Are you all right?" Sam rubs my shoulder. "Did you see the medical tools they carried out?" She looks worried. "What did you do to them?"

"Wasn't me." I look over my shoulder and Hologram Turner appears in a cloud of hazy electrical dust near the far wall, adjusting his shirt in the reflection of the window.

"Turner?" Sam stiffens.

"Hologram Turner," I correct. "He doesn't know," I whisper.

"Oh." She deflates a little as she walks over to give him a hug.

"What was that for?" Turner holds his arms out in question.

I walk to his side and grab his hand, weaving my fingers tightly with his without thinking. He looks down at our joined hands and back to Bishop and then me. "Sera? What's going on?"

"Do you think you could give us all a few moments?" I ask Turner, smiling and acting as normal as possible.

"Of course. Meet me in the gym later?"

"Prepare to be whipped," I say. He laughs so loud that the huskiness of his voice fills the room. The sound is so warm and rich that it makes my heart ache. Everyone reacts, bodies shrinking just slightly at the voice that represents the full life he used to have.

After his hologram disappears into a cloud of sparkles, I scoop the Animate from the ground, cupping it in my palm, and hold the machine up to Bishop's face.

"How did you do this?" I demand. "And more importantly, why?"

No 11

OLD WOUNDS

"I THOUGHT—I THOUGHT IT WOULD MAKE YOU happy?" Bishop steps back, and I see in his expression that he's questioning his own actions now. He grabs the Animate from my hand and places it on the floor. The arachnid creeps across my foot, dodging away.

"Are you literally trying to rip out my heart?" I rail at him.

"Sera." Sam touches my arm. "You know he didn't do it to hurt you."

"But that doesn't mean it was the right thing to do," I insist. She understands; I can see the teary heartache in her eyes too.

She turns to Bishop. "You should've asked first. You should've known better," she says firmly.

"I thought it would make things better between us, Sera. We aren't together anymore but that doesn't mean that I want to see you so sad. I thought a little piece of him would make you happy. I'm sorry." Bishop's lips press in a flat line as he digs his hands into his pockets.

I've spent the last two weeks consumed with losing Turner, fighting with the burden that he died for me, because no matter how much he loved me, I'm not worthy of that sacrifice. And with Hologram Turner here, I'm just not ready to face his ghost. It's too soon. The hollowness I feel from crying and sadness may never heal.

"How did you do it?" I latch a hand on my hip.

"It was Turner who designed it, actually. I stumbled upon the mechanical drawing of the Animate in his room—after." He drops his gaze to the floor. "The scorpion's body is made from Turner's old dreamdrive. As you know, the crystal carries his dreams, the essence of his soul. He merely invented a new way to incorporate the hologram into an Animate."

My jaw drops. It's as though Turner planned for his death and found a way to never leave me.

"Anyway, I found the mechanical drawings and took them to Professor Raunnebaum. He built the Animate to Turner's specifications for me—for you."

"Oh." I deflate a little as I stand down.

"I suspect Turner meant it for you all along." He rocks

back on his heels and frowns.

"But how will we tell him that his real self is dead?" Sam crosses her arms in a challenge.

"Dead!"

The three of us turn to see Hologram Turner's eyes wide with shock. All of us were so busy fighting that we never noticed his return.

I rush to grab his arm, trying to soothe him as my own heart breaks again, reliving that day in my head. His brow furrows in question, but he quickly reins in his emotions and his face stiffens. "When?" He crosses his arms, muscles hardening beneath his shirt, and my hand falls away.

Bishop steps between us. "Two weeks ago in Gibeon we fought Cece and the Underground. You protected Sera, engaging Cece in a battle. As the battle was happening, Gibeon had an earthquake and began moving through time, causing a large gash to open in the earth. While you were fighting, you and Cece accidentally rolled over the edge. Your bodies were never recovered. I'm sorry, brother."

Turner gauges each of us as though he's testing the truth of Bishop's words from our faces. Sam breaks first and looks away, crying softly. Her willowy body shakes as I reach an arm around her shoulder to pull her close.

"It's true, then?" Turner stiffens and stands taller.

I tighten my lips and nod.

Bishop reaches for him but Turner steps back. And in response, the hologram immediately simmers, zaps, and retreats. He's gone so fast, there's no way we can stop him.

"Turner?" I step from Sam and turn in a circle, looking for him or the Animate and can find neither.

"See?" I turn and yell at Bishop. "This is what I'm talking about!"

"He'll be okay, Sera. He just needs to let the information settle," Bishop offers.

Obviously too upset to hear any more, Sam runs past Bishop, clipping his shoulder, escaping to her room and slams the door.

"That's the most ridiculous thing you've ever said. It's bad enough that it happened, and now he has to deal with it too. And on top of that, we have to tell him about your family!"

Bishop stands frozen, jaw tight, his gaze drilling into my eyes. He's so angry he doesn't speak. Instead of responding, he storms out of the apartment, slamming the front door as he leaves.

I take a deep breath and collect my thoughts because everything is falling apart. My team is falling apart, and I'm not sure if there's any way to put us back together. Not the way we were, at least. I sigh and rub my forehead.

Hearing Sam sobbing in the next room, I knock on her door. When I do, the wailing relents and I peek inside. She lies on her stomach, facedown in a pillow, and when she slowly looks up, puffy skin encircles her red eyes. "How can he be so insensitive?" she asks and sits upright with her legs crossed, hugging a pillow to her chest.

I walk across the room and drop next to her on the bed. "I know that you're right; he didn't mean to hurt us. But still, it's just going to take some time getting used to seeing Turner this way." And knowing that from now on, this is the only way I will ever see him, my chest pangs with heartache.

"Yeah, but the problem is that I could sense Hologram Turner's emotions, Sera. Not quite hear his thoughts like Bishop. He was so scared and heartbroken."

"Can you sense him now?"

"It's all hazy, but I think he's mulling it over, like Bishop said he would."

"Well, I'm sure he needs to get used to the idea as much as we do."

Sam nods. "What did that doctor do to you?"

"He was trying to determine if I was a Chosen or not."

"A Chosen?" She scoots closer.

"Bishop hasn't shared with you yet?" Though they can tap into each other's minds whenever they want with their Protector and Seer connection, he probably wanted to give her the bad news in person.

She shakes her head, so I tell her all about what happened to me in Nocturna, about Perpetua, Terease, the prophecy, the key, the contacts, and the Reapers. When I reach the part about Bishop's family and how they are rapidly aging in Nocturna's fast-forwarded time, her tears begin to fall again, so I remind her that there's a way to set the inhabitants free through fulfilling the prophecy.

"Let me get this straight. You're a Watcher at this moment. You have the gifts of both a Wanderer and a Protector?"

"Yes, according to Terease."

"Considering how you can totally kick butt now, that makes sense." She pauses. "And if you become a Chosen, you will have all three abilities?"

"If I do, and apparently, that's a big fat if. We'll only know for sure after I've been anointed at the Oaths. At that point, if the Masters choose me, I'll make the transition to Chosen."

"Oh." She falls into her pillow.

Her disappointment causes me to backtrack. "I mean, I'm sure it will happen, it has to happen. I'll do whatever I need to do to save everyone." The last thing I want Sam to do is lose hope, so I change the subject by telling her about Dr. Shockey.

"He thinks he knows that I'm a Watcher and will become a Chosen, but at the moment he has no proof. There's a good chance he will, though, when the blood test results come back." I rub my palms down the length of my thighs, trying not to think about what that means because it's one more thing to worry about.

"And we have to find your mom's journal so you can learn more about the prophecy?"

"Yeah, and to do that I need a favor from you." I pull the key on the cord over my neck and hand it to her. "This is supposed to open the Member Archives. Terease said that my mom's journal might be there. Can you investigate a little, find out where the entrance is in the Academy?"

"Of course." She dries her tears. "It's about time you use me for what I'm here for."

"I will from now on. I promise."

"Have you told Bishop everything?"

"Yes, for once."

She rolls her eyes. "Shocking."

"Ha, ha." I give her a playful push.

Relieved that Sam seems to feel better and is on board, I glance at the clock on her nightstand. Not that I can think about school with everything that's going on, but we've already missed our morning class. Any more absences and I might receive another visit from the doctor. "Why don't you go to lunch, and I'll meet you in a bit?"

She nods and wipes her face with her palms.

No

12

TEAMWORK

OF COURSE, BISHOP IS NOWHERE TO BE FOUND when I leave Sam's bedroom. He's either still angry, or off explaining our morning absence to our teachers.

I take a quick shower, pull my hair into a braid, and dress in my school uniform. When I look in the mirror, the truth is that I actually do look sick. My cheeks are gaunt and colorless from either crying, being tortured, or just coming back from the depths of hell. Which option or maybe all, I'm not sure.

So much has happened in a short amount of time, but with all the uncertainty, I'm happy to have a task—anything that will change our lives for the better. I need to deal with finding my mom's journal today. The Oaths are on Saturday, just days away. I may become a Chosen that day and have no clue what that means.

When I leave the apartment my best friend, Macey, sneaks up behind me, then settles into step with me.

"I thought you'd never feel better. Can you believe that Bishop wouldn't let me see you? We had serious words. I may never talk to him again. I think I hate him." She flicks her hair over her shoulder in a dismissive gesture, reminding me how much I've missed her.

I give her a tight smile. "I'm sure he just did it to protect you from my toxic germs." If she only knew what I'd really been up to, she would die. But I can't bring her into my mess. Keeping her in the dark is the best way I can protect her and her team.

"Ick! You still look awful." She steps back. "Maybe you should sleep it off for another day. Seriously, chick, you look like patient zero."

"I feel a little better and I'm tired of my room."

"Suit yourself. Just don't get too close." She holds up her palm.

We stroll down the hall, past groups of students who are sharing all the recent purchases they've made with their new credit cards. Some kids sport new watches, tiny dogs, or the latest phones, but what they don't know is that each shiny new object comes at a steep price—their soul.

We walk into the main arcade, and the lunch bell rings.

All at once everyone makes their way down the stairs and to the floor below. We enter the dining hall. Boxy ceilings reach high and a large fire cracks and pops in the enormous fireplace. The room smells of a divine mix of sweet and spicy, making my stomach grumble, but not with hunger. It feels sick with the unknown.

Sam and Bishop sit at our usual table with Macey's teammates, Quinn and Xavier. Macey and I drop down on the long bench and greet everyone. Bishop looks away when my eyes find his. Instantly, guilt surges through me. Perhaps I was too hard on him earlier. With all that's happened, his entire family being taken away and not knowing how long they'll live, it really wasn't fair for me to be so upset. We're all affected, him just as much, if not more than me.

Determined to make things right, I stand up with a sigh and walk over, then lean close to him so no one can hear our exchange. "I'm sorry. I know you didn't do it to hurt me." In fact, after further thought, though it was a bad idea, I realize his reasoning was extremely selfless considering the circumstances. He's always so generous, never thinking of himself, which makes fighting my love for him that much more difficult.

He spins and faces me, then takes my hand. "No, I'm sorry. I wasn't thinking. It's not right to put Turner through this." He looks down. "Even if it's just Hologram Turner. He seems so— real."

I nod. "Has he come out of hiding yet?" Curious, I look around.

"Not yet. He will when he's ready. This is how he was when we were little." He smiles, looking off in the distance. "Once he became so furious that Mum allowed me to put the star topper on the Christmas tree instead of him that he hid in the attic for two days and wouldn't come out until little Charlotte cried for missing him." A sad smile transforms his face. "He was a good brother. I wish I'd been a better one—to both him and Charlotte. And poor Father, he's taken Turner's death the hardest. They were extremely close. And though you would never know it, we were extremely close before we came here. This world, who we became, ruined us in so many ways."

Without him explaining, I understand what he means. They were close before they met *me*—before I became the crack in their foundation. The realization stings but I put it aside to comfort him.

"First off, you're a great brother. And whatever the prophecy requires, I will do. I'll do anything to save them. I promise."

"I believe in you, Sera. More than you know." He removes a handkerchief from his pocket to dry his eyes.

While I rub his back, I say softly, "Please don't be so hard on yourself."

"I wish it were me, Sera. It should have been me who saved you, and who died."

Appalled, I lean over and wrap an arm around his shoulder, pulling him closer. "No, don't ever say that."

His head falls against my chest, and I hug him and drop a kiss on his messy hair. Clearly we're all still devastated over our new circumstances; all the more reason to accept the little bit of Turner that's survived. Sam relocates nearby and pats Bishop on the arm. The others at the table must realize we're going through something personal, and they give us space, chatting amongst themselves.

"I'll be okay. Let's just deal with this one day at a time." Bishop pulls away. He nods with a ghost of a smile. I settle next to him on the bench as the waitress drops the menus on the table. Scarlett, Atticus, and Agnes join our group as we order lunch.

"Today, I'll do some research on the key relic you gave me," Sam says, speaking normally as though we're investigating a class project. There's no need to alarm our friends.

"Sounds good," I say and take a sip of water.

Bishop places his hand on my arm. "Thanks, Sera."

"For?"

"For finally trusting us."

I nod without responding. Honestly, it doesn't feel right to include them and potentially put them in harm's way, but now that I understand the reason for my feelings, that Watchers do this, instinctively push their teams away, I'll do all that I can to resist the urge.

The lunch group discussion turns to the Oaths.

"I still have no clue what we'll be doing at the Oaths," Macey admits, picking at her blue nail polish.

Bishop waves us close and we lean in. "There's not much literature on the actual ceremony, the Society keeps that part very secret. Of course, what we do know is that it takes place in the Grand Lodge in Gibeon and that we'll be anointed. But," he says confidentially, "I've heard whisperings of sacrifices."

I kick him under the table. What is he doing?

"Sacrifices?" Macey's eyes widen.

"Yes."

Scarlett nudges Atticus. "Pay attention. This is important." Atticus looks up from his new phone and pulls out his ear buds with a disinterested sigh.

Everyone huddles closer.

Macey leans closer. "Who or what is sacrificed?"

"Wanderers."

I grab Bishop's leg and squeeze. We're heading into dangerous territory. The Society threatened Mona just for telling me this very information.

"What? That's insane. They would never do that," Atticus challenges.

"No, quite true. The students who decide not to take the Oaths."

Bishop keeps talking and I can't stop him; I realize what he's doing, and he's right. We should all be running around warning everyone of the truth. I've seen the repercussions for myself in Nocturna with Perpetua and Stu. When he finishes, our group naturally separates into teams, each having their own individual discussions. A moment later Macey jumps from the table, seeking another group to relay the information to.

I pull Bishop aside. "Are you sure this is the best way to warn everyone?"

"I didn't plan on it, but if someone is planning on rejecting the Oaths, they may think twice about it. And we can save them from Nocturna for now."

I nod. My gaze follows Macey and her bouncing dark curls as she slowly and systematically pollinates the room with gossip. With her disseminating the news, everyone will know by Saturday.

Our food arrives and though I'm starved, I only pick at it, nibbling here and there. My stomach clenches with the realization that I'm in a position to save every Wanderer here from the awful life that the Society's created for them. I can free them from the lies, the mind control, the theft of our dreams and being blackmailed with them. I can give them the freedom to choose whom they love, and to choose a life other than what the Society dictates for them. I can prevent them from being forced to sacrifice their children. Yes, the first step has been taken, but it's up to me to set everyone free, completely and irrevocably.

The bell rings and all the students migrate to their next class. I lag behind Sam and Bishop, deep in thought and scheming. It's ridiculous to go to class today. I can't keep up this charade any longer.

Sam looks over her shoulder as she whispers in Bishop's ear. They stop and wait for me to join them.

"What?" Sam's blue eyes assess me.

"I have a plan."

"Of course you do." She folds her arms.

"I can't wait around, going to class and pretending everything's okay. I need to do all I can now!" I gesture wildly, overcome with frustration.

"Sera!" Bishop hisses through clenched teeth. "Not so loud." His jaw tightens and he slides in front of me, blocking one of the E.Y.E.S., the school security cameras that watch almost every move we make.

"Listen up, here's the plan: Bishop's going to skip Animate Anatomy and research the prophecy. Sam and I are going to find the Member Archives." I point my finger at each of them in turn with authority.

I don't allow either to respond; this is how it has to be. Divide and conquer.

"We'll meet up later and fill each other in on what we've found," I say to Bishop. Then I grab Sam's arm and shuffle her down the hall to our apartment.

Nº
13

SEEING MORE

WHEN WE REACH OUR APARTMENT, I STRIDE into Sam's bedroom and she follows, locking the door behind us.

"I want you to teach me how to see the life path of a relic." I plop down on the floor, legs crossed.

She regards me for a moment, pursing her lips as though considering if it's plausible. "Okay. We'll try." She shrugs. "I guess it can't hurt."

She removes the archive key from the cord on her neck and places it on the ground in front of us, and then she settles on the floor facing me, folding her long, graceful legs to one side. This is her typical meditation stance: body poised, shoulders back, chest out, neck elongated, and chin lifted. She closes her eyes and speaks. "First, find your most comfortable position. It should be the spot that you could sit in for hours without readjusting."

I think about it for a moment and instead of sitting, I lie down, flat on my back, arms relaxed at my side. "Okay."

"Now, do everything that I say, starting with clearing your mind of any chatter." She pauses.

"You must relax every muscle in your body, and as I say each body part, release the tension that resides there." She pauses between each item on the list, pronouncing each one in a slow, soothing manner. "Jaw—shoulders—chest—arms—stomach—knees—feet. Allow all the weight of your body to sink into the floor. Sinking, sinking, heavier and heavier. Press all that tense energy through your body and out through your toes, squeezing every bit out until you're completely relaxed."

She pauses, then says, "Now, slow your breath, inhaling and exhaling quietly."

I do as she asks.

"That's right, softer and softer with so little movement that your shallow breath settles on the bridge of your nose."

She allows me to work through her suggestions, and when my breath turns so shallow that my lungs barely move, an unexpected twinkling spark of warmth settles between my eyes.

"You've got it. Now, allow the heat to grow, pulsing larger until you can hold one focused image."

With a flash, an image emerges from the haze of speckled fog. I push into the image, stretching it, searching to define the edges and lines, building it up from a sketch to a completed drawing. But as hard as I try, it remains fuzzy and indistinguishable.

"Focus on the warmth radiating from the vision, allowing it to gently glide toward you."

My brow furrows as I try to focus, but instead of clarity, the image flattens, discolors, and slides out of my field of mental vision. I've lost it. It's slipped away, and now I'm painfully aware that I've failed.

"I can't, it's gone." I squeeze my eyes tighter, coaxing the image's return.

"Relax and open your eyes."

My eyelids flutter open and I gasp, a sharp breath hitching in the back of my throat. Above my face, midair, hovers the key to the Member Archives. As soon as I understand that I'm controlling it, the brilliant light illuminating the key fades, and the relic drops to my face with a *thunk*, slides over my cheek, and tumbles to the floor.

I turn to Sam with wide eyes.

"It's true," she whispers. "You really won't need Bishop and me soon."

"What do you mean?" I sit up and frown at her. "I'll always need you."

"It won't be the same," Sam says sadly. "I can feel it now. The connection, it's not the same, not as strong."

"It's not certain. What I just did was nothing. I haven't been anointed yet. This could be as far as I ever develop. We won't know for sure until Saturday."

"You may not know, but I already do."

I grab her hand and glare at her fiercely. "You'll always be my sister. Always."

She forces a wan smile. We've been crying so much today, these last few weeks really, that I don't think either of us could force another tear, but to my surprise, her eyes glass over and she sniffles.

"Your turn." I snatch the key from the floor, returning it to her.

She reaches for a tissue, taking a moment to compose herself.

"Let's try something a little different," she says. "Sit here and face me, legs crossed." I do as she requests as she lays the key on the floor between us.

"Not sure if this is gonna work." She reaches her hands out to mine. Our fingers clasp, locking, forming a circle with our arms.

She relaxes into her graceful pose. I attempt to mimic her, but give up and settle in a hunched position.

"Now, let's follow the same routine from before."

"Okay."

I recall Sam's earlier instructions in my mind with my

perfect Wandering memory and follow each step systematically. I relax at the same time Sam relaxes, and our arms hang limp. No motion, just focus. Though my body's shutting down, there's a strange sensation between us. Like it did before, energy and warmth blooms between my eyes, but this time the energy travels with a sense of mission, follows the curve of my cheek, slides down my neck, and oozes into my arms, rushing like hot lava to my fingers. It collides with Sam's energy and a blast of light behind my closed eyes opens the door to the life path of the Member Archives key relic.

Images quickly flash, reeling by like the pictures presented by the relicutionist. In my mind, I sense that this is unusual and everything should be playing out quickly, yes, but at a reasonable pace so that I can make sense of it. One image that sticks in my mind is Terease stealing the key from the Academy office, only a day before she was arrested.

The flipping images grind to a halt and then play smoothly like a movie. To me, this view is real. Amazingly, I'm seeing like a Seer.

In this vision, the hand that reaches out to the door and inserts the key in the lock might as well be my own. Of course it's not because I sense that this hand belongs to a man. The shirt cuff winds in ruffles around the arm, and I deduce that this arm belongs to Gabe Garcia, the Academy's activities director.

When the lock clicks and the door creaks open, the point of view switches and I'm floating out of the body, looking down at Gabe with a bird's-eye view. I remember the outfit he's wearing from several weeks ago, and knowing Gabe, he would never be caught wearing the same outfit twice.

Gabe steps into the room, turns on a switch, and a buzz accompanies the illumination of the room. It's the size of a square walk-in closet, lined with a metal coat of steel ribbons, rivets, and rusted mesh.

Gabe shuts the door behind him and turns his attention to a panel on the wall. It's a typical Wandering apparatus, upcycled with various metal machines from the early twentieth century.

He cranks several dials like a combination to a locker. At each click a number appears on the panel's screen until the red digital combination reads 111896. Next to it, a second number appears: 30. This number immediately begins to count down. Something's going to happen in thirty seconds, and honestly, even though I'm merely watching this like a warped movie, I'm scared at what that something might be.

No

14

THE VISION

AS THE SECONDS COUNT DOWN, GABE UNFOLDS a seat mounted to the wall, sits, and drags a seatbelt around his lap, clicking it securely around his waist. But it seems that isn't enough because he unwinds a harness for his chest and buckles himself into place. His hands reach down by his thighs, where handles protrude from either side of the seat, and he clutches them so tightly his knuckles turn white.

What is he bracing for?

Anxious, I quickly scan the room. If I had a body I might be screaming and banging on the walls, trying to escape.

The numbers on the digital countdown reach ten, and the

caged room trembles and bounces. Fiery streaks of electricity race along the longitude and latitude of the steel ribbons, crisscrossing every wall.

Five.

Four.

Three.

Two.

One.

The box free-falls like an amusement park ride and I disconnect from my sense of the floor, fly upward through the ceiling, catapulting away from the scene, losing my stomach. For a brief moment, I have an outside view of the box dropping through the air below me. Shimmering sparks zap and pop, circling around the outside of the compartment and dragging me along with its light-speed decent. Then, like a rubber band tethered to the key relic, I snap back inside the room and everything slams violently to the ground, coming to a halt.

Even with no body, in this vision my heart races, and I still have a sense of tension melting away from my muscles.

Gabe removes his harness and belt, flips the seat upright, and steps through the door. Unwillingly, I follow, leaving the elevator. Though I'm not sure if I can call it that, maybe a transporter?

The new space is dark. Dirt crunches beneath his shoes on wood planks. It's cool here, smelling of cedar and earth. He walks through a passageway and enters a large room. A makeshift string of lanterns shines weak dots on the walls, revealing a cavern, high-reaching and twisted with dusky hollows and jagged columns of natural rock formations. We pass over a wooden bridge spanning a pond of peacock-blue-colored water.

Reading his actions and the ease with which he moves, I understand that he's been here before, many times. We continue weaving around stalactites and stalagmites, and finally the environment changes to, of all things, brick.

This section is easier to label. It's a very old train station. Exquisite brick patterns and barrel-vaulted ceilings whisper of another time period. Possibly Victorian. But it's what's beyond this room that is the most interesting part, and most likely the reason he is here—the Member Archives.

And though I've never questioned what they are, I instantly understand in seeing them, because I've seen something similar before, in the attic of the Academy last summer when I snuck out to visit Bishop in London. But this—this is nothing like that, in size at least. The attic of belongings I saw before is like a tiny cell of a much larger body. Perhaps a staging area before belongings move to their real home—here.

This area is open, possibly larger than the Relic Archives, which I estimate to be a football field in length. Iron fencing wraps in the largest labyrinth I have ever seen. Corridors and crossways disappear in right turns and curves. But it's what lines this maze that interests me most. Storage pens, each labeled with a framed number.

Gabe doesn't waste any time. He's looking for something specific, and it takes him thirty minutes of navigating the field of belongings before he reaches his destination. When he arrives, the label on the door matches the number he set in the control panel of the transporter that we arrived in: 111896. That number looks familiar, so I stare at it, breaking it down into smaller parts. It's my birthday, November 18, 1996, or 11-18-96.

Gabe unlocks the new door and when the gate swings open, he steps into the storage pen. Relics from my entire life line the walls in neat, tidy compartments. Clothes, everything from those for an infant to my current size, hang on another wall. My favorite long-lost toys, schoolbooks, childhood drawings, shoes, and personal knickknacks occupy every space.

Gabe walks to the wall of shelving and retrieves a purple suitcase. Stickers cover the surface, each representing one of the many places I lived with my dad, Ray. This is the bag I lost at the airport on the day I moved to Chicago, before I ever found out I was a Wanderer, before I moved to the Academy. Now I understand—the airline didn't lose it like I originally thought. The Society stole it.

A pink stuffed rabbit sits nearby. I remember dragging "Bunny" at my side as a toddler, never sleeping without it. This and many of the other items here were supposedly burned in a house fire when I was very young. Images of my home emptied and burned to the ground immediately consume my thoughts. The Society burned my home and took everything from my dad and me.

The list of reasons to despise the Society just keeps growing, and my anger rises along with my temperature. Watching Gabe here sends my mind racing to piece everything together. Gabe appears to be in charge of this space. He's in charge of making relics. He makes new relics for every student, every single year, by changing out their wardrobe. What I thought was just a bribe of lavish new clothes and an endless supply of material gifts is really much more sinister than that. The Society continually creates a safeguard of objects to watch and inspect our every single move—to keep us in line, to record and catalog our entire lives through relics.

Hate. It rumbles from my Seeing consciousness in heated swirls.

Gabe rolls the purple suitcase to a clear spot on the floor, drops it on its back, and kneels down. He unzips the top and flips it open. On top, just as I left it for easy access, sits my winter coat. Bishop's photo, the one that Turner sent to me, is tucked inside the front pocket, along with my old cell phone.

But what worries me more is what happens next. Gabe shuffles through the clothes, looking for something in particular. When he finds the item, his eyes light up with the kind of happiness that makes me sick to my stomach.

№ 15

A HOLOGRAM

From the suitcase, Gabe removes a framed photo of my mom and me at Easter when I was just a baby. He holds it up and smiles.

I want to reach for the photo and hide it away, so he can't use it for whatever the Society is planning, but here in this state of Seeing consciousness and no body, that's impossible.

In my mind someone whispers, "It's time to go. Wake up."

The voice pulls me, tugs at me, dragging me out of the vision even though I don't want to leave, and the image of Gabe returning the suitcase to its original position slips away, fading to dark red. I'm looking at the inside of my eyelids, becoming aware of my true reality, that I was only seeing the life path of the Member Archives key. Everything that I watched happened several weeks ago.

"Sera." Sam shakes my arm. "Open your eyes."

When I do, she looks worried. It takes a moment to orient myself, to allow the life path of the key and all the new images to rush over me, settling into an understandable state.

"Did you see everything too?" I look to Sam with wide eyes.

"Yeah. Did you know about that place, what they kept there? I'm assuming that all those belongings are yours, right?"

"Yes, they're mine." I allow the memories to wash over me again and have to close my eyes for a second to push away the anger. Then I open them again and shake my head. "And no, not in my wildest dreams would I have imagined that the Society tracked us like that."

"Why do you think Gabe wanted the photo of you and your mom?" She plays with her braid, looking as concerned as I feel.

"I don't know, but it can't be good." I pause in thought. "Can we go back and see more?" I pick up the key, ready for round two.

"Yes, but we should wait." She takes it from me and laces it back onto the cord as she talks. "We were under for a long time. It's not safe to stay away from our bodies for extended periods for a relic. Especially for you, you're too new, and we should go and find it for ourselves. We need to find your mom's storage unit, that's where her journal will be." She loops the necklace around her neck. The key dangles at the end, settling on her chest.

"You're right." I lift myself from the floor and offer Sam my hand.

"And we should meet Bishop to see if he's uncovered any-thing about the prophecy." She reaches to clasp my grip, and I tug her from the floor.

"There's one thing I have to do first." I blow a flyaway strand of hair from my face and lock my hands on my hips. "I'll meet you in an hour, okay?"

"Sounds good." Sam nods.

.

The door to the training room slides open, but the lights don't pop on. I walk to the center of the room and drop to the floor, draw my legs near my chest, and rest my chin on my knees. I'm exhausted from our Seer session, and glad Sam pulled me out of the meditation.

I promised to meet Turner here to spar, though I'm not sure if he will show. But as if he's been waiting for me, it doesn't take long before he speaks, appearing from within a twinkling haze of electricity.

"The last thing I remember is setting up Gabe's party, the Underground attack, being in the hospital, and that night, here with you, when you told me to find someone else to love," Hologram Turner says.

I look up and into the mirrors that line the walls, and his reflection sparks in blue hues as he paces. Dark locks of hair fall forward, hiding his chiseled face as he looks at the floor.

"You died after Gabe's party. You didn't sleep again that night, so your last dreamdrive memories are from the days before." I watch for his reaction, then I sigh out loud. Since it happened, I've forced myself to only remember the good parts of our last day together—specifically finally understanding his motives, the way he held me, and the way we kissed.

Hologram Turner places a hand on my shoulder. I grab it and twine my fingers with his, pressing his skin against my cheek. Even though he's a projected image, his hand is still warm, his skin thick and rough, exactly like the real Turner.

I give his arm a tug, and he relents and drops to the ground, settling close, too close. His slate-colored gaze cuts through me. "Has something changed between us?" He corrects himself. "Did something change—before?"

Of course he senses the shift in my feelings. How could he not with the way I'm acting? After his death, I promised myself that if I ever had the opportunity to look into his eyes again, I wouldn't look away, pretending that there was nothing between us. But this is different; though my heart still yearns for him, I have to remind myself that he's only a hologram, not truly real. I take a deep breath, unsure how to act or what to share. How do I tell him that I know about Bishop cheating him out of his role as my Protector, and about how we probably belonged together all this time? His months of torment, neglect, and hurt were for nothing.

My voice shakes before I decide how to answer but I panic. "No, everything's the same," I mumble, lying to protect him. To profess my love would only hurt him more. Besides, we're a lost chance that can never be resolved. He's only a hologram, and I'm a Wanderer.

His hopeful look diminishes. "Still lying to yourself, huh?" He pulls away and laughs.

I can't help but smile. He knows me too well.

Turner leans in, moving close, speaking in low, raspy tones. "I don't regret dying to save you because I would happily do it again." He coils a strand of my hair around his finger, and then presses his lips near the sensitive skin of my ear as the heat of his breath teases. "But I do regret never kissing you."

At his confession, my face turns hot and I know it must be red. The real Turner never slept the night of the gala before he died, never had a chance to download that day's events into his dreamdrive for storage, so his hologram never experienced our kiss that night. If he only knew; if I could only show him, and tell him everything.

The thought of the steamy kiss causes my body to stiffen and I jump to my feet to keep our distance. Now that I've had time to absorb everything, I've been able to put this situation into perspective. I can't let my heart be crushed again—and by a hologram, no less. There's no future for us. He's an illusion, merely a glimmer of the real thing.

I walk to the weapons rack and glide a finger over the head of an ax, tracing the shape. "Fight me?" I ask, wanting to return to what's familiar and comfortable between us.

His hand covers mine faster than I can turn to him. The length of his body presses against my back. "I'd prefer not to." He pulls my fingers away from the weapon, guiding me to the center of the dark room.

"Close your eyes." He gently slides a palm over my face, covering my eyelids.

"Okay." I squirm.

He leaves for several moments, and I hear him tinkering with something, though I don't know what.

Turner walks back to me and warns, "Keep 'em closed." I giggle out of nervousness. He grabs one of my hands and places it on his shoulder; the other he laces with one of his own. His free hand slides to my waist, pulling me close, causing a current of energy to run between us as we begin to sway.

"The thing is," he starts, voice heavy, "I'm not sure if I ever had the opportunity to dance with you at the gala. So I thought we could do that now, instead of fighting, that is."

When I open my eyes, we're standing in the same exquisite ballroom he designed for Gabe's gala. Hologram machines mounted around the room project the new holographic image, veiling the training room. Bright gold leaf carvings and paintings cover every surface. Rows and rows of columns and arcades run along a first and second floor. Red-and-white-striped curtains drape every wall, mimicking a circus tent. Beautiful holographic animals walk around: strutting peacocks, roaring lions, and graceful giraffes. In the corner sits a string quartet of women and men dressed as half human, half circus beast, performing the most romantic string music I've ever heard, so lovely it makes the small hairs on the back of my neck rise to attention.

Hologram Turner twirls me, and I realize that I too have been transformed. A creamy lace ball gown billows around me. The fabric flirts with his legs and ankles, wrapping around them as we dance. Even Rhett Butler would have a hard time competing with him in his black cutaway tuxedo and his hair slicked back into a low ponytail.

He smiles and it's so devastatingly beautiful that I melt in his arms, but he holds me up, strong and firm, just the way a great dancing partner should as he spins me around for several songs. We laugh and smile in this fake beautiful world. If only it were real; if only he were real and my life were this lovely, this perfect. This is what I dream of.

"You never told me what you thought about my design work." He looks around the projected ballroom and then back into my eyes, eager for my opinion.

"You know it's amazing."

"The hologram design, it was always for you."

I drop my gaze. "Do you think you'll ever stop flirting with me?" I look up from under my lashes.

In response, he quickly twirls me and pulls me to his chest, breaking our dancing form. "Apparently not even death can stop me." He smirks, steps away, and bows at the end of the song. Leaning over briefly, he kisses my hand at the knuckles. His soft lips linger there, brushing back and forth against my bare skin, warming just that spot with electricity, with love.

He stands, lifting my hand to his cheek and drops another kiss on my palm before starting to dance again. And in this moment I understand, Turner will always find a way to me. He prepared for it by designing the strange little scorpion hologram machine, which scrabbles across the floor behind us to a new position. Dead or alive, there will be no keeping us apart. It's impossible, and that makes me incredibly happy and sad all at once, because there can never truly be something between us.

Someone clears their throat nearby. I look over to see Bishop, eyes downcast as he kicks at the ground with one foot.

"Sorry to interrupt," he says without meeting my eyes. But it's easy to see from his expression that he's not. Knowing that he's witnessed this intimate and special connection between his brother and me—even though his brother is now only a hologram—I feel ashamed. And more than a little sad myself.

No
16

GABE'S GLAMOUR PALACE

"HEY," I SAY TO BISHOP AS I PULL AWAY FROM our dance. The ballroom fades, returning to the training room. Hologram Turner hesitates for a moment, looking between Bishop and me before dissipating into sparkling electrical dust. The scorpion Animate crawls across the floor and onto the top of my boot, then rests there.

"Sorry. I guess you and he haven't talked yet, huh?"

"No, but I will make an effort later. Does he know about—"

"No." I cut him off, a little unsure if Hologram Turner can hear us in the Animate state or only as a hologram. I haven't gotten that far with him yet, to tell him that his family has been exiled to Nocturna and that Bishop and I have broken up. "For right now, it's better if he doesn't know, I think. It's too much," I add.

"Perhaps you're right." Bishop averts his eyes and shifts from foot to foot.

"Let's find Sam and see what she's found." I pick up the scorpion Animate from my shoe. The machine turns in my hand several times before I tuck him gently into my pocket.

"I believe she's in the attic." Bishop squeezes his eyes shut for a second, the way he does when he's trying to locate her with their mental connection.

"Did you find any info about the prophecy?" I ask as we walk.

"None. The Society has most certainly wiped history free of anything related, or has hidden it elsewhere."

"Probably."

We hike back through the gym, down the dark tunnel, and into the underground city of Olde Town, which sits directly beneath the Academy's courtyard. A life-size puppet show is in progress across the plaza. Gabe sits at the top of the small, intricately-designed theater, acting as puppet master, pulling the strings of a real-life marionette. A petite ballet dancer in blush pink hangs on strings, spinning and stumbling at his bidding. To the students gathered and watching, this visual is truer than they will probably ever understand, and the irony of this fuels the hatred inside me. I will not let the Society define me; I will not be their puppet.

The enclosed walls of the Victorian city buildings reverberate with the chords of a piano, which serves as musical accompaniment for the show. Students laugh and cheer for each slapstick joke as we make our way to the Lion's Gate bridge.

After all this time, the lion Animates still stand at attention when I cross the bridge—nothing has changed there. But today they're a little more irritable than usual. Both snarl and retract as though they're ready to attack me. Maybe they've sensed my slipping loyalties to the Society, or perhaps they always knew this day would come with their Animate intuition.

Quickly, we load into the caged elevator and ride it to the top floor, the attic. Sam meets us as we exit, but this is a different part of the attic than I visited several weeks ago. Instead of a lopsided and unfinished dusty room, this area is finished off with elegant architectural details.

"Act normal and follow my lead," Sam whispers as an E.Y.E.S. security camera turns in our direction, surveying our moves.

"Glad you guys finally arrived," she says normally.

Though the E.Y.E.S. can't hear our conversation, I understand that Sam's acting for the cameras. She's trying to appear normal as a way to secretly find the transporter we saw in our vision, which will lead to the Member Archives.

"Come on." She beckons with a wave of her hand.

We follow down the hall lined with tiny arched windows.

Each looks out onto the obelisk in the courtyard. Outside, the wind blows through leafless branches, a dark and gray Chicago day. Normal life passes by in yellow taxis and pedestrians bundled up, walking home from work. They don't know how lucky they are to be Normals, to go home to their normal families, and to have normal problems. My new life, though incredible from the outside, makes me look back at my lonely life with Ray and think it extraordinary for its utter simplicity.

We reach the end of the hall, ending at a pair of ornately carved doors. Sam reaches up and grabs the brass knocker, letting it drop loudly three times.

"Gabe," she hollers. She reaches for the doorknob and twists but it's locked. Obviously, Gabe's not here; he's in Olde Town performing the marionette show for the students. And I wonder again with anger what he's done with my mother's photo.

Bishop moves around her. "Gabe." He knocks again, continuing the show. He twists at the handle, surreptitiously breaking it with his Protector strength and pushes in as though we've been invited.

Sam and I file behind, hiding what he's done. We shut the door but it won't latch, so Bishop drags over a small chair to hold the door closed.

I take a deep breath and look around, nervous about being here. If we're caught, how would we explain ourselves? What would our punishment be?

Gabe's apartment is an explosion of color and textures that I can only liken to a Las Vegas or Broadway show dressing room. Feather boas and sequined outfits hang over furniture. Everywhere. Shelves containing rows of colorful wigs sitting on busts line one wall, and on another, there's a display of shoes, both men's and women's, neatly arranged for optimal display on glass shelving. Yes, there are the normal elements of an apartment: a kitchen, bath, and bedroom, but Gabe has made his home into more of an extravagant dressing area rather than a living space.

"I think the Member Archives door is behind the dresser." I point to the lavish art deco dressing table sitting against the wall. A large round mirror reflects the three of us, staring at it.

"I sensed the same from the vision," Sam concurs.

"The same?" Bishop looks between us.

"Long story." I wave him off. I haven't had the chance to tell him all the fun news of how I'm slowly coming into my Seeing abilities, like Terease suggested. And I'm sure Sam isn't looking forward to that conversation with him either.

"Um, okay." He looks at Sam and they lock gazes for a few moments. I roll my eyes, knowing they're talking mentally with each other. Thankfully, I can't hear him myself—yet. Bishop grimaces and looks back at me with a frown.

Avoiding the awkward conversation to come, I step forward and peek behind the mirror. "It's attached to the wall. There must be a hidden trigger to open it."

I immediately scour every inch of the room, looking for that super special item that might open the secret door. In a movie it would be a novel on a bookcase, tipped forward, unlocking a secret passageway, but here there are no bookshelves, only an overabundance of Gabe-fabulous glamour.

Sam sits at the dressing table, systematically moving the items resting there: a brush, a comb, makeup, and two small lamps, but nothing works. Nothing sets off a trigger to open a secret door.

"I'll meditate on this to see the life path." She holds up a perfume bottle. "Maybe it will reveal the door."

At my nod of encouragement, she settles back into the chair, cupping the bottle in her palms. Falling easily into a meditative state, her body relaxes and the bottle hovers above her hands. Light illuminates the crystal exterior, shooting bright prisms around the room, but it isn't long before she emerges, eyes wide and alert. She places the relic on the dressing table's surface and says one word, "Marilyn."

"What Marilyn?" I ask.

"*The* Marilyn." She points to a framed black-and-white photo hanging on the wall. Platinum-blonde Marilyn Monroe kisses Gabe's cheek at a dinner party. Both are dressed to the nines in gorgeous attire from the 1950s as balloons and confetti flutter around them.

I stand before it, taking the image in. Oh, how lucky Wanderers are; if only we could play nice all the time. I grab the frame and begin to pull it off the wall, but of course it doesn't budge. I try to turn it, to open it like a medicine cabinet, but nothing happens.

"It's this, it has to be." Sam stands.

"Let me try." Bishop pushes past us and places his hands at the edges of the gold frame and pushes. It sinks into the wall, activating a series of cranking noises, which immediately make me think that the room is rigged with booby traps, Indiana Jones style, and we should run. But while I'm waiting for arrows to skewer us, the only thing that happens, thankfully, is that the dressing table pivots slightly away from the wall, revealing an opening.

As we step forward to inspect the opening, the elevator door in the hallway outside clanks open and shut. Collectively, we look at each other, eyes wide in horror. Someone is on this floor. Footsteps walk this way, becoming louder as they close in on our location.

"Hurry." Bishop ushers Sam and me through the secret door and into a dimly lit corridor. He shuts the dressing table behind us, and a lock clicks shut.

"My stars! What's happened here?" The words are muffled, but I can still make out Gabe's voice and anticipate his actions as he pushes through his broken front door.

We're not safe. He may check the secret passageway. I visually sweep the hallways that lead in many directions and the walls, looking for E.Y.E.S. Thankfully there are none.

I nudge Sam and Bishop, who have ears pressed to the wall, listening. I jerk my head twice, signaling quietly that we must leave. They nod and follow me around the corner. Just in time, each of us presses back against the wall as the trigger activates. Above us, a grouping of pulleys and levers crank and grind, and then I hear the door to the passageway creak open.

I imagine Gabe popping his butter-colored curls through the secret door, peeking inside. I hold one finger to my lips and look back at Bishop and Sam.

Gabe steps into the hidden hallway and shuts the door behind him. His footsteps slide over the many years of dust and dirt and then he walks quickly in the opposite direction, away from where we're hidden. I peek my head around the corner only to see him disappear, descending a set of stairs.

We creep back to one of two transporter doors, which are directly across from Gabe's apartment.

"Do you know where the passageway leads?" Sam whispers, pointing after Gabe.

"No," I whisper back. "But considering all the secrets that the Society has, this one doesn't surprise me. There's probably a huge network of hidden passageways. They could lead anywhere."

Sam removes the cord from around her neck and slips the key in the transporter's door lock. It opens easily, revealing the same room we saw in our vision. We quickly step inside, shutting the door behind us. I eye the dials on the wall, and then look over my shoulder. "You guys should strap in."

Bishop and Sam glance around and pull down seats mounted to the wall, then strap themselves in with both a waist belt and chest harness as I set the dials to my mom's birthday.

"How do you know what numbers to pick?" Sam asks as the machine starts to count down.

"The numbers Gabe used to find my storage unit make up my birthday. So if I choose my mom's birthday, I hope it will lead me to her unit."

With the digital clock set, I jump into my own seat and quickly strap in. By the time I'm secure, the room jumps, buzzes, and rumbles with electricity.

As the red digital numbers count down, the box jolts erratically. Blue electrical currents flutter and pop, igniting a wild display of magical energy.

Five.

Four.

Three.

Two.

One.

The box drops in a free fall, and now that I have a real body, my stomach immediately races up through my chest, throat, head, and presses into the top of my skull. If this afternoon's lunch doesn't make a reappearance, it will be a miracle.

I look down to the floor and see that it's an open mesh grate, which explains the wind rushing up past our faces. It blows my hair away and rushes into my eyes, making them water. There's nothing below, only blackness for which I'm thankful, because if I were to have some real perception of how far and fast we're really falling, I may pass out.

Bishop's complexion turns green, and Sam's eyes roll back into her head. Stiff with fright, both grasp the handlebars at their sides, gripping them for dear life. When I think we can't take any more, the box grinds to a sudden and jerky halt, landing with a resounding thump. With the air knocked out of me, I allow my heart rate to decelerate, muscles relax, and take comfort in the stable ground.

"Whose idea was this, anyway?" I ask to lighten the mood.

"I know you hated every minute," Sam chirps and shrugs out of her harness.

"No, I think we should do it again," Bishop says sarcastically with a smirk.

"I think we will, maybe on the way back," I remind them.

"Blast, I forgot about that." He cringes and drops his head between his knees, breathing heavily. When he stands back up, I pat him on the back as we step out the door and into a space much different than I anticipated.

"Um, Sera?" Sam looks at me in question.

"I just assumed we'd travel to the same place, but that's stupid, I guess. We did just travel in a transporter." I look back at the box. "I suppose we could be anywhere right now." Underground in the Antarctic, on another planet, or in an alternate universe.

"Well, what we're looking for must be here, so we should get going," Bishop says as he climbs out of the transporter.

No
17

THE MEMBER
ARCHIVES

THIS SPACE IS NOT LIKE THE OTHER; IT'S NOT
A cavern with beautiful earthly formations or a long-lost
train station. It's a jail. A real one with sturdy iron cell doors,
but old, dark, wet, scary, and abandoned.

Each cell serves as a storage unit for a Wanderer. They
must not be as important here because items are stored open
to the elements. Water seeps in through the faulty structure
and puddles at our feet. A chilled breeze rushes by, and I shiver in my school cardigan.

"Doesn't look like anyone comes here." Sam finds a lantern and lights it.

"If I had to guess, these storage archives belong to the outlawed and the dead—like my mom." I turn to them with a grim look.

"She's not an outlaw to the other side," Sam offers helpfully.

I nod, still a little sad that her belongings would be treated any different from my own, as if they're somehow not as important.

"Let's start there." Bishop waves his hand to the nearest cell.

"These aren't labeled as well as the others." I look for some sense of whom the cell belongs to, but there's no nice framed number here.

Sam bends down and squints. "Here, look close. Numbers are scratched into the lock panel."

We separate, checking each cell one by one, one floor at a time, but it's the third floor and feels like a million cells later before we find the correct one.

"It's here!"

Bishop and Sam run to my side.

"But it's locked."

Bishop squeezes his face between the bars, peeking inside. "And empty."

"What?" I follow Bishop's lead, sticking my cheeks between the bars, visually searching the room for anything at all.

"It's hard to see, but it does look empty," Sam agrees,

holding the lantern up to illuminate the darkened cell. All we can make out are three stone walls, a ratty old bunk attached to one of them.

"We need a flashlight, why didn't we think to bring one?" I shake my head in disgust at our lack of foresight.

"Or a lock pick for that matter," Bishop adds.

Sam lets out a little huff. "Now what?"

"Wait!" Giddy with sudden inspiration, I remove the scorpion Animate from my pocket and place him on the ground. "Turner, we need your help."

The machine crawls a short distance away, stops and turns, and shoots a beam of light from its crystal face. Hologram Turner appears in an electrified dust storm.

"You rang, my lady," Hologram Turner drawls with a smirk as his body coalesces into hologram reality.

"Do you think you could go inside and see if there are any relics?" I gesture toward the locked cell.

"Where are we?" He looks around.

"I promise, I'll fill you in when we return."

He crosses his arms and tightens his features, the way he does when he's protesting, and says nothing.

Dipping my head in a gesture of sincerity, I give him a piercing look, then grit out, "I promise."

Hologram Turner looks us over, his gaze barely skimming Bishop, but finally relents. He steps through the bars. Since he's a hologram made of light, he can walk directly through anything.

"Good idea." Bishop joins my side. We watch him check every nook and crevice.

"Not looking good in here." Hologram Turner kicks over a piece of wood, then sticks his hand in a crack in the wall. "Nothing here either." He looks up. "And the roof is missing." He holds out his hands, palms up, catching the spitting rain. Lightning cracks above. "Storm's coming."

"Great, we came all this way for nothing. Terease told me it would be here."

Hologram Turner kneels on the floor to sweep the area below the bunk. "Wait. Found something." He reaches under the bed and slides out a wooden box.

My heart leaps in my chest. This is it; it must be. He lifts the box as he stands, brings it forward, and slides it sideways, passing the box between the bars.

"Thank you." I smile, catching his blue-gray gaze with mine.

"You're welcome. And I'll expect answers soon." He steps back through the bars, then disintegrates into thin air.

Sam crouches down and the scorpion Animate crawls across the floor and into her palm. She sets him on her shoulder, and he perches there, tail poised and curled.

Placing the box on my raised knee, I lift the lid. Inside, within a nest of weathered crushed velvet, sits a leather journal. I remove it and hand the box to Bishop, who places it aside.

On the cover is an infinity symbol that has been burned

into the leather, and I run my fingers over it before flipping the book open. "The end is at the beginning," reads the words inscribed on the first page.

Sam leans closer with the lantern as I flip to the next page. Loose pencil lines, dark smudges, and cross-hatchings reach across the paper, forming a drawing of a desert. The scene is familiar because I've seen it before—twice, though never in a drawing or photograph. Once was in a dream, the night Aunt Mona told me I was a Wanderer, and then again this scene was presented to me on the hot air balloon ride, the one at Gabe's gala dance that revealed my future like a crystal ball. I look over to Bishop, who was with me at the time, and his eyes glint with recognition.

"So you'll be going there," Sam says, apparently reading his mind.

"I guess so."

Excited, I flip again and again. Beautiful and detailed sketches of our beginnings, specifically of our collective beginnings as Wanderers in Egypt, adorn each page. Each matches very closely with a story Mona told me long ago.

I press my lips together as I recall the story's details, re-capping for Sam and Bishop what I know of King Unika. The king took over the kingdom of Egypt after his brother's death, wanting to return his ailing city to greatness, especially the grain fields, which had grown barren. To please the gods with a gift, he ordered his architect to construct a golden obelisk in the middle of his fields. It is said that because of this, after some time the god Amun-Ra appeared to him, revealing how to irrigate the fields to better his crops. It's believed that the king was one of the original Wanderers, and that's how the obelisk became the symbol of our people. Though it's just a story, part of our mythology. Until now, I wasn't sure how much of this story I truly believed, because how much truth can survive this length of time?

"So, what else is in there?" Sam points to the book. "Isn't there a prophecy somewhere?"

I flip through, but there are only notes below the sketches, mostly names of portraits and locations on hand-drawn maps.

"Well, what do they say?" Bishop leans closer and squints. "The pencil is smudged here. Can you read it, Sera?"

I clear my throat, following each word with my finger as I say them aloud. "A child, born unto a mortal and a Wanderer, will set off the cycle of the Chosen, for this union is not meant to be and can only mean the undoing of the Wanderers." I hold the book to my face, trying to read the rest. "It's smudged, I can't quite make any more out," I say with a huff.

"What does that mean, anyway? Why would they even care who married who?" Sam asks.

"I can tell you what it means." But it isn't Bishop or me who responds. The voice comes from someone standing behind us, hidden in the darkness.

No 18

MISS SWIFT

VOLTA SWIFT, OUR DEFENSE ARTS TEACHER, steps out from the hallway's shadows. Today she's wearing a security uniform that somehow can't hide her elegant, yet muscular form, or how striking her looks are. Her short and spiky white-blonde hair contrasts with her dark skin and the unexpected light color of her eyes. I relax a little, knowing she will be on our side. With her violet eyes, she's one of the Watchers who never transitioned into a Chosen, according to Terease.

"'A child, born unto a mortal and a Wanderer, will set off the cycle of the Chosen, for this union is not meant to be and can only mean the undoing of the Wanderers,'" she repeats.

"I, myself, found bits and pieces of information on the prophecy when I found out I was a Watcher. From my studies, I believe the Masters saw this union as an act of treason, a dilution of the purity of soul we possessed in the beginning of our time when Gibeon was a utopia, a paradise, and long before the city was set into motion. By mating with humans, we'd take on their humanity, though good in many ways, we would also inherit the bad, which would bring about abuse of our gifts and cause us to deviate from the enlightenment that they wished for us to achieve. We simply wouldn't be able to help it. The Society scholars call it *necesse corruptionem*."

"Inevitable corruption," Bishop translates.

"Yes." She nods. "The Masters saw the future for themselves. So a child from this union, once matured into a Wanderer and later the Chosen, would have to fulfill the prophecy and end us. But as you know, that never happened, and since then, every so often, new potential Chosen have been born."

"But how? How does a Chosen end it?" I step forward.

"It's not certain, but Society scholars believe we must go back and kill the queen and the king before they bear a child."

"'The end is at the beginning.'" Sam recites the line from the journal. "If that's true, you would end us at the beginning." Sam flips to the front of the book and points to the handwritten line.

"Unfortunately, that's as much as I know on the subject,"

Miss Swift says, "and I need to sneak you back into the Academy. Gabe's sent out the alarm to the staff, reporting one of the transporters stolen."

"Oh God, the E.Y.E.S. video," Sam squeaks. "They'll know it was us."

"Now that's where you're extremely lucky." Miss Swift crosses her muscular arms and smiles. "I was on security watch when you pulled your little stunt, so the proof has been erased. But you know, Sera, you need to be more careful. Grand Master Levi is already sniffing around."

"But I had to come and find the journal. It must have the answer to how I will Wander back in time to carry out the prophecy in here somewhere." As I flip through, one sketched image in particular stops me.

I hold the book up, flat and open for the others to see. It's the crown of Unika, a sketch similar to the one Stu showed us a year ago when I put together the sundial bracelet to take me to my mom.

"That again!" Sam cries out. "Please, no." She rolls her eyes.

"But where is the bracelet now?" Bishop asks. "It holds the gem that belonged in the crown. We'd have to put the entire thing back together."

"You're right and that could take forever," I add.

Sam frowns. "Do we even know where to begin?"

"Terease took it for 'safekeeping.'" I sketch the quotation marks in the air with my fingers.

"We could just go back in time and steal it back," Sam offers.

"But where would we even begin to look?" I ask Miss Swift.

"I wish I knew," she says. "But first, we have another problem—I need to sneak you back into the school. Bishop and Sera, I think you should skip through time, back to your apartment." She waves us away. "And I'll take Sam with me. We'll leave your transporter here."

"Fine, let's meet back at the apartment in fifteen," I say. Everyone agrees. Sam exits with Miss Swift via her transporter. Bishop and I stand on one side of the long corridor between the jail cells. With one hand, I clutch the journal to my chest; the other I extend to Bishop and he grabs it tightly. Together we run, leaping over fallen debris and splashing through water puddles to activate our supernatural gift of time travel. That, along with holding a keyword in my mind, will send us back to the Academy.

We travel through a sparkling gateway back to the Academy via skipping—the simultaneous movement in time from one point to another.

Bishop and I fall through the wormhole and land in our apartment. We tumble, entwined, onto the couch. His elbow jabs into my side, and I groan as he clumsily untangles himself. When he stands, he reaches out his hand to help me up.

"Let me go hide this really quick," I say, holding up Mom's journal. I bound into my room and slide the journal under my mattress. Maybe it's not the most ingenious hiding spot, but if someone really wants to find it, I suspect that they will no matter where it's hidden in this apartment. I may have to remove it from campus to truly keep it safe.

I return to the living room. "Let's go out to the murals in the main arcade. I want to see something."

"Sure," Bishop says.

We walk out of the apartment and down the marble corridor. A group of students walk past with shopping bags filled with more new items. Their purchases are nonstop since they received their credit cards a few weeks ago—a perk of becoming a new member of the Society. Maybe they would think twice about their new stuff if they knew they were creating relics that mapped their entire life. My stomach grumbles with anger, or maybe it's hunger. As I reach up a hand to rub it, I wonder if we can scrounge up some food in the apartment because I think we missed dinner.

In the main arcade the ceiling reaches six stories, arching over our heads. An ironwork roof of Victorian stained glass details allows the evening late fall light to settle, casting a dark gray hue over the space. As usual, birds fly from one colonnade to the next, playing in the space above us. One lands on the frame of the Seraphina Angel painted by Leonardo da Vinci. It's the one that Bishop often stares at and claims it look like me, but it's the painting nearby that I'm here to see. "Unika's mural." I point at it, then lean to him and whisper, "I wanted to look at where it is I'm meant to go."

In the painting, a golden obelisk stands in a field of grain. A river flows nearby. In the foreground, a king stands with two field workers at his feet, kneeling with harvest baskets. Stylized geometric sunrays beat down from a cloudless sky.

"I don't think I could kill someone." I take in Unika's lean figure. It's not his fault he was the first. And even in this painting he looks like a ruler, yes, but fair, familiar even. I lean back on the railing, taking in all the details. "Here I am, supposedly this special person, someone who's going to save everyone from this craptastic life, set Nocturna free, and I have to do something that makes me no better than any of the Society. I have to kill someone—two someones." I look to Bishop. "In my heart it doesn't feel like the right answer."

"Well, maybe we shouldn't think of it like that. What if you were to just stop the actual meeting of the king and the queen so that they never fall in love and have children?"

"True." I think for a moment. "But if I stop the beginning of our race, then where does that leave everyone we know? Do we just disappear from time, cease to exist?"

"I don't know, but I honestly don't like what's expected of you." He turns to me with a look of desperation and grabs my arms, taking me by surprise. "We could leave, Sera. We could run away from it all." Bishop's expression is sincere and earnest, and he's shaking, he's so upset. "I could keep you safe. We could live as Normals, the way you've always wanted. I could give you the life you deserve, the love you deserve."

My heart wrenches at Bishop's plea. With his all-consuming love for me, he'd rather run away to make me happy instead of saving his family. This is part of our curse. Wanderers love so intensely that it rewires ours brains to react irrationally. "I know you don't really mean that." I give him a sad look as I brush away the hair that's fallen messily on his forehead. "What about your family? They're still wasting away in Nocturna," I remind him. "This is the reason I was born, to set everyone free." I take a deep breath. "Maybe after this is over we'll become Normals? Or maybe none of us will be. I'm sure the world wouldn't miss me too much." My gaze drops to the floor.

"But I'd miss you." I look up and he pulls me closer, giving me the expression that I love. His eyes come alive with upside-down smiles, his lips curve, and his cheek punctuates with a dimple that's always stolen my heart.

"Thank you." I can't help but smile back at him, and he leans down and kisses me on the forehead.

"Hey." Sam joins us. "I just got an earful from Miss Swift. Be glad you didn't have to deal with that or ride in the transporter again. It's even worse the second time." Sam reaches out, places a hand on my shoulder, and the scorpion Animate crawls across the bridge of her arm, settling in the crook of my neck.

"Lucky you." I laugh, pulling away from Bishop.

"She begged us to lie low for the next day. She said that because the transporter was stolen, the Society officials have to be notified. So they'll be arriving to watch everyone, and target number one will be you."

"Figures." I rub my forehead in thought. "But did you happen to mention to her that I'm kinda on a deadline? The Grand Master will have the results of my blood tests soon, and he'll know exactly what I am." Has it only been this morning since the awful examination by the doctor? "At this rate, I may not even make it to the Oaths on Saturday."

"We won't let anything happen to you, Sera," Bishop assures me, but the truth is, I'm not sure if anyone can save us all now.

"I'm going to my room to scour the journal for any helpful info."

Nº 19

THE GUINEA PIG

SAM AND BISHOP RANSACK THE APARTMENT refrigerator. I'm tempted to stop and eat, but in truth, my appetite seems to shrink the more I think about what's ahead for me. Instead, I hide away in my room.

Leaving the lights off, I strip out of my school clothes and slip into my pajamas. Sleep would be nice, but too many thoughts scream around inside my head. Why me? And can I really be this hero, if you can call it that? Can I change the past when I have no idea what the outcome will be?

I feel guilty for thinking even for a millisecond that I could run away with Bishop. Once upon a time, the thought would have been very enticing. Bishop and I could easily blend into any time. Would they hunt us down? The Underground? The Society? And how would I save Bishop's family or protect Sam? They could send her or anyone I've ever met to Nocturna, just for knowing me.

I collapse on my bed, surrounded by a fluffy cloud of bedding. Even with the weight of this task pressing down upon me, I can't allow myself one second of peace, so I lean off my bed and reach under the mattress to pull out Mom's journal.

I sit up and settle the book as a bridge between my crossed legs, studying the cover. Around and around, I drive the tip of my finger, tracing the infinity symbol like a racetrack. If you look closely at the details, you can see that it's a snake twisted into an elongated figure eight. The mouth of the serpent devours its tail. This is the symbol of the Underground. I remember it from the presentation Terease, Principal Evans, and Professor Raunnebaum gave after the Underground attacks several weeks ago. But at the time, the coiled snake was engraved on a shield.

Flipping open the book to the first page, I read the words out loud to myself. "The end is at the beginning." When a voice responds, I jerk with surprise.

"Can you tell me what's going on with that?" Hologram Turner points to the journal. The scorpion Animate has climbed up and settled itself on top of my headboard to project Turner's image on the other side of my bedroom, and now he's returned for answers.

"I figured you would have heard everything by now. So you can't hear anything when you're stuck in that thing?" I gesture to the scorpion.

"No, not really, only if you beckon me." He laughs. "It's quite like a genie bottle, actually."

"I like the sound of that. My personal genie."

"Tell you what." He sits on the bed, facing me, one leg bent beneath him. "I'll grant you three wishes, but then you have to set me free."

"Is that how it works?" I say, willing to play along.

He smirks back. "So, what will your first wish be?"

I stare into his eyes and immediately know the answer, but I could never say it out loud. *For you to be alive.* I drop my gaze and play with the edge of the comforter, rolling the fabric between my fingers.

"And you can't say the obvious," he clarifies as he leans back on one arm.

"And what would that be?"

"A make-out session with yours truly." He waves a hand across his body.

"Ha!" I laugh out loud. A real laugh, in a way I haven't laughed since he died. Despite the pressure that I'm feeling, he manages to make me feel better. My face burns with embarrassment but I continue to play because ironically, Hologram Turner is the one thing in my life at the moment that feels real. "Well, now that you mention it," I say. His eyes light up. "No, we aren't making out!" I smack him on the leg and laugh again. "That's not what I meant. I want to show you something."

"Okay." His brow furrows and he tilts his head.

"I think that there's something special I can do, and I want you to be the first person I try it with."

"Now, this is getting good." He rubs his hands together with a grin.

"Do you ever stop?" I giggle. "Just calm down, Casanova, and give me your hands." I grab each of his hands. The electricity that they're composed of radiates with warmth, shocking me with pins and needles. "I haven't really done this before or even attempted to do this yet, but I think it will work."

"I'm a guinea pig, then?"

"I'm afraid so. Do you trust me?"

"I'm putty in your hands, love."

My lips quirk. "Good. Just close your eyes, relax, and be quiet for once—if you can."

He raises an eyebrow but does as requested.

"Look into your mind," I suggest.

I settle into a comfortable pose the way Sam taught me, close my own eyes and relax all my muscles, but I'm not looking to see the life path of an object, I'm looking to share my thoughts and memories with my Protector, just as if I were his Seer.

Then I focus on the evening of the gala, letting him see exactly what happened between us from my point of view.

He deserves to know the truth. I don't want him to regret anything from his Wandering life.

Bishop makes his way through the crowd, disappearing from view. Now I finally have a moment to do what I've wanted to do this whole night. I scan the crowd. When I find Turner alone I march over to him, where he's pouring punch for himself. Perpetua chats with a group of friends across the room.

I stand next to him, practically burning out of my skin. With quick movements, I grab a cup, swipe the ladle from his grasp, and pour a drink for myself. I take a quick swig, casting my disapproving gaze over the rim, and then I slam the glass on the table. My opinion can't be held in any longer.

"I can't believe you brought her with you!"

"Are you suggesting you have a problem with my date?" *He smiles, acting innocent.*

"She's a horrid, back-stabbing witch!"

He shoves an arm under mine and hisses, "Aren't you the one who told me to move on, Seraphina? What was it you said exactly? 'Find someone new,' I think it was." *He drags me out a set of ornate doors and onto a veranda that overlooks a holographic city. Turner kicks the doors closed behind us. The party and music disappear, leaving us in silence.*

"Ugh!" *I grunt and stomp away, but he grabs my arm.*

"No! We're having this out now! You aren't going anywhere!" *He swings me back to face him.* "Why don't you ask yourself why you're so jealous of her?"

"Jealous? I am not!" I scream. "You're out of your delusional mind!" I pull away.

But he isn't done with me. He pulls me back again. My body lands with my chest against his. Before I can react or even say another word, he crushes his lips into mine and kisses me. I struggle to get away, but he holds me there, letting his hungry fingers skim over my shoulders and down my back. His kisses are frantic, hot, and out of control. I lose my mind, because suddenly, I kiss him back.

All the tension that has built up between us explodes into fireworks. They sizzle through my veins, shooting throughout my body. The kiss, heated with passion, is the consequence of the raw and careless emotional disturbance that's been building for months. His scorching lips work mine over. I reach into his dark hair and twine my fingers into its roots, pulling him closer, gasping for more.

Turner kisses the line of my collarbone and bare shoulders. In a frenzy, he lifts me from the floor and staggers backward. I land seated on a ledge and lock my legs around his hips. Then I grab his collar, jerk him closer, and lose myself in absolute delirium. There's passion—so much more intense passion than I've ever felt before.

"Sera!" The veranda doors fly open.

We pull away from each other. Turner's wistful eyes lock with mine. I drag my wrist across my wet lips, breathing heavily. I want to jump back into his arms and devour him when he steps away.

Sam rushes forward. Her beautiful taffeta gown sweeps behind her. She slaps Turner in the face and grabs my arm, quickly dragging me away. I only look back over my shoulder, staring at his silvery eyes. I want to return and allow his kisses to consume me. A ghost of a *smirk reaches his lips as though he can read my mind. Then he's gone from my view.*

The image fades, and I open my eyes.

"Whoa," Turner says and squeezes my hands.

I blush and look up into his electrified eyes. Reliving the moment brought it all back: the feelings and the passion. Nothing's changed. Looking at Hologram Turner now, I know in his living life that we belonged together, even if it's impossible for us now.

"I could have done without the slap," he says and releases my hands.

"You aren't happy?" I read his expression. "I thought that's what you wanted? Your only regret."

He stands without saying a word and paces the room. With each step he rakes his fingers through his long, wavy hair. He stops and rubs both hands over his face and drops his hands to his side, clenching his narrow hips.

"I'm sorry. I shouldn't have shown you." I stand and cross my arms, feeling vulnerable and wanting to take it all back.

He quickly steps forward, picking me up and crushing me to his chest, burying his face in my hair as he says softly, "It's just that it shows me everything that I lost, and that hurts more than you can ever imagine."

"There's more." I lean into him and close my eyes as I hesitate, knowing that what I'm going to tell him won't be easy. "You can't know the one thing without the other."

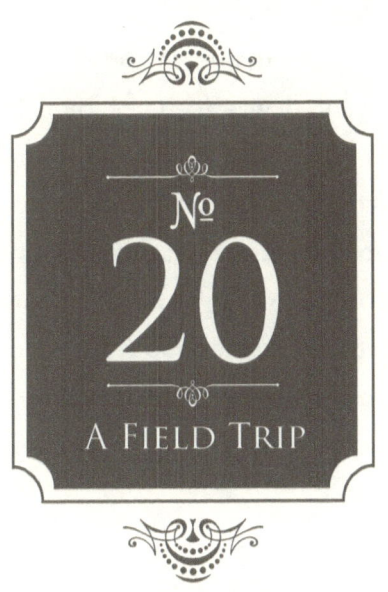

No

20

A FIELD TRIP

HOLOGRAM TURNER LOOKS AT ME SKEPTICALLY. "Go on." He sets me back on the floor.

"Well." I clear my throat. "I know about how Bishop cheated you out of a team. And what you are to me—that you were meant to be my Protector."

He has the same reaction as the first time I told him that I knew. Through a bright red blush, relief flashes behind his eyes and his demeanor changes. His hardened macho shell dissolves.

"I'm so sorry. I wanted to tell you for so long, but I've been forbidden." He hangs his head, saying exactly the same words to me as he originally did as a real person.

"It's not your fault. It's the Society."

"All I ever wanted was to be recognized by you. Now, tell me how you did what you just did. How's that possible? Does it have anything to do with what we found in that jail?" He examines me as though the answer is on my face.

I fill him in on everything that's happened since he died. Honestly, he takes my stories about his "hero's funeral" better than expected. To my horror, he loves every minute of the attention, the parades, the pomp and honor of being recognized as a hero.

"Is there to be a statue in my honor?" He poses, flexing his muscles.

"You'd like that, wouldn't you!" I smack his leg and he laughs. In response, I roll my eyes but then continue the story, relaying the events of my trip to Nocturna, what Terease told me about my destiny, the prophecy, and that if I'm the Chosen, I'll fully manifest the gifts of all three team members—Protector, Seer, and Wanderer.

At that point I pause, deciding whether to tell him about his family. It doesn't seem right to go there when you have to deal with knowing about your own death too. I leave it out because Bishop and I agreed not to tell him and if we do, we'll do it together. Besides, there's nothing Hologram Turner can do about it anyway. Technically, he's dead.

"What is it," he says, eyeing me. "I can tell you're hiding something from me, I sense it. Like, Protector sense it."

Of course he can, because he now knows that I can share thoughts with him. Without even realizing it, I've opened the door for him. Will he be able to read all my thoughts now? My mouth drops open in horror.

"Don't worry, I can't read your mind. Not yet, anyway." He smirks.

But he wouldn't be smirking if he knew what I was really keeping from him, so I continue talking. "Sam taught me how to see earlier today and it worked. She thought that I wouldn't need my team any longer, but the one thing I realized after, was that I'm drawing from the energy of my team—all of you. I'm pulling from Sam to see, pulling from Bishop to protect, and even though you're not really here anymore, I believe that you were meant to be part of our team. The fact that I can do this with you proves it's true."

I lean toward Hologram Turner and capture his gaze as I say meaningfully, "Just because there's never been a four-person team before doesn't mean it wasn't meant to be. And how would the Society ever know anyway, since they normally kill off one of the twins that may make a four-person team? They've been messing with the true order of life for a long time, and this is one of those situations."

"What are you saying?"

"We were all meant to be together for a reason. Everything happens for a reason. And there's something more to it that I haven't pinpointed yet, but I will."

He narrows his eyes and places a protective hand on my

knee. "You realize that traveling back to the beginning is ridiculous. I can't allow you to do that."

"How can I not with everything that's happened? This is my destiny. I can set everyone in Nocturna free, I can stop the brain manipulations, the sacrificial murders, the bribing of all the students, and the way we're controlled by our genetics. What we're doing isn't living. It's just existing."

"You have a choice. You can walk away." He pulls his hand away and his posture stiffens in that way I know so well, and I sigh inside. That stubbornness that makes Turner such a great Protector is making this so much harder. He wouldn't argue with me if he knew the entire story, that his family is wasting away in Nocturna, but this is the best I can do to protect him.

"No, there's no choice because there's only one right thing to do."

Turner and I argue early into the next morning. By the time I lay my head on the pillow, we've reached no middle ground. He sits on my bed with a perturbed look on his face until I fall asleep, and then he cuddles with me like we never argued. When I wake in the middle of the night, I find that he's gone. Even the Animate is nowhere to be found.

Morning arrives too early with a knock at my door. I roll over to see Gabe prancing into my room with a long garment bag. I'm on edge for a moment, thinking he knows that I've broken into his penthouse of glamour, but he seems to be acting normal, so I act normal.

"Ugh, I forgot." Today is a Wandering field trip. I rub my sleepy eyes.

"I'm offended, my little pot pie. Do you know how hard I work to put these fantastical adventures together?" He hangs the bag on the door, turns, and places a hand on his hip in exaggerated Gabe fashion.

"No, but I'm afraid you're going to tell me, aren't you?" I lift my head, hair nested and ratted on one side, and throat dry from arguing with Hologram Turner all night.

"For now I have to finish my costume deliveries, but I'll make a note to come back and school you."

"Awesome, I'll put it on my calendar. 'Meet Gabe for a snooze fest.'"

"Sass me all you want, sweet cheeks." He waves a painted fingernail. "I'll only haunt you more." He shuts the door behind him, and I smile with satisfaction for getting under his skin. Our beloved activities director deserves a much worse punishment for what he's apparently involved with, but it's a start. I sit upright, legs dangling over the side of the bed, and yawn before I stand and stumble across my room into the bathroom.

I lean into the mirror, inspecting the "contacts" in my eyes, which I assume I'm leaving in since I don't think there's a way to remove them. Red veins feather from my irises from lack of sleep and stress, reminding me that the clock's counting down. I have to find the relic to take me back to the beginning—to free us all, I hope.

After I've showered, I unzip the garment bag Gabe left. On any other day this would be like opening a present. What girl wouldn't want to play dress-up in these gorgeous historical gowns? But today I grumble through fastening each button of the bustled blue day dress. Then with a few more huffs, I fix my hair, following the instructions that he provided for hairstyles of the late 1800s. I should be focusing on finding Unika's crown, which would take me back to our beginning, rather than lying low like Miss Swift suggested.

There's a knock on the door. When I open it, Sam stands at the threshold. "What's up?" I ask and allow her to enter.

"Wanted to make sure you were here and following orders."

"What's that supposed to mean?" I turn to her as I'm slipping on a pair of earrings.

"Normally you'd be off on your own, Wandering through time to solve everything yourself."

"That was the old Sera. This is the new and improved Sera."

"I like her. She should stick around." Sam begins making my bed and I snicker to myself. She's such a neat freak; it's like she can't help it.

"Good, 'cause you're stuck with her." Until she dies trying to save the Wandering world as we know it, came the unbidden thought. My mood dips briefly before I force myself to be cheerful. "Besides, why would she leave when she has you to clean up after her?"

"I'm always good for something." Sam fluffs the pillows. "Now if I could only coax you into cleaning up the rest of your crap." She eyes my room, which looks like a wrecking zone.

"That's the part of old Sera that you're stuck with. Sorry." I stick out my tongue and one side of Sam's mouth twitches in response.

"Bishop's made some tea, and I think you'll want to watch the morning news."

"What now?"

"More attacks." She frowns.

I follow her into the living room where Bishop sits in front of the TV, slouched on the sectional sofa with an arm hung over the back pillows. He's watching frightening video coverage of an explosion at a Wandering university in Russia. Then additional videos of similar scenarios play out in different cities around the world. In every one, people run and scatter, screaming frantically for their lives. Plumes of smoke and debris fly through the air.

At the end of the terrifying footage, Gabe's face appears on the screen. This newscast is prerecorded and runs on a loop on the Academy's TV station from early in the morning until lunch. "Even with the unconfirmed death of the Underground leader, Cece, all signs indicate that the rebellion has brought the fight between us to the Normals' world. Grand Master Levi indicated that it will be increasingly difficult to hide our secret organization from the outside world with such brazen attacks, singling out our Society facilities."

Slowly, our magical world is leaking deeper into the Normals' in ways other than manipulating time. My gut twists and pinches more with each new revelation.

"Casualty reports are still coming in, but we know at least two hundred are injured, and forty-eight are confirmed dead. Most of them Normals." Gabe flips the note cards in his hand.

My heart drops at the news, and I slouch back into the couch next to Bishop in shock. "Everything really is falling apart, isn't it?" I look to my team, whose faces mirror my own sadness.

Bishop flips off the TV. "I can't take any more madness." He stands and without another word retreats to his room, shutting the door behind him. If I had to guess, he's probably sitting in his favorite reading chair with his headphones on, blasting classical music. If I wanted, I could try to check his mind and see, but I'm not ready to share that ability with him, and opening that door would mean that he would realize we had that connection. For now, I like having my thoughts to myself.

"He's just upset because he can't stop what's happening to you. He can't protect you from your destiny," Sam says, leaning over my shoulder as she grips the back of the couch.

"I don't think anyone can."

"Did you find anything else in the journal last night?" She walks around the couch and seats herself next to me.

"No, just what we found before, the hint about the prophecy and a lot of drawings. But it didn't help that Hologram

Turner argued with the me the entire time."

"Nothing's changed between you two, then."

"He's as annoying as ever." And I still can't have him.
At that instant, the scorpion Animate crawls across the floor
to my feet, and I bend down and scoop him up. "Where have
you been?" I say as I lift my hand and the machine skitters up
my arm and onto my shoulder.

I stand up and backtrack to my room to retrieve the
journal. When I return and sit back down on the couch, Sam
scoots close as I flip through the yellowed pages.

Inside, maps show cities, rivers, and structures. Portraits
of people are scattered among the drawings, with names
scratched beneath each. One page shows several portraits of
King Unika, drawn from different angles in great detail. Then
there are interior sketches of the palace. Rooms with statues and columns that hold up majestic ceilings painted with
constellations of stars. One such room has a large fountain
centered in it with an obelisk on top. A facade of a building,
one much like one I've seen in my dreams, is depicted on another page. Where could my mom have found all this detail?
Perhaps she saw it through meditation on a relic's life path?
Or maybe these are from her imagination. I'm not sure.

"I just had a thought," Sam says suddenly. "You could Wander back in time with this book to visit your mom. Allow her
to explain everything to you."

At Sam's words, I feel myself stiffen. Before these past
few days, I had promised myself that I would not go there,

that I would never look into the past at her or Turner's death, so that I could move forward in my life and finally heal. But I might not be able to keep that promise.

"I suppose it's a relic whose life path could lead me to her." Finally, and the journal was here all along, so very close for me to pluck from the Member Archives. "Maybe tonight. I'll go after our class trip." Mom's so close again; it's so tempting.

"You don't seem so sure." Sam places a hand on my arm.

"Ghosts, they'll always haunt me with the temptation of seeing them again. Makes it impossible to grieve and heal normally."

"We'll try to see the life path first. It'll be good practice for you, and then you can decide if you want to Wander back."

My body trembles at the thought, and the threat of tears burns my nostrils, but an announcement over the school's intercom saves me from having to think about it right now.

"Will the junior class students please report to Olde Town. We'll be leaving early for our Wandering Trip," the announcer requests.

Bishop exits his bedroom only a few seconds later dressed in a day suit from the late 1800s, and together we head to Olde Town.

Our entire class gathers in the courtyard, mingling together and chatting in small groups. When we reach the obelisk in the center of the square, Sam hands me our relic. WORLD'S COLUMBIAN EXPOSITION reads the title on the antique flyer.

"It's in Chicago in 1893. Despite all that's going on, this

should be a fascinating trip."

"If you say so."

"I read about this one." Bishop taps his finger on the paper. "They built an entire ancient city for the event. Very lovely, from the photos I've seen."

"Okay, kiddies, let's line up, please." Gabe flutters from team to team, clapping his hands and directing us to the proper positions.

"That's my cue to leave. Off to the meditation rooms," Sam says with a wave and gracefully walks away.

Bishop nears me as we line up two by two with the other students. Every time we're near each other, I can't help but feel the tension surrounding us. We're still strongly connected but fighting our feelings. He catches my hand and wraps it around his arm.

"Maybe you should tuck your Animate in your pocket while we're out in the real world?" His tips his head toward the scorpion.

"Almost forgot." I grab the arachnid from my shoulder and shove him into my crocheted wristlet purse, then clear my throat. "And thanks for the present, I never properly thanked you. It was a thoughtful gift."

"You're welcome." He smiles with his eyes. And though I understand that this doesn't make everything okay between us, it helps to know we're working things out the best we can.

Ms. Midgenet interrupts. She's at the front of the line, barking out instructions like a drill sergeant to teams before they Wander.

We step to the front.

"Do you have your relic in hand?" she asks.

I hold up the flyer.

"Your key word is 'World's Columbian Exposition, Chicago 1893.' Gabe's already there with the other students." She recites the prescribed instructions, then hands us a map of the fair buildings and exhibits, an old map of Chicago, and a wad of time-appropriate currency. "We ask that if you see or hear anything strange, you immediately report it to Gabe."

"Is there something we should know?" Bishop asks.

"We're sending all the students out on Wandering trips today. Trying to keep everyone moving in time to keep you safe from the Underground attacks. Just watch your back." This is the most comfort I can ever imagine receiving from her. She's rough around the edges and anything but warm and fuzzy, which makes me worry.

"Break a leg!" She waves for us to run.

No 21
21

THE WORLD'S COLUMBIAN EXPOSITION

B ISHOP AND I TAKE OFF RUNNING ACROSS THE courtyard of Olde Town with our hands locked together. With the keyword in his mind and the relic in his hand, Bishop unlocks the gates of time.

The ground rumbles and the brick patio cracks beneath us, rolling high into the air. Like a wave, it reaches all the way to the ceiling, six stories up, and hovers for several moments as it builds energy. And finally, when it's done teasing our safety, it crashes down and catapults us back into time.

We launch into the glittering wormhole, which radiates and bleeds leftover colors from the scene and warmth of Olde Town. Then new colors invade, mixing and meshing, fading us into our new reality—a brilliant white, the World's Columbian Exposition, Chicago, in 1893.

The time warp spits us out, depositing us behind a building near Lake Michigan. As I regain my bearings, I immediately notice the lack of high-rises. This reality is very far removed from the Chicago where I live in my true time.

Students gather, waiting for everyone to arrive, and Gabe urges Bishop and me to step aside. We comply, shuffling over to Macey and Xavier, who are joined with entwined arms.

"I looked for you guys after class yesterday. Wanted to warn you about Professor Raunnebaum's pop quiz on paradoxes," Macey says.

"Yeah, I decided to go back to my room and lie down," I fib.

"Did you hear about the break-in at Gabe's penthouse?" She leans down to feed me the newest gossip.

"What happened?" I feign interest to hide my guilt.

"Who knows, but I'd break in there just to look at his closet," Macey says with a giggle. "Can you even imagine the awesomeness of the shoes alone?"

"I think I can." I laugh and Bishop nudges my arm.

After the final Wandering team pops through the wormhole, Gabe positions himself in front of the group, calling for everyone's attention.

"Today, I'd like very much if everyone sticks together. With the recent attacks by the Underground, I'll be keeping you safe and giving the guided tour of the buildings and their exhibits. This is my ruffled pink umbrella, and though it will block my flawless skin from the sun"—he pops open its canopy and holds it high above his head—"it will also act as a beacon, and I want you to follow it at all times. *Capische?*"

He calls out "Follow me, my lovelies!" almost like a battle cry, then prances to the front of the group, twirling and pumping the umbrella in the air, looking more like a majorette in a parade than a tour guide.

We march dutifully behind, following him to the front of the building and into a swarm of tourists lingering before the facade of a stark white building.

"Holy wow!" My mouth drops open.

I glance around, instantly visually overloaded by the scene because this is, without a doubt, the most gorgeous city I've ever seen. Thousands of spectators stroll along great promenades lined with neoclassical-style buildings facing elongated lagoons, but it's the details here that are special, and those details come in the form of statues. Stone-like figures dot the top of buildings like birthday candles, or stand guard regally at canal edges and basins. Angels, sea warriors riding waterhorses, and human mythological creatures and gods such as Poseidon rest at the bases of exquisite fountains that feature water spouts as high as geysers.

"Too bad this doesn't still exist in our time. I bet most people don't even realize that this was ever here." I turn in a circle, taking everything in with amazement.

"I certainly agree. Quite spectacular," Bishop says. "Look, Sera." He points to a nearby basin. "Gondolas."

Several elongated boats glide past and I blush, thinking back to our first "almost kiss" in Venice, Italy, during a school Wandering trip last semester. "Those were the days when I thought anything was possible. When I was excited to be part of the Society."

"You and me both."

For several hours, Gabe leads us through buildings with endless exhibits: the Liberal, Music Hall, Agriculture, Manufacturers', Horticulture, Women's, and Choral buildings, and too many small structures to count. Though the six hundred acres are beautiful, I desperately want to leave to deal with the issues at hand. I won't solve my problems here. Frowning, I look at Bishop and groan.

He leans in and whispers in my ear. "I know what you're thinking, but we must lie low. Remember?"

"Easier said than done."

"For you, yes, it's certainly a challenge."

I'm about to smack him on the arm for the remark but then I stop in my tracks. "Oh. My. Gosh. I can't believe it."

"What?" He glances around.

I point across the sunny promenade. There, running and weaving in between tourists is a petite girl with dark hair and an eggplant-colored day dress—she's me—another version of me, a future me. "What in the world is she doing?"

"I haven't a clue." He scans the area, then points. "Look!"

My gaze follows the direction of his finger. Not too far behind, several people chase her.

Without thinking, I take off running in their direction, leaving our class behind.

"Sera, wait!" Bishop follows, but I keep moving until I catch up with them and hide behind a statue. From a distance, I can see her stop and face the gang. They're part of the Underground; I recognize them from last semester. Closest to her at the front stands Drake, the boy with wild hair and dark eyes. Once upon a time, they wanted to kill me, and I still don't understand why.

Future Sera grows agitated and yells at them, waving the crown of Unika.

"She has the crown!" I yank at Bishop's arm excitedly.

"You're right!"

It gleams in the sun and tourists stop and stare at the scene she's causing.

"Can you make out what she's saying?"

I step forward, wanting to know; just a few feet closer is all it takes to hear everything.

"You're lying!" Future Sera yells to Drake and takes a step away.

"I'm not. In fact, if you come with me, I'd be happy to supply more information," Drake says, attempting to bargain with outstretched arms.

She glances my direction for a fraction of a second, and I can see her eyes glass over. Whatever Drake's trying to convince her of has made her upset. But with each step I take forward, she steps away, and before long, she's off and running again. The gang follows her as well but they're no match for her speed, and before long, she's disappeared to Wander through time.

Drake and his gang catapult into their own sparkling window of time, exiting the scene.

"What was that about?" I turn to Bishop, hardly able to believe that I've run into myself here and with the crown. What are the chances?

"Not sure, but at least we know that you secure the relic in the future."

"Yes, but now I have to worry about when that's going to happen." I gesture to the lingering spiral of Wander dust, where they just stood. "It won't be today. She had on different clothes. I've never even seen that dress." I cross my arms with unease.

"Yes, I suppose it will be on another trip then. But still, I think it's a positive sign."

"I guess." Realizing there's nothing I can do about it now, I relax, allowing my arms to fall to my sides.

Bishop looks around until his gaze lands on our school group and he grabs my hand to pull me toward them. "We better hurry back. Gabe may freak if he finds us missing." That's my Bishop; always too worried about breaking the rules.

"Wait." I grab his sleeve, pulling him behind a crowd.

"What now?" Bishop scans the crowd but his tone changes when I point out who I've seen.

"There." I gesture to a familiar man walking across the plaza—one that I imagine he's as shocked to see as I am.

№ 22

THE GRAND MASTER

"WELL, THIS TRIP JUST KEEPS GETTING MORE curious." Bishop lifts his hat and fans his face with the brim as we watch Grand Master Levi step inside the massive Machinery Building.

"Let's follow him." I tug at his arm but Bishop stands his ground.

"I don't know, Sera, he's already set his sights on you. And spying on him doesn't exactly fall under 'lying low.'"

"And what does Sam say?" I raise my brow.

Bishop's face crinkles; he's mentally conversing with her as team rules dictate. She's been following our trip through her Seeing meditation. He chuckles and responds to me, "She says, and I quote, 'Follow that turdwaffle.'"

I laugh too. That is the dirtiest word she's ever said.

"He's the enemy. Consider this reconnaissance," I offer to make him feel better.

Bishop relents with a grunt, and we dash across the walkway and into the opening beneath towering archways. Inside the building, the ceilings soar several stories high, lined by a tunnel of steel structural frames. Immediately my gaze drifts to an exhibit of a stone obelisk farther away that nearly touches the roof over the clerestory.

Not surprisingly, the Grand Master heads in that direction, so we follow closely. He finally steps into an exhibit booth next to the obelisk and slips behind a velvet curtain, letting it drape closed.

We shuffle inside the booth too—after all, no one is there to stop us—and I pull back the curtain to peek in.

"Contraptions. Several of them," I whisper to Bishop who is keeping watch. "All like the ones we use at school, the relicutionist, the contrapulator, and some others I don't recognize."

Bishop's curiosity must get the better of him and he looks behind the curtain too. "Yes, you're right, though they look like older models than what we use in our true time."

Grand Master Levi reappears behind a machine carrying a box of tools, and disappears through a back exit. At the same exact moment, a strong hand from behind me pinches my shoulder, and I yelp and turn. Bishop does the same.

"Sera?" The man's hand falls away. "And Bishop!" He looks us over, but I don't recognize him. "My goodness, I haven't seen you two in ages." He pauses, scanning us again. "But apparently not for you; you appear to be nearly the same age as when we originally met."

I try to place him in my mind. His eyes do look familiar with that soft tinge of violet. Who have I met in the past on my time travels that would fit into this puzzle?

My brain produces only one name. "Elijah?" Elijah Vanderpool, the founding father of the Academy, an important figure in our Wandering histories. "Oh my gosh, I can't believe it's you. The last time we met, you were just a boy." And at the time, he'd told me that I was "like him," and now I understand what he meant. He's a Watcher too.

"Nice to see you again, sir." Bishop steps forward to shake his hand.

"You, as well! Yes, I remember it well, the London Exposition of 1862." He chuckles. "Very fond memories of that family trip. Father and I made real strides in our inventions after that." He opens the curtain to the back room and ushers us through.

I quickly glance around, searching for Grand Master Levi. Only the Masters know what he'd do to me if he found me here, following him. Luckily, the room appears empty and when I look to Bishop, he seems as nervous.

"I should've known you'd be here, exhibiting your inventions," Bishop says. "Showing anything new for the exposition?"

Elijah turns and gestures over his shoulder. "An improved version of the unfragmentation machine." He steps to its side. "This version fixes fragmented Wanderers, rather than fixing fragmented relics."

Fragmented relics are broken or with missing pieces. Using them to Wander through time can be dangerous because the life path may send you to random places in history, leaving the Wandering trip uncontrollable.

"Really?" Bishop steps forward with interest.

"Yes, in fact, we've had episodes of self-fragmentation among several members who've Wandered too far back in time or Wandered with a broken relic. In several curious cases, those subjects lost their mind, their memories, their humanity, and in some unique situations, they themselves split apart into several people."

"Intriguing. So you place the fragmented individual in the machine, and when you turn it on, they meld back together?" Bishop asks and places a hand upon the contraption's wheel.

"Exactly. It's still in the testing phase, but early experiments prove positive." Elijah puffs out his chest and pats the contraption with pride.

The machine is similar to the previous version, but large enough to fit a Wanderer within its glass box, which sits on two sets of wagon wheels. Control panels line its sides, with a tangled mess of various cranks, pipes, and levers jutting out haphazardly.

In the beginning, when I first learned what I was, Mona

warned me it was dangerous to Wander without knowing the rules. Perhaps this is what she meant. How awful would it be to lose your mind, or even split apart? This concept adds a whole new dimension to the term "split personality."

I walk around the machine, inspecting it, and I think back to yesterday when I was in Nocturna. Stu mentioned that the Time Reapers had been split apart. When he tried to explain, I had blown him off, but perhaps this is what happened to them, their bodies were fragmented along with their minds and their humanity.

As I make my way back to Bishop and Elijah, a man slips into the hidden room with us. It takes only a millisecond to register the image of Grand Master Levi, and I turn cold as the blood drains from my face.

No.
23
A Return

FACE-TO-FACE WITH GRAND MASTER LEVI, I expect him to start yelling but instead, he smiles at my reaction. "Sorry, miss," he says and tips his hat, continuing past.

"Replacement pieces came for the unfrag machine. Boys bringing them over now, sir," he says casually to Elijah, seemingly having no idea who I am. Bishop appears at my side and grabs my hand. Like me, I'm sure he's perplexed.

"Excellent, Levi. I'll be right with you as soon as I finish here." Elijah gestures to us. Levi nods to Bishop and me, then disappears again. We look at each other in shock.

"Who was that?" I ask even though I know the answer, because I'm looking for an explanation that might make sense.

"My very smart assistant, Phineas Levi. Has political aspirations in the Society. Perhaps you've read about him in your Wandering History books?"

"Actually, sort of." I cringe.

"Ah-ha! I knew it. Always thought the ol' chap would do well, but don't tell me another thing." Elijah raises his palms. "Don't want to know what lies ahead. Gets very tricky when you do."

"But——" I begin to speak and Bishop shakes his head. I understand; it's not our fight, and in changing the past, who knows what we may find when we return to the future. It's better to leave things as they are, just as we're supposed to.

"Bishop, we should leave," I say weakly, waving my hand toward the exit.

"May I suggest taking the stairs to the roof? There's a nice stretch for running up there." Elijah smiles brightly, seemingly delighted to be able to help.

"Lead the way," Bishop says.

Elijah guides us to an open spiral staircase that leads all the way to the roof. Up top, the sun shines and the breeze rustles my hair. From here, the entire exposition stretches out in every direction below us. It's far-reaching and grand in every sense. When someone uses the phrase, "They don't build them like that anymore," I believe this is what they're referring to. I can think of nowhere in the world or in our time as beautiful as this place. It has the beauty, mystery, and grandeur of the Trevi fountain, the finest streets of Paris, and the Taj Mahal all compressed into a few hundred acres.

If I weren't trying to fulfill the prophecy, I might come back here and enjoy this place further. Bishop and I grasp hands as he holds our flyer relic, and we run across the roof to open the time travel wormhole that will send us back to the future.

We Wander back to the Academy, returning to our true time. Just like the time-traveling rules dictate, our classmates arrive at the same time, a fraction of a second after we originally left from the Academy. Though it's still early in the morning, we still have an entire day left. The time we spend in the past doesn't affect our true time's reality. Even so, that doesn't mean I don't feel like I just spent six hours walking through exhibits. My body remembers, even if the clock doesn't read correctly.

Happily, Gabe never even realized Bishop and I ran off on our own. Perhaps he was too busy parading his pink umbrella, or more likely, he was consumed with being the center of attention for the day.

A short time later, Sam meets us at the apartment where Bishop and I sit in the living room discussing Unika's crown.

"I did some quick research in the library on the Grand Master before coming back." Sam drops on the sofa. "Seems he's been in power since 1894, just a year after you met him at the exposition."

"Are you saying that he was in his true time in the late 1800s? How's that possible? He'd be over a hundred years old now, and he still looks like he's thirty." I turn toward her.

"Well, that's what the history books suggest." She raises her hands as if to suggest that she claims no responsibility for the accuracy of the information. "I'm not sure how he's been doing it, but because he doesn't age, the higher-ups in the Society believe he's been chosen by the Masters to lead us. In a way, they think he's holy, like a pope or a saint."

"That would explain why he didn't recognize either of us. We had not technically met yet," Bishop adds.

"One more puzzle to solve." Sam folds her arms and sinks back into the cushions with a huff.

"Let's just focus on what we do know," I say. "We know that if I'm to be the Chosen, I will complete the transition to Seer, manifesting all three gifts after I take the Oaths and become anointed on Saturday. By that time, I need to have Unika's crown so that I can travel back in time and prevent the meeting of the king and queen."

"And now that we've seen your future self at the exposition, we know that you do retrieve the crown. But when?"

"Hmmm." I settle back into a pillow. "Today's Thursday. We only have a day and a half before the Oaths. So I believe whenever it's going to happen will present itself to me in an obvious way."

"Maybe we can research where the crown is at the exposition to start," Sam suggests.

"Assuming that's where I found it. At least it's a starting point. We'll do that tonight."

"And have you found any clues about what will happen to our kind after you thwart the meeting of the king and queen?" Bishop asks.

"Not in the journal, there's so much smudged text, it's nearly impossible to read, but there could be a way to find out." I look to the floor. "I can use the journal as a relic to travel back in time to ask my mom. She must have the answers."

"Did you want to check the life path of the journal before traveling back?" Sam asks. "Maybe we can gain some info there without forcing you to face your mother again so soon."

If she were asking this question just a few weeks ago, I would have jumped at the chance to see my mom. But now, knowing what her future holds, can I really see her and not tell her she's going to die? Especially when there's no way to save her. Death in the Wandering city of Gibeon is final. There's no coming back from that.

Bishop pats my shoulder. "I realize it won't be easy for you."

"No, it won't." I sigh, and Sam slides into the seat next to me.

"Is it wrong that I don't want to see her again? At least, not right away." I look down at my hands, twisting nervously in my lap.

"You wouldn't be normal if you didn't have reservations,

but you'll do what you always do," she says forcefully.

"And what's that?" I lift my gaze.

"You'll get the job done."

"No pressure." I laugh but as I think about it, I realize that I can do this. "Will you see the life path with me?"

No
24
THE JOURNAL

I RUN INTO MY ROOM TO RETRIEVE MY MOM'S journal, but when I reach my hand beneath the mattress I find nothing. Frantically and with all my strength, I lift the box spring and heave. The mattress slides away, revealing my worst nightmare. Mom's journal is gone; someone's taken it. I run back through the apartment. "Do you have it? It's gone."

"No." Sam stands and looks at Bishop.

"I didn't even know where it was." He raises his palms in defense.

"Well, who did?" She steps forward with concern.

Instead of answering, I pull the scorpion Animate from my

purse and place it on the ground. "Turner!"

Within seconds, a beam of light shoots from the Animate's face, landing on the opposite side of the room. Hologram Turner appears in a cloud of electrical dust particles.

"You rang, my lady." He's smiling, but he wouldn't be if he knew what I was about to accuse him of.

"Did you move the journal?" Last night Turner paced my room for hours, spouting off all the reasons that I should not fulfill the prophecy. The discussion turned into a heated screaming match where no one won.

Turner crosses his arms and stands straighter. "No-o-o," he says, narrowing his eyes and drawing the word out at the accusation.

"Then who did? You were the only one who knew where I hid it."

"I don't know if you've noticed, love, but you've seen me almost every time I've become a hologram. When would I have done it? And it would be quite hard to carry a book away on the back of my Animate." He waves to the scorpion on the floor.

"He's telling the truth," Sam says. "I can sense it."

I can too, but I don't mention it. I haven't revealed to her that I'm connected to our Protectors too. At least to one of them. It might scare her to know how far my Seeing skills have developed. It seems the closer I come to the Oaths ceremony, the stronger I become in all aspects of the team.

My body seems to sink in on itself in defeat as I rail inside with frustration.

"You're forgetting, we can easily see the life path of your mattress to discover who took it." Hologram Turner moves nearby and places a calming hand on my shoulder, showing more affection than necessary. The energy from him activates my skin like static electricity. It's even worse than having the real thing around.

Before I can say, "You're right" and apologize to everyone, Bishop groans out of nowhere. "We're not doing enough. You're not doing enough!" He points to me, his face turning scarlet. His gaze lingers on Hologram Turner's hand, where it's touching my shoulder. "Sera, I know I gifted the Animate to you, but I didn't realize he would steal all your focus. And now, because of it, the journal's been stolen!"

"I'm not doing enough? I'm not focused?" My jaw drops. Where is his attitude coming from? "I haven't stopped working on this since I returned from Nocturna!" I move into his personal space in challenge. "I haven't been to school in over a week. I've barely even eaten! This prophecy is all I've been thinking about. It consumes my every thought!" By the time I'm done, I'm screaming in his face.

"Except the times when you're flirting with a hologram," he bites out. His words have a serious edge, the blade of them cutting through my soul, splitting me further.

We've had fights before, yes, but not like this one. This is different. I sense that Bishop's finally hit his limit and instead of running into his room to hide and listen to music while sucking up his feelings, he's finally cracked and exploded. Realizing this calms me and I take a deep breath before adopting a gentler tone. "Please, let's not go there. This isn't you." I wrap my hands around my stomach. "There's only so much we can do in a twenty-four hour day."

"It's not enough, Sera." He stiffens. "While you're doing God knows what with him," he says with a sneer, jerking his head toward Hologram Turner.

"Hey, now——" Hologram Turner steps forward to defend me but Bishop keeps going.

"They're withering away; they're on a deadline. If we don't move fast enough, they'll die!" Bishop stalks around the room, waving his arms in the air for emphasis. At least this part of his argument I understand. Even I can't move fast enough to save his family.

"Who's going to die?" Turner asks quietly.

I cringe at those words from the person it seems I can no longer protect. I hadn't explained this part to Hologram Turner. I had every intention but it's only been a day since he learned about his own death. It just didn't seem right to bring him in on the most pressing part of this venture. Not yet.

I look to Bishop, whose face is now pale with the realization of what he's done. We'd agreed that we wouldn't tell Turner yet, but in his anger, he's changed everything. We'll have to hurt Turner again with more awful news.

"Who, brother?" Turner steps forward with crossed arms. His biceps bulge and his lips tighten.

Bishop approaches Hologram Turner carefully, finally

somewhat calmer. He places a gentle hand on his brother's shoulder and looks him directly in the eye. "We had every intention of telling you, but wanted to give you time to digest your new"—he looks Hologram Turner over, seeming to search for the correct word—"form."

"Go on." Turner relaxes slightly, adjusting his stance.

"It's the Society. They've taken Mum, Dad, and Charlotte." He swallows, his Adam's apple bobbing as if he can't abide the taste of the words that must come next. "And exiled them to Nocturna."

Turner stands rigid at the news, never dropping his gaze from Bishop. His brow furrows before he collapses into his brother's arms, crying. With each tear, the hologram sputters a zap, like water and electricity mixing. My heart breaks seeing the two this way. Vulnerable. But the cries soon escalate into rough slaps and angry pushes. "You should have told me. You should have told me!" Turner wails.

Sam and I run to them and wrap our arms around them, hugging them tightly. It's all we can do to contain the emotion. We press into a huddle, arms clutching each other as we grieve together, collectively feeling the pressure, the pain, and the loss.

"We can't let this tear us apart," Sam says, her face red with emotion as we pull apart. "We have to work together. It's the only way."

"Agreed." Bishop sniffs deeply and runs a hand over his face.

"Let's go see who took the journal." With determination, I return to my room. The others follow quietly. When we're gathered around my bed, I sink to my knees, settling them on the box spring and lean into the mattress that still lies teetered off the opposite side.

"Do you want my help?" Sam offers.

"No thanks, I think I need to do this myself." I close my eyes.

With my fingers splayed and palms facing down, I focus on the mattress, preparing to see the life path. My entire body relaxes, every muscle, every breath until the spark of warmth settles between my eyes. It's easier to pull the image from the cloudiness in my mind, now that I've practiced a few times.

The information I'm seeking appears quickly in reverse chronological order, starting with where we are now, my outburst, and before that, lifting the mattress to find the journal missing. A thousand other useless images scroll behind my eyes in vivid detail until I arrive at the one that matters—the intruders who took the journal.

When I see their faces in my mind, my mouth sours with hate and I shake my head to cease my meditation. Slowly my eyes clear of the vision, until my true reality returns. Sick to my stomach, I turn to face my team to tell them the grim news.

"Who was it?" Bishop asks.

№
25
AN EXPLANATION

I STAND UP TO MEET MY TEAM MEMBERS' GAZE and reveal who stole mom's journal. "Grand Master Levi and his security team."

Sam gasps. "Oh no, Sera!"

"When?" Turner's expression hardens.

"This morning, after we left the apartment for Olde Town, waiting to leave for our field trip." I look between them.

"Bloody hell!" Bishop throws his hands in the air and then slaps them at his side. "Now what?" He paces in a circle. "Why in the world did he steal it?"

"I'm not sure but it probably has everything to do with the doctor's exam."

Bishop glances at me over his shoulder with a defeated expression.

Sam steps between us. "Let's not freak out. It's a setback, yes, but let's talk about where we are. Technically, all the pieces are coming together. From the journal, we've learned the prophecy and determined what relic will allow us to fulfill it, and in general we know what we'll have to do. At this point, we only need to research the crown. Maybe we should take a breather, get some food, and regroup before moving forward," Sam suggests.

"What about the journal? What if there's important information in it that I missed?" I adjust my stance.

"We'll get it back," Turner assures me. "But if we don't, it doesn't matter. We have everything we need to succeed." He looks at me. "We have you."

I can tell he wants to come to my side for comfort, but remembering Bishop's accusation, I step away. Instead, I cross my arms, wanting to remove myself from the situation. "Sam's right. I'm starved. Who wants food?"

Everyone agrees. Hologram Turner dissipates, returning to Animate form, and I pick him up from the floor and place him on my shoulder. Sam and Bishop make their way through the front door of the apartment and that's when I pull Bishop aside to deal with the unresolved tension building between us.

"We need to talk." I tug at Bishop's arm. "Sam, we'll catch up to you in a bit, okay?"

"Sure." She nods and practically runs away.

I close the front door and face Bishop. "Let's talk this out."

He sighs, letting his gaze roam the room, but when he finally speaks, it's very controlled, unlike earlier. "How can you show your love for a hologram and not me? I don't understand the difference."

"He's not real. That's the difference. I understand there's no future with a hologram. Hologram Turner isn't going to become real no matter how much I flirt with him. So you shouldn't be jealous or think for one second that it lessens my resolve to help your family. Even though Mona and I have fought recently, she's still my family too, and I'll do everything within my power to free them and free us." I grab his hands. "I'm not choosing him or you, I'm choosing all of us."

"I know. I'm sorry." He pulls away. "I'm not sure what came over me. I'm mentally exhausted and frustrated on so many levels. I'm not sleeping, and all I can think about is everyone that I'm losing. My parents, my siblings, and now you. And you want to know the really sick part?" He rubs his face and paces, groaning, then he turns to me. "A small part of me, the competitive part, was happy that I didn't have to share you with the real Turner anymore, and I hate myself for it." He looks away in shame.

"But that's the part you can't control." I rush to his side. "That's the part of us I hope will change, so we'll have a choice who we love." I embrace him and he wraps his arms around me, holding me tight.

"I hope you're right," he whispers.

"You know, why don't you go ahead to the dining room with Sam, and I'll meet you guys later. I think I need to clear my head and decide how to deal with the Grand Master."

"Later, then." He grabs my hand and kisses it gently, and then leaves, running to catch up with Sam.

I go back to my room, change clothes, and then head off on my own, needing some time to think because the stress has become too much to bear. I step inside the elevator, close the gate, and rotate the ancient crank. When I exit the elevator car and stroll into Olde Towne via the Raptor Gates, the sight of the charming Victorian buildings don't excite me the way they used to. The colors, the warmth, and the scent of charcoal in the secret underground city used to awe me, with its sharp contrast to the windy city of Chicago above. Especially now with the seasons changing from fall to winter. Magically, everything always remains colorful here with machines controlling the weather and atmosphere.

Walking into one of several tunnels that exit away from the city, I find myself at the gym. It feels like forever since I trained. When I stop to really search my memory, the last night I practiced was with Turner, before he died.

The training room door slides open, sensing my presence. Lights automatically pop on and I shrug out of my hoodie, dropping it on the floor near the wall, and place the Animate on top.

At the center of the room on the mats, I stretch each limb and warm up with a few jumping jacks. With clenched fists, I throw several punches in the air, and after I've sufficiently pumped myself up, I activate the hologram training machines.

"Volta Swift, hologram 38." Turner wiped out my training programs before he died, so from now on, I'll fight Miss

Swift's holograms. They're always meaner and nastier, and that's exactly what I need to relieve this anxiety so I can think clearly.

Five machines mounted around the room activate, turning on at the sound of my voice. Their lights blink green and then the machine speaks. "Hologram number—38—choose any weapon. Prepare for street fighting. Training starts in thirty seconds," the robotic voice says and begins counting down. Needing a challenge, I decide on no weapon.

After hearing the number one, a haze of electrical waves appear in a swirl. The particles swarm, forming three holograms. At the sight of the group, my heart rate accelerates. The trio is half beast/half human in form—two male, one female. One man carries a crowbar, which he spins on his palm. The woman holds a long chain that drapes at her side and heaps in a pile near her feet. The other man doesn't need a weapon because his scaly hands curve into long claws.

The training holograms always know their mission, to destroy. And without any words of dispute, the group steps forward to challenge me.

The fight begins when the larger male attacks, taking a swipe at my face with his hand daggers. I easily duck out of the way but the girl tosses the heavy chain around my neck and pulls tight, restraining me, my back against her chest.

Readjusting my stance and steadying my feet, I twist to the side to release myself, grab the chain, and kick her in the stomach. She flies backward into the man, and they launch across the room, slamming into the wall. But by the time I turn my head, the third member of their group charges me.

I quickly realize the problem here isn't that they're especially gifted at fighting, it's that I'm outnumbered. Fighting all three at once is not only complex but extremely tiring. Or maybe, by missing just a few weeks of workouts, I'm already out of shape. The thought worries me because I have no idea what I'll truly be up against to fulfill the prophecy.

The fight continues, but I struggle to keep all three at bay. Honestly, my heart isn't in it. Soon I'm pinned beneath one man's foot while the girl pulls at one leg, and the other boy pulls at both arms, twisting them so far that I'm waiting for one to break.

"You win!" A voice across the room yells the safe words that turn the machines off. The three holograms fade into twinkling particles and disappear, allowing my limbs to flop to the mat in relief.

From my location on the floor, I push up with my palms and sit to look around. Hologram Turner rests in the corner, relaxed.

"I think you've lost your touch," he says with a sad expression.

"Maybe if I still had my training partner, I'd be better," I snap with irritation because I really wanted some time alone. "Why are you here?"

"I don't want to be alone and I needed to distract myself too. Seems we have that in common."

I can tell by his glassy eyes that he's fighting with his sorrow of the news of his family, but in typical Turner fashion, he tucks his emotions away, puts on his macho facade, and confidently strolls forward.

"I'm standing right here and you didn't ask me to come out and play." He holds out his palms.

"Just needed some time to think. And clearly, I need a lot of work." I stand and look around, annoyed and breathing heavily, and place my hands on my hips.

"I know, I read your mind."

I look up, my eyes wide.

"It's a two-way street, love. You slip into my mind, I slip into yours."

"But——" I start to protest but that's how this works with Protectors and Seers. Now that I'm slowly manifesting all three states, and showed him we could connect, he knows now. Thank goodness Bishop and I have not connected. The less people in my head, the better.

"It took a bit for your thoughts to become clear but now that they are, I can't look away."

I cross my arms.

"But don't worry, all your secrets are safe with me. Even the juicy ones." He wags his brows playfully, hiding his feelings behind his charm.

"All?"

He nods. I can see he's happy to have the upper hand. "But you're wrong about me. You don't give me credit for being what I am. Even as a hologram I can help. You should have told me about my family. I'm still living my life, just in a different form. And I know for a fact that when you told me about Mum, Father, and Charlotte, my heart slipped away and disappeared with despair, but by standing in front of you here, alone, it eagerly returns to remind me just how much I still love you."

I pause, thinking back to his zapping tears and my immediate need to console him. "And I still love you. I always will, but there can never truly be something between us. You're still not real." I look away. I know deep down that I'm lying to myself. Pretending that he's not real is the only way I can justify the flirtatiousness between us. I've analyzed our unique situation from every angle. No matter what his form and as much as it kills me inside to push him away, I need to protect my mutilated and manipulated heart.

"That's what I'm saying, I am real. This is real." He hits his chest with passion. "And this is real." He touches my hand, allowing electrical current to pass between us. The tingles ascend my arm and race across my chest, and my heart literally skips a beat at the shock. "And this." He moves closer and wraps his strong arms around my back, gathering me into an electrifying embrace. His persuasion is impossible to resist. I relax against him, curling into his broad chest, enjoying the sizzling warmth of his love as it consumes me along with all the hurt we've been feeling. "And this is real." He tenderly presses his lips into my hair, nuzzling his nose from side to side, and I want to melt into him right here, right now.

"Mmm-hmm," I murmur as every nerve in my body activates. Automatically I return the embrace, sliding my hands along the defined muscles of his back, pulling him so close that no air separates us. Every molecule of my soul desperately wants to give in. There's no denying it. The more our hands explore, bodies shifting against each other with friction, the more the heated energy builds between us, somehow propelling my need to consume him. I lift my face to drag my nose gently along his collarbone and he groans with pleasure. He dips his head to near mine and presses our cheeks together, and his expedited breathing rushes over my shoulder like a raging waterfall. My raw and unresolved feelings, though tampered with, are ones that I've suppressed for months. And now here he is, back from the dead, ready to be kissed with the same intense passion that we once shared before, and I still can't allow myself the joy of loving him. I have too much guilt for loving two boys at once.

At the thought, I place my hands on his chest. No, I definitely can't allow this. I have to do everything within my power to fight it, just as I do with Bishop. If I look up, he'll kiss me. I know it. We can never be. My heart can't take any more. And even though he acts tough, neither can his, regardless of whether it's a real heart or not.

He's not real. He's not real!

Finally, I break away from the intensity of our connection and he sighs above me. I'm sure he's read every word of the conflict in my mind.

"You know, some physicists think that the entire world, everything we experience, is an intricate hologram. It's called the holographic principle."

Now I look up at him with crossed arms, considering the possibility. "Okay, if the entire world is a hologram, then why do you look different from me?"

"Maybe because I'm only operating with the partial essence of my soul, the part that's recorded on my dreamdrive." He nods to the scorpion Animate on the floor across the room. "I'm just missing some of my mojo, but that doesn't mean I'm not real. I can promise you, I feel real even if I don't look the same as you."

I hesitate to mull over his explanation. Yes, he did feel real; better than real. I shyly look away, heat rising through my body, and call him a nerd for his hologram lecture.

"But I'm quite a sexy one."

"You wish." I press my lips together to hide my smile because being here alone with him is exactly what I needed. "Let's fight," I suggest to break the tension.

"Your wish is my command."

With a new bounce in his step, he walks away and turns to face me, crouching down, ready to attack. "You only have one left, you know."

"One what?" I charge him, ramming my shoulder into his gut, slamming him into the ground. We roll several times until he lodges his knee in my stomach and flips me over, and we're both standing on our feet again.

"One wish," he says as he swings a high kick at my face. I lean away, enough that he doesn't make contact, but so little that the whoosh of his foot passing by ruffles my hair. "You better make it a good one." He turns and kicks again with the other foot. I duck down, twist, and sweep his leg from under him, making him fall on his back with a thud.

"I don't think I recall the first wish." I rush him in his vulnerable position on the floor. His arms circle my knees, forcing me to fall forward, tumbling onto him. Now chest to chest, faces inches apart, he locks me in a scissor grip with his legs, a wrestling move that's nearly impossible to escape.

"I think I granted that one before I kicked the bucket," he

says as I struggle. He manages to capture my wrists and continues. "I seem to remember a vision of a very heated make-out session on a beautiful veranda on gala night." I thrust forward to head butt him, but he easily avoids it. "You've already tried that move on me, remember, love?"

"Haven't you heard, history always repeats itself?" I smash my elbow into the side of his cheek. The blow distracts him enough so that I scramble out of his grasp. With another elbow to his face, his legs release, and we grapple and roll until I manage to maneuver him onto his stomach. With our positions reversed, I'm sitting on his back with his arms pinned behind his hips.

"Do you give in?" I yank his arms. In retaliation, he kicks his leg, but I have him pinned for good.

"Give in, love," I say, mimicking his British accent.

"Never. I'll always fight for you."

Even in the heat of battle, his choice of words doesn't escape my notice. So I let him go, stand up, and step away.

"Let's start again. This time with swords." I walk to the wall of weapons, selecting a nice set, and turn and toss one blade to him. He easily catches the grip as he stands.

"Oh, now you're in trouble," he remarks with a twinkle in his eye.

"Why's that?"

"My favorite movie as a child was *The Princess Bride*."

"So?" I walk to face him and lunge into *en garde* position, pointing the blade of the sword in his direction.

"Just call me Inigo Montoya."

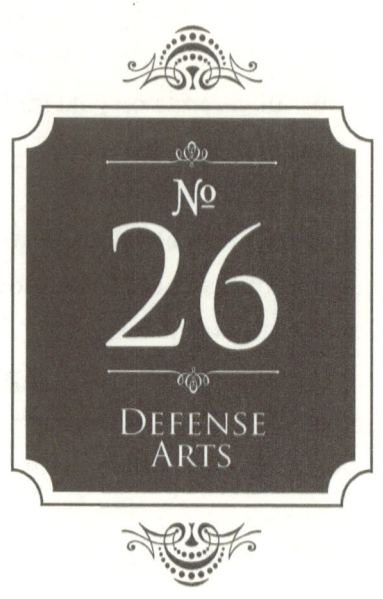

№ 26

DEFENSE ARTS

Turner and I train together, blowing off steam until late evening. And I try desperately to forget my feelings for him. With each uppercut, kick, and leg sweep, I'm building confidence for whatever I may tackle on my quest to fulfill the prophecy.

That's when Sam and Bishop find us and tell us the news. They've skipped lunch in order to research the location of Unika's crown at the exposition, but were unable to find any info.

"How do you suppose I discover where to travel back?" I ask, breathing heavily.

"There must be some clue we run across in the next day," Sam says.

"I propose that we rest up for whatever happens next. We know you're going to go back and find it. We've witnessed it for ourselves." Bishop seems less emotional, more clear-headed than before. I hope he's feeling better now that all of our feelings are on the table.

"True. I suppose it will present itself at the proper time."

Even with the suggestion, we all stay up late talking about the issues at hand, and my head doesn't hit my pillow until three a.m. Though I have no intention of waking early, I do when Sam knocks on my door.

"Come in." I rub my eyes and face, and roll over on my back, pushing the comforter away.

The door cracks open, and she tilts her head in. "I think we should try to go to class. Today's only a half day, and we have to at least pretend to be interested." She comes in completely, closing the door. "And I've heard that the Grand Master's returned." She cringes.

I sit up, my sleepy eyes now wide open. "Oh no, the blood test. I totally forgot. I wonder if they know."

"Well, they haven't arrested you, so that's something, right?"

"True." I rub my arm to soothe myself. "And we need to figure out why he stole the journal. With him here, maybe we can get it back."

"Let's feel the situation out. Then we can better determine what we're up against." She looks at her watch. "You've got fifteen minutes to pull yourself together for breakfast."

"Okay, I guess you're right." I sometimes wonder what I'd do without Sam. Just when I need it, she's here to kick me in the rear, reminding me that I need to make it to the Oaths tomorrow and stay off the radar until then.

She nods and turns to leave, shutting the door behind her.

I take a shower and dress. When I emerge from my room, I find Bishop at the counter reading an old book and sipping a cup of breakfast tea. Gabe's morning show blares from the TV in the background, spouting off about the Oaths and the parade in Gibeon in our honor, which is all taking place tomorrow.

I've had only a few hours of sleep in the last two days. Last night, without the journal to study, I had nothing else to do but live with my thoughts. Why would the Grand Master take it and what will he do to me for having it?

The scorpion Animate crawls across the floor to my feet. I pick it up, place it in the pocket of my hoodie, and approach Bishop, who pours me a cup of tea.

Bishop looks tired and worn, but slightly better today. Still, there's no doubt he's worrying about his family, just as I am. How old must they be now in Nocturna's fast-forwarded time?

"Did you sleep?" I place my hand upon his arm.

"A little. I keep worrying about how old my family is

now. In Nocturna, Charlotte could be in her twenties."

I hold back a smile, thinking how closely our thoughts parallel each other. "Everything will be okay. I promise." Simple words, I know, but I give him what little encouragement that I can.

After we're done, we leave for breakfast in the dining hall. Together, we sit at our usual table. Our friends Macey, Xavier, Quinn, Scarlett, Agnes, and Atticus straggle in one at a time, but they aren't the ones that concern me. It's the Society soldiers. We passed at least twenty of them on the way to the dining hall. The number has increased steadily since we broke into Gabe's apartment.

"Why so many goons?" Macey asks and settles next to me with a plate full of breakfast food from the buffet.

I shrug. "Maybe because the Oaths are tomorrow. Don't we have some preparation ceremony tonight?"

"On the contrapulator, in our sleep. They give you the details in your night classes, I've heard," Bishop says.

Subliminally. Figures. They wouldn't want you to realize they're brainwashing you at the same time. Maybe I'll actually have to stay up and listen to it, so I'll know what to expect.

"Oh gosh, there he is." I stare across the room. It's Grand Master Levi. He strolls in and sits at the main table with Mr. Evanston, our principal. The teachers' tables sit on a dais, looking out over the students.

The Grand Master's gray fur coat hangs over the back of

his ornate high-backed chair, and his skull cane leans against the table. Special tuxedoed butlers bring them food and drinks as soldiers stand at attention behind him.

I'm half waiting for him to lift his eyes to meet my gaze, to give me some kind of sign as to what he's up to, but the two remain in deep discussion.

"Don't stare, Sera," Sam chides me.

"If you ask me, he's kinda cute, in an older guy kinda way. A nice dresser and all those muscles." Macey stares at him. "Did you hear about how he saved those kids from one of the Underground attacks?"

"You must be thinking of the wrong person." I look up, confused. That man wouldn't do anything that he wouldn't benefit from.

"Oh no, it was all over Gabe's news this morning, before they talked about the Oaths."

"Must have missed that." I look over at him. "If you ask me, I think he's a real creepster." I turn my attention to my plate and push fruit chunks around with my fork.

"How can you say that? He's amazing," she says insistently. I give her a strange look because I can't understand why she's defending him this way. She and Quinn fall into a discussion of his awesomeness and I turn to Sam with a sigh.

"Sera, it'll be fine. Remember what I said," Sam whispers and places a hand on my arm.

"Yeah, you're right. It's just hard not to worry. There are so many things to worry about." I let out a nervous laugh.

"Thank goodness we only have to survive one class today."

"I can't tell you how excited I am about the Oaths," Macey says. "Jenn told me that Michelle told her that Tabitha said that our credit cards will officially have no limit as soon as we're anointed. I'm thinking about buying a car. Can you buy a car with a credit card?" Macey's mounting excitement is matched by her speech, which ramps up to warp speed.

I stare at her. Is it fair that she has absolutely no clue what she's getting into? Can she really not see how corrupt the Society is? That they are bribing her with material gifts that will track her entire life path? That the love she shares with Xavier is carefully crafted and manipulated? That if she doesn't take the Oaths, they'll send her to her death in Nocturna? Did she not care when we told her about the sacrifices at the Oaths? Or maybe she doesn't believe it, or more probably, they've brainwashed her during her night class on the contrapulator to overlook events that would normally set off alarms. Whatever it is, it's clear that all my classmates are moving forward in their lives while mine is falling apart.

"What?" She raises an eyebrow, fork stopped in midair, full of waffle and syrup. "No buying cars with credit cars?"

"No." I sigh heavily. The sad thing is that just for one second I wished I were Macey, and that I didn't know how awful everything really is. It's nice to be blissfully unaware of the danger that surrounds us. Disgusted, I push my plate away.

"Sera, you need to eat." Bishop nudges the plate back. "Don't make me force-feed you."

"Fine." I relent, scarfing all the food down without tasting a thing, all while listening to the group chatter about the Oaths, how thrilled they are, and how amazing it is to have all this money to spend however they want. Of course, Sam and Bishop remain quiet. When I think I can't stand another moment of this, the bell saves me by announcing the first class.

The three of us slip out, heading to Defense Arts. When we arrive at the large gym, Miss Swift is rearranging several large blue mats and covering the floor with them. We join in, helping, and so do other students as they arrive.

Professor Raunnebaum walks to Miss Swift and she stands to meet him. "All the training machines are set up and ready to go. Here's a remote control. Just press the red arrow and the holograms will appear," he explains.

"Thanks, Professor. This will be a real treat for the class."

"And if there's anything else at all that I can do for you, don't hesitate to ask," he says with a nod that jolts his head of wild black hair.

As he walks away, I look around until I see why we're practicing here, rather than in one of the smaller training rooms like we normally do. Through an open door, I see Grand Master Levi sparring with a beastly hologram. It's the first time I've seen him in clothing other than an expensive suit. I move closer for a better look, and notice several intricate tattoos winding around his arm beneath his white tank. They're unexpected, considering his clean-cut persona. But seeing him in this new way doesn't give me ease because I can see he's dangerous, strong, and despite the fact he's fighting a hologram minotaur that's five feet taller with two hundred additional pounds of muscle, he's still going to win.

"Okay, class. Let's begin, shall we?" Miss Swift blows her whistle. "Let's stretch and warm up."

She leads the group in sprints. In a line, we run back and forth from one side of the gym to the other. Then she sets up cones, and we run backward and weave around them, run forward, and jump over hurdles. It's thirty minutes of hard workouts before she allows us to stop, grab a drink of water, and announces the next lesson.

By this point I'm sweating profusely, but it feels good to work out again, just like last night. I drag my wrist across my forehead and pull my drenched hair into a low ponytail.

"Okay, I'll need help with a demonstration." Miss Swift looks around. Her gaze passes over her usual sparring part-ners, Atticus and Bishop, and then lands on me. "Sera, would you mind?"

I hesitate, surprised, but then agree. "No problem."

Students encircle us, giving us a wide berth, as I walk to the center mat. Miss Swift removes the remote control from her gray jumpsuit, points it at a nearby machine, and presses the button.

The lights in the cavernous gym dull on cue and one by one images appear, scattered around the room. But these aren't images of beastly half humans or warrior/zombie holograms, these are objects: rusted-out shells of cars and trucks, refrigerators with doors hanging open, and garbage and other debris litter the ground in massive mounds that soar into what used to be the ceiling of the gym. The entire class now stands in the middle of a holographic garbage dump.

Though the students have seen the holograms in action, they ooh and ah with excitement.

"This class will be dedicated to learning how to use your environment while fighting." Miss Swift slips the remote in her pocket and walks around the newly configured space. "Look around. Take in all the elements and strategize how you would use these items if you should ever encounter an attack. In this new uncertain Wandering world that we live in, and with the resistance of the Underground, this could be a real scenario."

Unexpectedly Grand Master Levi joins our class, standing at the side of the hologram. Students look in his direction and become uneasy; I sense it in their postures. Many are in awe of him and his power.

"Carry on." He waves. "I'm interested in observing the students." His gaze immediately finds me, but I hold my face rigid and unreadable, determined not to give in first in this staring battle.

He struts forward, barking orders. "Rex, I'll need a chair." In a matter of seconds, his meathead guard presents a chair and the Grand Master sits down. Another guard hands him a towel and a bottle of water. He takes a deep swig and pats the towel over his sweating forehead.

"Sera!"

My head turns in the direction of my name, and the class giggles.

"Are you ready?" Miss Swift raises a white eyebrow.

"Sure."

We walk to the center of the room and she whispers, "Try not to look too experienced, Sera. It will only pique his interest more."

"Right." I agree, but only as my first reaction. Of course, she's right; I should do everything within my power to keep him disinterested in my abilities. I can do this to protect the people I love, at the very least.

Miss Swift crouches into position, and though I should have already surveyed the space better, I let my gaze quickly roam around. She blows her whistle and the confrontation begins.

She approaches me first, fighting in a typical street manner, hard punches and uppercuts, intense pushing, and high-flying kicks. We grapple and I fall to the ground, which is now dusty and dry red earth. The grit covers my entire body, and I reach into a pile of trash to pull out a piece of wood. Rushing forward from the ground, I take a few swings. I have to make this fight look somewhat real—like I'm not a complete wuss.

Miss Swift easily evades the swings. With her foot, she kicks the lumber from my grip and it flies through the air, landing with a loud clunk and sliding across the floor near the Grand Master.

Behind me, I hear him laugh. The sound causes my shoulders to tense, but I need to focus and forget that he's even here, watching my every move.

I run to grab the board, but Miss Swift catches up and pushes me from behind so that I fall to the ground. My face lands at the Grand Master's feet, so close I could kiss his boots, and I grimace at the mental image.

He laughs again, but this time the sound is too much for me to take and I lose it. Pushing up with my palms, I jump upright and before the guards can do anything, I kick his chair and it flips backward. He falls on his back with a thud, arms sprawled out to the sides.

"Sera!" Miss Swift grabs my arm. "What are you doing?"

I should be scared, but the sight of him below me, embarrassed, reaching for his bloody lip and covered in the clay dirt, makes me happy. It only takes seconds before the guards restrain my arms but I don't fight them, there's no point. He's responsible for everything—corrupting the Society to the point where my world has fallen apart. I blame him for everything that's happening.

Grand Master Levi reaches for his face, dragging the top of his hand across his skin. Blood drips over his chin and down his shirt. With his arm muscles flexing and pulsing with rage, I expect him to scream, ordering my arrest. Instead his anger boils inside, carefully controlled from the looks of it.

His guard, Rex, extends a hand to help him, but he refuses with a flattened palm and he rises on his own to meet my gaze. "You may be too young to realize this but in our world, what you've done is challenge me to fight."

Before I can respond, or even think of a way to answer this, he leans closer and says, "I accept your challenge with pleasure."

No

27

A
CHALLENGE

THE CLASS ERUPTS WITH CHATTER AND FRANTIC
yelps of concern. Miss Swift rushes between us. "Surely
you can't be serious, Grand Master. Sera's just a child. You're
much too skilled for this young one," she says in an attempt
to placate him.

"It wasn't I who did the provoking, Miss Swift. I'll ask you
to stand down or my guards will do it for you."

Her face crinkles with concern as Rex moves in behind
her.

"I've got this," I say.

Grand Master Levi throws his head back with a cringe-worthy guffaw. "It's settled then. We fight." He waves the guards away, and they release their grip from my arms.

Bishop rushes to my side and huddles close, pulling me from the commotion. "Sera, have you gone absolutely mad?" he says through gritted teeth.

Miss Swift joins us. "What I said earlier still applies. Even more now than before." She gives me a stern look, encouraging me to lose.

"Listen to her, Sera," Bishop agrees.

"Sorry, I'm just not built that way." I ball my hands into fists, trying to control the anger, and turn to walk away.

This time I take an extra moment to really survey the hologram space. There's a high-reaching industrial crane with an arm that swings across the room, a junkyard magnet at the end to pick up metal. Several crushed cars sit scattered around, along with many jagged and pointed items easily re-purposed as weapons.

"Rethinking your bravado, Miss Parrish?" the Grand Master yells across the space.

"Just thinking about what I'll do to celebrate after I'm done with you." I turn to face him.

"Then bring it, child," he says wickedly and crouches into a defensive move. Confidently, he waves me forward with his fingertips.

All I see is an evil man, one who sent Bishop's family and many other innocent people to Nocturna, and the one responsible for my life turning to crap.

My face heats with emotion and I crouch too, getting ready to attack. I take off running across the room, screaming a battle cry at the top of my lungs.

As the distance between us closes, he lunges forward in a sprint, mirroring my action. Our collision course crashes shoulder to shoulder, fingers digging deep into each other's skin. He's much larger in height and muscle, and when he tosses me over his side and I land with a crash into the debris, I instantly wonder if I misjudged the playing ground. Can I beat him?

He turns and leaps. When he's about to land on me, I jump, lifting both legs and using the bottom of my feet to launch him in another direction, throwing him off to allow me time to regain my footing.

He jumps to his feet and pivots to face me, adjusts his stance, and whips a kick in my direction. His foot makes contact, pummeling my side. Snapping his foot back quickly, he does it again before I can even think to respond, and I tumble away.

With the next switch kick, I scurry away and set up a kickboxing stance. I manage to land a few punches to his face. When my fist connects with his jaw, it's as solid as rock, which sends pain spidering over my knuckles.

I take off running, looking for anything to help me gain the upper hand. Up ahead there's a ten-foot partial concrete wall. As I near, I take several running steps forward, launch up the side of the wall in a parkour move, and flip over the

Grand Master. He doesn't see it coming because when I land facing him, he's turned away.

I strike him between his shoulder blades and he flies forward, slamming his jaw into the concrete wall. Blood spatters like red paint and he groans, immediately boosting off with his palms. The veins in his forehead pulse with rage. A mixture of dirt and sweat paints his bulging arms. But now that I've had a decent hit on him, I'm positive I can land more.

We fight intensely for many minutes, kicking and punching in what seems like endless repetition. I bend and pick up some trash and throw it in his face to distract him while throwing a heavy punch to his gut. His posture caves but with his lightning reflexes, he captures one of my wrists, somehow crushing it with his grip. In retaliation, I bash my knee into his arm.

He's wearing down and now it's my turn for some banter. "Looking a little tired, old man." I spit the dirt from my mouth, remembering how old he truly is, and how impossibly wrong that info has to be. No one more than a hundred years old would look or fight this well.

"It's about time you spoke up. I was starting to think you were all looks and no brain."

My eyes widen at the remark.

"Creep." I punch him again, but he kicks me first and I fly away, landing at the bottom of the mountain of trash. I flail about in the garbage, trying to stand, but not before I grab a steel rod, sharpened into a point at the end. Whipping around,

I drive the spear into his bicep. It pierces the skin, penetrating the muscle, and exits from the opposite side.

For a moment I can't believe what I've done; I've seriously injured him. It was my intention, yes, but now that I've followed through I'm in shock. He pauses too, stumbles backward, staring at the impalement. I think we're finished, surely he can't continue like this, but he grips the rod with his good hand and pulls it slowly from his arm. There's no blood, only a puncture. My brow furrows in confusion.

He laughs, seemingly unharmed by what's happened. "I should kill you for that." He steps forward to continue our fight and throws the spear back at me. It nearly slices my leg as I scramble away, rolling under a bombed-out vehicle for cover. He jumps onto the hood and bounces, his weight pressing the car down and sending a rain of dirt, rust, and loose engine parts over my face.

"Come out, Sera. It's no fun without you."

He's insane.

I slide out and make a run for the pile of garbage. When I reach it, I rapidly crab-walk up the hill, slipping and sliding. He leaps from the hood and races in pursuit, but when he follows, I realize that this is one thing I have on him—I'm smaller. His large frame disturbs more of the debris, causing an avalanche of garbage everywhere he climbs. I scurry to the top and race across the ridge of the mound, leaping from one precariously placed piece of trash to another. That's when I head for the junkyard crane.

I climb the open metal ladder with beams that crisscross high into the sky like an erector set. At the end, I struggle to climb into the control car, trying not to look down or even think about how high I am. Sweat drips over my skin, making my hands slippery, and I almost lose my grip and fall to my death as I crawl into the driver's seat. The students below scream with excitement or fright; I don't know which.

Grand Master Levi continues to climb the mountain of garbage. Once he makes it to the ridgeline, he'll be able to move faster, so I hurry.

I turn the key in the ignition and the crane rumbles to life. There are a few levers, just like that arcade game with the crane and the silver claw; I just have to pretend that the Grand Master is the prize.

Peeking out my cab window, I adjust the levers, lining up the junkyard magnet with his body. When I think I have the two aligned and just when I'm about to drop the ten-ton magnet the size of a smart car on his head, the Grand Master mysteriously lifts from the ground. He's not flying exactly but shooting upward, drawn toward to the magnet until he's stuck to the bottom of it.

The hateful man hangs there by his damaged arm, screaming profanities and pointing in my direction with his free hand.

From my perch, I look down and see students, Society guards, and Miss Swift gathered below and pointing up, though I don't understand what's happened.

Confused, I climb out of the cab and shimmy down the metal ladder. When I reach the bottom, I scramble across the mountain of garbage until I'm standing directly below the Grand Master. He's attached to the magnet with several other bits of trash and garbage; black droplets leak from his magnetized limb and a few land on my forehead. I run my hand through the goo and pull it back to find black oil oozing over my fingertips.

Trying to connect the dots, I look back up to inspect him. The flesh hangs from his arm like a wet and ripped towel that's dripping wet. What lies beneath doesn't look like anything human; it's not muscle or bones. It looks remarkably Animate—metal and obviously highly magnetic.

"Should have known you were trash," I yell to him.

"You little witch," he screams, flailing about wildly.

A piece of me wants to end him. I eye the crane, thinking I can rush up and drop him, crushing him to death. But behind me, Society guards yell for Professor Raunnebaum's help, who has just reentered the room.

"Turn the hologram machine off!" they scream.

I look down at them and realize I'm still twenty feet off the ground. If they turn off the hologram, removing the hill of garbage, I'm going to have a nasty fall. So I scramble back down, sliding most of the way on my backside.

Bishop and Sam rush to my side, crushing me into a group hug, and I feel every bruise forming on my body. When I moan, they quickly pull away.

"God, Sera, you were incredible. Absolutely insane but incredible."

"If you weren't worried about what he was going to do to you before, you should now." Sam takes a towel and drags it across my cheeks, the touch burning on impact. I'm bleeding and didn't even realize it.

"What happened to lying low?" Miss Swift asks tersely as she joins us.

I cock an eyebrow at her as Sam continues to dab at my face. "He deserved worse."

"Maybe so, but this isn't your destiny. Your energy is meant for more than him, something greater. You really should learn how to control your anger," she shoots back.

With just her frosty words, I instantly feel guilty for letting my emotions take over. I'm not perfect on so many levels, and I'm unsure why the Masters would pick me as a Chosen, or even a Watcher for that matter. I don't deserve to be either. I sigh, angry with myself when I remember Bishop's family.

"If he didn't know what you could do before, he certainly does now," Sam says meaningfully.

I look around, surveying the room. The Society guards scamper to release the Grand Master from the crane.

Macey appears from the class group. "Sera, if I were you I would take off. Grand Master Levi is pissed, and rightfully so. I don't know what's gotten into you lately," she says, her eyes open wide with concern. "Is there anything you wanna tell me?" She looks me over.

"I'm sorry, Mace, I can't." If she knew, maybe she'd understand, but I can't really fault her if I don't let her in on what I've learned. Sometimes it's safer to be clueless. For once, I'm glad that not everyone I know is involved with all the craziness that surrounds me.

At my words, she narrows her eyes, spins, and stalks away. Her team, Quinn and Xavier, fall into step behind her, rejoining the rest of the class to watch the Grand Master's ruckus. Others, not in our class, have joined the group. They must have heard him all the way down the hall in Olde Town.

"I'm leaving," I announce.

The others don't try to stop me. It's probably best that I keep a low profile for the rest of the day. For as long as I can, anyway. I stride across the room, which is still a junkyard, heading for the door of the gym. It's the only thing that remains of the real gym. But I don't make it that far because four guards stop me.

"You'll have to come with us, Miss Parrish. And your team too."

№ 28
THE CONFRONTATION

THE GUARDS BARRICADE US IN THE MEDITATION room, the room where Sam and all the other Seers gather to meditate while their teams Wander.

Oversized deep-cushioned chairs, sofas, and daybeds sit around the perimeter in front of golden-colored walls. Sheer curtains hang here and there, creating private nooks, while large multicolored pillows dot the wood floor. Normally several candles sparkle like stars, helping to create the most relaxing ambience for Seers, but now the overhead lights buzz brightly in the empty room, and the harsh light seems out of place.

I drop into a soft chair and drape my dirty, sweaty limbs over the arms, letting out a sigh. I should be worried about facing the Grand Master, but for some reason I'm not. Everything, even the bad stuff, happens for a reason, and each new event leads you down the road you are meant to travel. I never believed that more than I do now.

Sam and Bishop don't look as confident. When I see their worried faces, I feel guilty that I've pulled them into this. Sam stands rigid next to me, winding her hair through her fingers, the way she does when she's nervous. Bishop, on the other hand, paces the room, raking his fingers through his hair. Every so often he glances in my direction to give me the evil eye. Watching them both I feel guilty for being who I am, for being a possible Chosen, and for pulling them into this mess—my mess.

I stand up to apologize, but before I can open my mouth several more guards burst into the room, clearly angry, followed closely by Grand Master Levi. He's dirty and bloody from our confrontation, much like me, but he's not laughing. Not anymore.

Pushing myself from the chair, I stand up tall, lift my chin, and place my hands on my hips. I will not shrink away from him, especially now, but I can't help staring at his damaged arm, the one I impaled with an iron rod. It's hard not to when the skin's hanging there, dark and rubbery, dripping with oil.

"You think you're very clever, Miss Parrish, but if you knew what I had in store for you today, you would not have pressed me to fight." He reaches for the dangling skin with his good hand, tugs, and rips it from his frame like a rubber glove. The inorganic skin rips free with a nauseating wet snap, revealing the arm's inner workings. He throws the sickening piece of meat on the floor and it slides across the room, landing at my feet.

I don't look down because I know his movements are carefully calculated to elicit a response. Giving him what he wants, even just a glance at a mound of used rubber skin, gives him control. He will not control me.

Grand Master Levi's arm is a machine from shoulder to fingertips: metal rods where bones should be, cranks where joints should be, and a metal frame, shaped and sculpted like muscle.

He lifts his mechanical arm, testing its motion, swinging it from side to side and flexing all his digits. The arm halts, sticking to one spot in midair, and he grunts with disgust and glares at me. "You damn well ruined the thing."

Dr. Shockey, my tormenter from just days ago, walks into the room. He moves with purpose, drops his briefcase on a chair, opens it, and removes a screwdriver. From his hat, he lowers a magnifying glass over his eye and immediately turns to inspect the Grand Master's faulty arm. Stabbing the tool into the gears and joints, he goes to work, repairing the damage.

"In fact, I think you would have been long gone by now if you were smart." Grand Master Levi glances over, searching for a hint of fear, a retort, but I won't give it to him. Shoving all emotion aside, I dig deep and keep my face placid and unmoved.

"Nothing to say?" He lifts an eyebrow.

"What should I say?" He can't hurt me more than he has already. With all the betrayals I've suffered at the hands of the Society—the death of my mom, of Turner, the exile of Bishop's family to Nocturna, the brainwashing and bribing of my friends, and let's not forget, the sacrificial killing of innocent twin babies during the Oaths—what else can he do?

"Oh, sweet Sera. I think you'll have plenty to say in the next day with what I have planned for you." He pauses with a cynical smile, the same one he wore when he thought he could beat me in a fight.

"Rex!" he calls out. "Bring me the evidence."

Very quickly, Rex rolls in a flat-screen TV on a wheeled cart. The guard hands Grand Master Levi a remote as someone dims the lights.

"I think you'll all enjoy this." The Grand Master lifts the remote, pointing it at the screen, and the TV turns on. From a dark screen, an image materializes.

"It appears you've been a very naughty young lady," he proclaims with pleasure.

The images on the video are unmistakable. Bright security lights, like those you'd see on a football field, illuminate the scene. Three figures run from the edge of the pit of Nocturna and back to the line of shrubs and trees, disappearing. A figure reappears, running directly for the pit. Several Society guards, only little white dots on the screen, take chase. From this bird's-eye view, it looks as though the guard dog will attack the person before they leap. But I know better, because that person running is me. This video surveillance is from the night I jumped into the pit of Nocturna to find Terease. I should have known they'd have security cameras.

Bishop, Sam, and I scoot closer together, team instinct urging us to stick together for protection.

"Any of this look familiar?" He waves his good arm.

"No," Bishop says. "What is it that we're looking at?"

"Don't play games with me, child. I know for a fact that these intruders are the three of you." The Grand Master points to the scene.

"They look like dots to me," I say with a straight face.

"Well, let's fast-forward this, shall we? Maybe there's something on here that will be more interesting."

As the video fast-forwards, the doctor finishes his work on Grand Master Levi's arm and steps away. The Grand Master paces, tests his repaired limb, moving it from side to side, and up and down. He stops in front of the television, points the remote and presses a button, which halts the screen. We're looking at the same image of the pit of Nocturna, but this time it's daytime and the perspective is closer, making the image larger. A person appears on the field—a boy. Bishop.

I stiffen because there's no denying his identity.

"You see this young man here," the Grand Master says.

"Well, he looks quite a bit like our Bishop. Don't you agree?"

We have nothing to say to this. Bishop grabs my hand and squeezes. This video was taken the day that Bishop snuck into the pit to find me.

"Anything to say for yourselves—hmm?" The Grand Master pauses, clearly for effect. "No? It's okay, there's more to see. Let's move on." But instead, in a spastic rage, he slams the remote to the ground. It smashes into so many pieces of plastic, and the batteries roll across the floor.

"No," he shouts. "Why waste any more time on this! You know what you've done. Trespassing, illegally entering Nocturna, breaking into Gabe's apartment, stealing a transporter, and stealing this—"

He removes my mom's journal from the hand of one of the Society guards that have just entered the room.

"You've got a lot of nerve snooping around my room," I bite out.

"Is that what you're worried about? That I snooped in your room? Sera, Sera," he tuts in a show of fake concern. "That's the least of your worries."

The Grand Master paces back and forth, shaking his head with dismay. "Let's not mess with the piddling infractions. There's something much more important that we need to discuss." He turns in a circle, journal pressed to his chest. When he faces me again, his expression is serious but his eyes dance with delight as he raises an eyebrow and simply says, "The results of your blood test."

No

29

A PILGRIMAGE

M Y HEARTS SHRINKS AT THE MENTION OF MY
blood test.

At his cue, Dr. Shockey hands over a piece of paper.

Grand Master Levi holds it to his eyes, gleefully pretending to read the results. "Congratulations! It's positive!" He pinches the page playfully between his fingertips.

My lips tighten as I suppress a retort.

Watching closely for my reaction, he smiles and his eyes brighten with a manic light. "Wasn't what you expected?" He balls the paper and tosses it on the floor.

"I don't know what you're talking about; I don't even

know what you've tested me for," I lie.

"Sera." He sits on the arm of a sofa, one leg dangling, and sighs dramatically. "I think it's time we come clean with each other. I know you're a Watcher, a potential Chosen, and I know you know what that is. Okay?"

I take a moment to consider if I can even fight this, if I can play dumb any longer. With so many guards surrounding me, there's no way to escape. Maybe if I play along, I'll have a better chance of protecting Sam and Bishop. I don't answer quickly enough and he begins again.

"Do you think yourself so special?" His words turn to acid, and he springs forward, near my face. "Do you think you arrived at this point of potential Chosen above all others without my help?" His words come so forcefully they spray spit. Instinctively, I close my eyes to protect them.

"Look at me," he roars.

I open them and set my jaw.

"I made you!" He grabs my chin with his robotic hand and clenches my cheeks between the cool metal of his fingertips. "I made you and own you." He squeezes tightly, contorting my face.

Bishop shoves the Grand Master away. "Stay away from her!" he yells, taking a defensive position. His muscles surge with a primal instinct to protect.

Every guard in the room lunges forward and within moments, Bishop is restrained, kicking and yelling. We're outnumbered.

"Get rid of him," Grand Master Levi says with an annoyed flick of the hand. Several more guards wrangle Bishop as he fights frantically for freedom. Sam and I launch to his aid, punching and kicking guards away, but with so many we're easily torn away from him. The guards shove me into a chair, hold me down, and secure my arms and legs with plastic zip-tie restraints. They do the same with Sam so we're facing each other. When they're done, I'm still jerking and squirming with infuriation.

"Where are you taking him?" I yell as they frog-march Bishop out of the room, with Dr. Shockey following behind.

"It depends, really." He circles me.

"On?"

He stands behind my chair and leans down, almost resting his head on my shoulder. His breath disturbs my hair, warming my ear, and I cringe. "It depends on you, of course."

I lean away, drawing my shoulders to my ears in disgust because I'd rather have snakes slithering over my body than have that odious man anywhere near me.

Beside me, he sits back down on the arm of the sofa. I take note that he doesn't sit level with me; no, that would be beneath him.

"I think we need a history lesson so you can appreciate this amazing gift that I've bestowed upon you. How does that sound?"

I turn my head away, looking across the room. From the corner of my eye, I see him move as he continues to speak.

"I've heard that Samantha plays a lovely rendition of Bach's Cello Suite no. 1. Or at least, she used to," he says, and then with a crack, I hear her scream. I whip my head toward them and she's crying. He releases her hands from behind her back and I see two of her delicate pink fingers bend awkwardly, broken, and clenched inside Grand Master's large mechanical hand.

"Stop! Stop! I'm listening. Leave her alone!"

"Very good. That's all I wanted, of course." He strokes Sam's blonde hair with his palm. Her head tips to one side and she sobs softly, the sound causing my heart to sink.

"You see, I've been Grand Master for a very long time. Isn't that correct, Rex?" He looks over his shoulder.

"Since 1894 to be exact, sir." Rex folds his large arms across his chest.

Though Sam confirmed this, I still don't believe it. "Impossible." I shake my head.

"No, no, I'm afraid it's very possible." He waves his finger. "Ah, that was a grand year, brings back so many memories. I bet you were quite surprised to meet me that day at the exposition with Elijah."

"How? How have you lived so long?"

"Now that's better, interaction! Well, that's quite a fun story actually, and I'm positive you'll both find it very interesting. I'll just give you the highlights, not to bore you."

He clasps his hands behind his back and begins to pace, taking on a professorial air as if he's giving a class a lecture.

"Within every generation, I allow a fully developed Chosen to be created from a Watcher. Yes, created. The Society has known for a long time how to look for the signs. Early signs...not these things I had you tested for, Sera, blood tests and so forth. The earliest sign of a potential Watcher begins with the bearing of twins in a Wandering family."

I stiffen.

"We'll use Bishop and Turner as an example here. How's that?"

He wants me to nod but it takes all my might to just stare through him and not avert my attention. If I do, he'll probably break another of Sam's fingers.

"I'll take that as a yes!" He smiles. "Now, if I had killed one of them at birth, sacrificing him, I would have effectively smothered any chance that there would be a matured Chosen in their future team. And when Terease harvested your team, I knew from then on that either you or young Samantha was my Chosen. I only needed to wait and look for the additional signs to pick you out. Right on time, you showed signs of manifesting the skills of a Protector, and now I suspect you can see a relic's life path just as well as Samantha here." He places a hand on her shoulder and she tries to shrink away, but he clamps her shoulder tightly, holding her in place until she whimpers.

"The Society had been practicing this slaughter for thousands of years, but when I came into power, every so often, when I needed it, I allowed for one Chosen to be made. This time around it was you."

"You're lying," I spit out. The thought that this repulsive man is responsible for who I'm becoming sickens me. What I thought was a wonderful gift from the Masters to set our kind free of Wandering is nothing more than manipulation by the Society, sending me down a path where he wants to control me in a new, even more sinister way. The walls of my world seem to compress more tightly around my soul with each new revelation and I want so badly to scream. I grind my teeth and clench my jaw, holding back my cries. Only a deep tremble of hate alleviates this ceaseless pain.

"Oh no, I'm not lying. These are all my cards on the table. I'm leveling with you, remember?"

"Why?" I say through my teeth.

"Because there's something that I need to exist, something that I need in order to stay youthful and continue my rule, and a fully matured Chosen is the only one who can obtain it for me."

"So, what is it? This *thing* that keeps you alive?"

"Let's not get ahead of ourselves, shall we?" He pulls the chain on the information, drawing it back, so he can feed me little bits at a time.

"The question is, will you help?" he asks and stands behind Sam, bracketing her shoulders with his hands. She cringes and closes her eyes.

"I said leave her alone!" Of course I have no choice in whether I'll help him or not. Will I do it willingly? No. Will

I do it for Bishop and Sam? Yes. How can I not do everything he asks when he's holding the two most important people in my world hostage?

"You haven't told me what it is I need to do."

"First, I need you to run a small errand. Nothing major or out of the ordinary for you." He looks back to the TV, which is now playing video of Sam, Bishop, and me breaking in Gabe's apartment, the video recording I thought Miss Swift had destroyed. Apparently there are additional hidden cameras that even she doesn't know about.

"Go on."

"So that we're not wasting time, let's get you ready to go." He waves a group of people into the room. From what they're carrying—garment bags, makeup cases, and mirrors—I can tell they're stylists and are here to prepare me for my errand, an errand that will require Wandering.

They drag a curtain on a track in the ceiling between the Grand Master and me, and he disappears from view. Immediately the stylist strips away my grime-covered workout clothes and scrubs me with a washcloth, which she repeatedly dips into a bucket of water. I cover my naked self, wanting to fight, but I think of Sam and what he may do to her next, so I eventually just close my eyes, sending myself to my happy place, if I even have one of those anymore.

Grand Master Levi continues to talk from the other side of the curtain. "Your errand is to Wander back in time and retrieve the crown of Unika, where it's displayed at the World's

Columbian Exposition of 1893 in Chicago."

I perk up at this because it's finally happening. This is when I go back to retrieve the crown, but when I saw the scenario play out before, I had no idea I'd been coerced to do so.

"This is the last known location of the relic," he continues. "There it was shown as part of the Western Electricity Display in the Electricity Building. There were many things the people of the time were deeply fascinated with, among them Egyptian artifacts and electricity. Here's a map of the buildings for you to memorize before you leave."

He hands the map around the curtain, and I clutch a towel around my now-clean body and snatch it out of his hands. He retreats to the other side while the stylist starts blow-drying my hair and dressing me.

I study the map, holding it close to my face. The Electricity Building was one of the only exhibition halls that Bishop and I didn't see. Perhaps Gabe toured our class there after we ditched them.

"Why can't you just go back and get it yourself?" I ask him through the curtain. "You've already been there, lived in that time."

"Why would I when I have one of the most powerful Wanderers of all time at my disposal?"

I roll my eyes.

"I made you to serve, and now it's time to pay up."

Snorting softly, I mumble, "I should have killed you when I had the chance."

"I'm afraid you don't have it in you, Sera. If you did, I'd be dead. I imagine that in time, I'll break you down with whatever means necessary, and you'll be subservient to my every whim."

I tighten my jaw, ready to attack him with more words, but I imagine Sam on the other side, fingers broken, and Bishop, wherever he is with Dr. Shockey, so I hold my tongue.

"At any rate, pet, you'll need this little relic to move on to the next task."

The stylist pulls back the curtain, revealing my makeover to the Grand Master. I'm dressed in the clothing of the time, namely the same eggplant-colored dress I saw my future self wearing yesterday. Someone pins a wide-rimmed hat on my head and shoves my feet into a pair of boots. As usual, I'll fit right into the 1890s, and no on will know who or what I am.

"You look lovely. I knew that color would complement your beautiful skin." He scans me appreciatively and I want to kick that creepy look off his face.

From the corner of my eye, I see my scorpion Animate crawl out from my old pile of clothes, across the floor, and under my dress. The Animate mounts my foot, tangling himself within the laces of my boot.

Sam looks over at me and I search her eyes for confirmation that she's okay. I attempt to push into her mind to exchange thoughts with her, the way I have with Hologram Turner, and I'm surprised when it doesn't work. It seems I haven't developed this skill yet.

She nods slightly anyway, probably reading my face, and I cross my arms in an effort to keep them restrained and to myself. I wouldn't want a stray fist to fly at the Grand Master's gut.

"Any questions?" he asks.

I shake my head and avoid his eyes. "Let's finish this."

No.

30

A SHOW

THE GUARDS LEAD SAM AND ME OUT OF THE
Seer's meditation room and back into Olde Town. News
of what I've done to the Grand Master has apparently spread
faster than wildfire; everyone's buzzing. This is still high
school, after all. Should I expect anything less?

When we enter the city, they drag Sam away from me and
down the dark corridor to the library. That must be where
they're keeping Bishop. At least they'll be together, hopefully
safe from the ministrations of the evil Dr. Shockey.

The students gather in Olde Town to gawk. They huddle
in groups, stand on chairs, and hang from tree branches to
capture a better look at me. As I scan the faces, they boo me

in return—maybe because they don't know any better, or because they've been prompted to react. They're brainwashed, after all, but whatever the reason, they must see my act of challenging, fighting, and hurting the Grand Master as treason to the Society.

I hold up my head, knowing that the course I'm on is true, even if they don't realize they're on the wrong side. I scan the students and pick out Macey in the crowd. Her team stands behind her, and they're all booing and pumping their arms too. At this sight my heart breaks, but I can't blame her. If I were in her situation, not knowing the truth about the Society, I might be doing the same. My eyes burn as tears threaten, and I remind myself that I chose not to tell her everything to keep her safe.

When the Grand Master and his guards have sufficiently paraded me around the city for everyone to see as a show of power, they guide me to one side of the plaza beneath the shadow of the obelisk.

Rex stands on a bench chair, elevating himself above the crowd. He waves his arms, hushing the roaring group. "Students, I know you're as shocked and saddened as I about this afternoon's display of lack of respect to our gracious and generous leader." He gestures to Grand Master Levi, who drops his gaze to the ground in a nauseating display of humility. "But even in light of his serious injuries, he would like to say a few words."

Grand Master Levi leans on his skull cane, wobbling convincingly with uncertain footing across the way, and two guards lift him up and onto the bench beside Rex. His arm, the one I injured, is wrapped within layers of gauze with red blood seeping through. It's fake, of course, to hide the true nature of his arm from the students.

Rex braces the Grand Master's back to carry the weight of him. With the Grand Master acting like this, like he's truly been hurt, he's playing on the sympathy of all the students and everyone here as they wait quietly and patiently for his words.

I roll my eyes at the display, but keep my mouth shut, thinking of my team being held captive by Dr. Shockey.

"I speak to you this day about forgiveness," the Grand Master says, projecting his voice over the crowd. "Forgiveness of a child that lets her emotions control her. Even though you've disrespected myself, this Society, and all of the people here, I forgive you, Seraphina Parrish."

My mouth drops open at his words. The crowd erupts in applause and cheerful shouts. He's won them by leading them to believe he's humble, generous, and forgiving. Everything he's not.

Every muscle in my body tightens with anger and humiliation. His megalomaniacal manipulation will never end, not until I set us free. My goal to fulfill the prophecy entrenches itself deeper into my soul, and I decide that I will go on this errand only to retrieve the crown for myself. Then I will use it to set every one of us free from this life by fulfilling the prophecy.

"I'm sending Sera on a Wandering pilgrimage, where she will repent, seeking amends for her shortcomings."

"Such a freaking liar," I whisper, the words twisting from my lips.

Guards help the Grand Master from the bench, and he staggers to place a hand on my shoulder and smiles weakly. Very unlike the man who threw the remote control in the Seer's meditation room, or tortured Sam just a little bit ago.

"Sera, think long and hard about the mission I'm sending you on. I truly think it's a matter of life and death," he says loud enough for everyone nearby to hear, and I don't miss the double meaning. It's my team's life or death if I don't bring back the crown.

I nod because I have to. For someone who can't control her emotions, I'd say I'm doing a pretty darn good job. At least I manage to do it when it counts the most.

The Society guards clear a long path, and Grand Master Levi steps away with a look on his face that's more like a parent who's sending a child off to college. Seeing the students and teachers lapping up his playacting makes me feel sick to my stomach.

Rex steps forward and hands me my relic. It's a coin, one that passed through Chicago in 1893 during the exposition. I take it and close it tightly within my palm.

First there's a low rumble, but by the time I take off sprinting across the plaza, all those present chant the word "repent" over and over. The sound resonates deep within the city walls and awakens the Animate lions and raptors. They jump or fly to the fortified walls to watch the mayhem for themselves.

Finally I gain enough speed and the ground shakes beneath me. Historic buildings and walls snap and crush in on themselves as the plaza of stone behind breaks apart and rolls up behind me like a wave. It blocks the light above, just before it crashes down from the sky, catapulting me into a wormhole.

I fly, tumbling with no gravity to hold me in place, only speed, perhaps light speed, to send me back in time. The landing is messy because the wormhole spits me out on the shore of a lagoon where the ground is uneven and riddled with brush. I fall to the dirt, landing just a few inches from sliding into the water.

While I'm on the ground, I lift my skirt, unwind the scorpion Animate from my bootlaces, and place him on the rim of my hat. He walks across it and nests himself into the loopy bows in the back where no one will notice him.

I drag myself away from the lagoon and take in my surroundings. There's a Japanese structure behind me, which I remember from the map that Grand Master made me memorize.

I step out onto the walkway, slipping easily into the crowd. The day is sunny with a light breeze blowing off the nearby Lake Michigan, the same as it was yesterday when I was here with my classmates for our field trip. And soon, I will see myself with Bishop, but this time from a new perspective.

As I make my way through the exposition, I notice many people funneling into the opening beneath a soaring archway of the Electricity Building, so I follow. Inside, the ceilings reach several stories high, lined by steel frames. Several companies and inventors exhibit, many of which I recognize: Westinghouse, Nikola Tesla, American Bell, Thomas Edison, and General Electric. When I reach the Western Electric Company display, the one the Grand Master told me about, the exhibit resembles an Egyptian temple.

I follow a tour group inside. The interior is dark, but my eyes quickly adjust. When I turn a corner, I find several display boxes built into the wall that feature Egyptian artifacts. Looking for the crown, I walk quickly from display to display, but it's not until the final room that I spot it.

The crown sits on its own stand in the center of the room. A woman removes the glass box that protects it. Noting the box of tools at her feet, I make a quick assessment. She's merely a preservationist, cleaning the relic.

She holds up the crown in white-gloved hands and appraises it, and then her gaze flicks to me as I approach. "It took you long enough. Your mother said you would be here sooner," she says.

"My mother said..." My words drift off.

"Yes, Eliza Parrish." She nods.

I step closer to see the color of her eyes. Violet.

"Several months ago, your mother summoned me from my Society post. When we met, she tasked me with restoring

Unika's crown. She presented me with the emerald, the one that was set within a sundial bracelet, one Terease passed on to her, and with that and the help of Elijah Vanderpool's unfragmentation machine, I was able to restore the crown to its original state. Since then, I've been the Keeper of this relic, charged with its safety until the Chosen appeared. And here you are. You are the Chosen, are you not?" she asks.

"Yes, I think so. I mean, I should be after tomorrow, after the Oaths."

"So then, it's not done—not yet. The Masters haven't completed the promise of a Chosen." She continues cleaning the crown and looks down. "Come back when you've been marked," she says plainly.

"I can't come back; I need it now. You don't understand—"

"No, you don't understand. I cannot relinquish this until I see proof, no matter who you are. Eliza left me with strict instructions."

I cringe, remembering the tattoos Dr. Shockey tested me for with the electrified light saber, the ones I saw on the leathery skin. I've seen no sign of them on my own body.

Instead of backing away, I push up my sleeve, as if to show her the marks that I know aren't there. I'm not even sure where they'll be, if and when they appear. She raises an eyebrow as I step forward.

"So, you do have them." She meets me, and I raise my bent elbow. When she's close enough, I smash my limb into her jaw. Her head jerks back and her wire eyeglasses fly off her face, but she's barely affected.

"You should not have done that." She tips her head forward and her determined eyes meet my gaze. "You will not win." Her eyes narrow dangerously and she squeezes my arm, digging her fingers into my skin.

"I need that relic," I say through clenched teeth. "My friends, my team, they're in trouble."

"That's no concern of mine." She uses all her strength to push me away, propelling me into a glass exhibit that shatters. Bits of broken glass fall in a cascade and crash to the floor around me, causing tourists perusing the exhibit to stop and stare in shock, before several run away screaming.

"It will be if I don't make it to the Oaths. Then you'll never have your Chosen." I stand tall and straighten my dress, brushing off a few bits of glass that cling. "Or you can give it to me before I really hurt you."

This time she laughs. "Do you think Eliza would leave this relic for anyone to guard? Stupid child."

I hadn't considered that she might be as strong as me. It makes sense. "Yes, but I'm the only one with a Turner," I say, pronouncing the last word loudly.

She looks confused. "What's a Turner?"

"I'm a Turner." Hologram Turner appears in a sparkling blue dust cloud, arms folded across his chest.

The woman spins to face him and when she does, I take her out.

№

31

THE CROWN

THE WOMAN FALLS TO THE FLOOR AND HER blonde hair spills free from her coiffure. I feel guilty for what I've done. We're on the same side, and she's just doing her job. A job tasked her by my own mother before her passing.

I grab the crown of Unika and push the Animate back into the nest of bows on top of my hat before I take off running. Spectators gather around, so it's only a matter of time before the police become involved.

I haven't traveled very far from the scene when I'm met by a pair of familiar eyes. I pause for only a moment, knowing that running into the Underground gang can't possibly be good news, and I take off sprinting out of the building and into the Chicago sunlight.

The group is not nearly as fast as me but it's something that Drake, their leader, yells that causes me to stop, turn, and face them.

"Your Turner," he yells. "He's alive."

"What?" I step backward in surprise.

"He made it through the wormhole with Cece." Drake steps forward, and though I haven't seen him since last semester, he still makes me uneasy. To this day, I have no idea why they were ever after me to begin with or why they ever wanted me dead.

My face crumples with confusion. "Turner's dead. You're lying," I say and take another step back.

"I'm not. Cece is losing domination over the Underground because you took the dreamdrives. Without them to control the members, they've gone raving mad, rallying on their own, attacking random Society buildings."

"You're lying," I say, and begin to move away.

"I'm not. In fact, if you come with me, I'd be happy to supply more information," Drake offers, pleading with outstretched arms.

I glance through the crowd, trying to make sense of his words, and finally see my past self and Bishop not very far away, staring at me. I remember seeing myself from their point of view and what I looked like to them.

My eyes glass over as sadness creeps up on me. I have no idea if Drake is telling the truth or if he's trying to trick me. I firmly grasp the crown in my hand, remembering my task. I can't let the Underground detour me with their lies. I need to return to my true time and save Sam and Bishop. So without another thought, I pivot and dash away from them, opening the time travel doorway and Wander back into the future, back to the Academy.

With my mind, I bend the wormhole, and instead of landing in Olde Town, where the students still chant for me to repent, I land in my apartment, slamming into the refrigerator, where I press my cheek on the cool stainless steel and take in a deep breath of relief. My dress puddles around me as I slide to the floor in confusion.

I look down at the crown, clenched in my hand. It's exactly like I remember from Stu's drawing from last semester. A winged scarab holds the green emerald, flanked by two Egyptian-style Seeing eyes and two scorpions. Each side is a pictorial representation of a Wandering team: the eyes being the Seer, the Scorpion being the Protector, and the wings representing the Wanderer. My mom had this reconstructed for me, but how did she know this was my path?

It bothers me that I had to hurt the Keeper in order to obtain the crown, but at least it will help my friends and eventually fulfill the prophecy. I want nothing more in this moment than to control my own destiny, control who I love, and know exactly who my family and friends are in this life. I deserve at least that. All of us do. I can only hope that the prophecy will allow that. It has to be better than what we have now.

With a tug at the large hat pin securing it, I remove my hat and place it on the floor next to me. The scorpion Animate crawls out of the bow, over my thigh, and down the side of my leg, making its way across the tile floor. A beam of light shoots from its face and the illumination shimmers into the shape of Hologram Turner. Seated and facing me, he extends his legs, intertwining them familiarly with mine.

When he takes my hand and laces our fingers together, locking them tight, I lose it and begin to cry.

"You had no choice, you had to hurt her," he says.

"I know." I sniffle.

"Then why are you crying?"

"Because I ran away when Drake told me you might still be alive."

Turner stiffens at this. "What are you talking about?"

"The Underground gang, the one that tried to kill me last semester, they somehow found me at the exposition and tried to convince me that you're alive. They said you and Cece are alive!" I suck in a breath and exhale a sob, then begin to cry harder.

"That's ridiculous. If I were, nothing could keep me from you." He rubs his hand along my cheek, stroking the skin with his thumb. The electricity causes me to shiver and I hiccup suddenly, then swipe at my wet face and try to compose myself.

"Unless," I say uncertainly, "there's some reason. Maybe real Turner is hurt? Maybe he can't leave. Maybe Cece's holding him captive?"

He looks skeptical.

"It would explain why the Underground attacks continue. She's still alive," I say with more conviction. After further consideration, Drake's explanation of Cece losing control of the Underground makes sense. The dreamdrive she used to control her members is still hidden away at Mona's home.

"I know they never found their bodies, but still, their survival was impossible since a Wandering compass is needed to travel to and from Gibeon," he reminds. "And have you ever felt Turner in your mind, like you have with me?"

I shake my head. "I've only shared thoughts with you. In fact, I tried with Sam and it didn't work. I haven't completely developed that skill."

"But you're also forgetting the most important part." He squeezes my hand. "Real Turner can only travel through time with his Wanderer. That's with you and only you. Which means that he didn't make it, Sera. I'm sorry. No one wishes him alive more than me."

My chest hitches with new sobs and I bawl louder for my poor heart that's breaking again. Feeling emotionally and mentally drained, I go off on a rant. "I'm tired of being the strong one. Tired of being the one that fixes everything, and the one who will save everyone." He doesn't say anything and my blubbering continues. "I know it's selfish." I wipe the tears from my face. "I haven't even had enough time to grieve for Turner or my mom, and if I wasn't trying to save everyone in Nocturna, I'd be off investigating whether Drake's telling the truth—even if it's completely impossible."

"Sera, you have so much courage, strength, and resilience. Even if you tried, I know you couldn't control your determination, you couldn't slow down and do nothing because you're so strong."

"I'm only strong because of the people who support me. Because of you."

"Still, it's okay to cry. Even if you need to take a few minutes to recoup, you'll always strike back. I've never met anyone as amazing as you. Everyone needs to recharge, even if you're meant to be the superhero."

He lifts my hand and presses his lips to the base of my fingers. The warmth of the electricity that makes him live spreads over my skin, prickling the hair on my arms.

"The Grand Master has Sam and Bishop?" he asks.

I let out a snort. "Yeah. He's unbearable and manipulative."

"Then you just need to beat him at his own game."

I let those words churn, considering what I would have to do to beat him at his own game. I lift my head to Turner. "You're right, that's exactly what I need to do." I smile. And in that second I discover a wellspring of reenergized hope that can change our lives. If by some miracle Turner is alive and I survive this, then I will find him too.

"Let's go get 'em, love." Hologram Turner disappears, the image shrinking back into the beam of light that disappears within the Animate scorpion. The machine skitters across the floor onto my palm and I place him on my shoulder.

Then I stand up and ready myself to face my enemy.

No 32

THE GAME

INTEND TO MAKE A SCENE BECAUSE THAT'S EXACTLY what Grand Master Levi would do. I'm going to beat him at his own game, and with the help of Hologram Turner, I'll do it even better. As I think we're meant to, we make an excellent team.

First, I steal two hologram training machines from Professor Raunnebaum's laboratory. Next, I install them in Olde Town on the fortified stone walls that surround the city, being careful to avoid the Animate raptors and lions. And finally, after I'm done, I stealthily climb to the top of the six-story bell tower, and sit on the edge of the roofline. My stomach turns as I look down at the students gathered and gossiping in the town center below. They're completely unaware that I perch above.

Rex stands on the opposite side of the city at the tunnel entrance that leads to the library. He's probably waiting there, watching for my return. With a little wave on my part, he spots me and points, alerting the other guards. The group moves in my direction, cutting through the crowd as Rex takes off running back down the hall, disappearing in the darkness, hopefully to retrieve the Grand Master.

In the commotion, students abandon their chatter and look up. When I have everyone's attention, that's my cue to turn the tables and give the Grand Master a taste of his own medicine.

Students begin chanting "repent" as they did before. Their arms pump with each syllable as though they're beating the word into the air, pushing it into my lungs. As if breathing it in would change how I feel.

I stand with the crown in a bag, hanging from my waist. From this height, I can barely make out the Animate scorpion crawling across Olde Town through the piazza on his own mission. There's a gleam of light on his crystal body, and that's what my eye follows.

On the balls of my feet, I balance near the edge of the roof. Steadying myself, I raise both arms and shout, "Students, friends, Society members, and guards, I have an announcement to make—a confession."

The crowd quiets and stares. Grand Master Levi appears on the opposite side of the city, just in time to hear my speech like I'd hoped. The scorpion Animate dodges around him, sneaking down the now empty corridor. I smile inside, preparing to own this game and turn the tables.

"As you've seen in my action against the Grand Master today, by challenging him to a fight, I often struggle with this Wandering life, finding myself questioning the reason why we're here. And finally, after almost a year, with the help of the Grand Master," I gesture toward him across the square, "I've found the answers, ones that have given me a new perspective and understanding of our lives in the Society, and I have to publicly apologize and thank the Grand Master for his amazing gifts."

At my fake apology, the roar of the crowd is immediate, and students turn to look in his direction. For a moment he looks shocked at my words, then probably realizing he's on display, he smiles tightly and waves to me.

He moves to stand on a nearby park bench and rises above the crowd to speak. "Seraphina, child, I'm so glad that I've been able to help you achieve higher enlightenment," he says, obviously playing along but he can't possibly know where this is going. He brings his hands together in front of his body, as if in prayer.

I begin again. "In my pilgrimage to repent, and with the Grand Master's humble and forgiving ways, I've realized that I owe him my allegiance. And for him, as a gift, I've brought back this special relic." I remove Unika's crown from my drawstring bag and raise it above my head. The metal shines bright and golden in the false sunlight of the city, and the green emerald at the center glistens. "With this special relic, the Grand Master can serve us for as long as he sees fit. If I had my way, it would be forever."

The students go wild at my false pronouncement; even the guards clap at this. It's as though they're all programmed to react to any positive propaganda regarding the Grand Master, even if it doesn't make any sense, even if it comes from me. And their actions confirm that the Society programmed everyone in their night classes on the contrapulator, subliminally, without their knowledge. Now that Bishop, Sam, and I have stopped using the machines, we've been unfazed by the manipulations. As the students cheer, I slip my free hand into the pocket of my day dress and grasp the remote for the hologram machines that I've set up.

"And thank you, Grand Master, for taking care of my team while I was gone. I know they will be happy to be anointed tomorrow, and will pledge full loyalty to you. You should bring them out since you've been watching over them, and let them enjoy the honor of being in your presence."

The students can't hear enough; they're rowdy and becoming more amped-up by every single word of praise, but when I look at the Grand Master, he's frowning. Knowing him, he doesn't like being dictated to, and he surely doesn't like not knowing my plan, but he can't refuse when all of his people expect him to be accommodating and pure of heart.

"That's a fabulous idea, Sera." He waves for Rex to bring them out and at that moment, I press the button on the remote, activating the hologram machines that I rigged around the city.

Before Rex turns, Sam and Bishop appear from the tunnel. But they aren't really Sam and Bishop, only their holograms, made possible with the crystals from their old dreamdrives. The crystals carry the essence of them, visualized in light form, just like Hologram Turner. They've solidified enough so that no one will detect the switch.

The two stand at the entrance, half alert and squinting. Hologram Bishop has a blackened and bruised jaw, arms, body, and face, looking like a car hit him. Sam hunches, appearing limp, broken, and abused herself, her fingers bent to impossible angles. I've made the holograms look maltreated so that the students will think the worst.

At seeing them and their injuries, the crowd settles into an uneasy silence and quickly steps back to clear a path.

Hologram Sam looks up and sees me, and I wave her on. She nods, quickly grabbing Bishop's arm, tugging him forward. They lean on each other, walking slowly, looking into everyone's face as they pass, allowing just enough time for each student to take in their injuries.

Now the students can see for themselves what the Grand Master has done. How broken and bruised they are, how the Grand Master has "taken care" of them in my absence. Even if it's just planting the seed in their heads, hopefully they'll realize something is off. But I don't say anything further; I need the time to let the Animate scorpion do his part in this scheme, to rescue the real Sam and Bishop. So I stall, continuing my charade of loyalty.

I finally see the Animate scorpion crawl back into Olde Town. His return is my sign that the real Bishop and Sam have escaped safely, and I can finally say what I really want to. "Look at them! Look at their injuries. Grand Master Levi hurt them. He punished them for no reason!" I point, punctuating my accusations.

Students gasp, looking very confused at my words. Grand Master Levi breaks his composure and yells, "Grab them! Shut her up!" Guards descend on Hologram Sam and Bishop and when they jump them, I turn the hologram machines off. The two dissipate into a cloud of blue electrical dust, and the guards land in a pile on the ground.

Now that I have every student's attention, I tell them the truth, warning them. "Don't listen to anything Grand Master Levi says, or anything that the Society tells you. You've all been brainwashed through the contrapulators, through mind control. They're building an army of time travelers who will manipulate time in their favor, so that they will be the most powerful beings on earth, and they will kill anyone they need to in order to achieve this. And if you don't comply or choose not to take the Oaths tomorrow, there is no out, there's no going home to your families like they've promised you all along, there's only death. They'll exile you to Nocturna, just like they did to Perpetua, Stu, Jessica, and my aunt Mona and her family!" By the time I finish I'm screaming, the words spilling out in a panic. My heart races, pulsing with each new accusation.

The Grand Master's face turns bright red; he's so apoplectic, I can only hope he has an aneurysm. He's screaming, waving his arms erratically, calling for my death. Society guards crash through the front double doors of the bell tower building and race up the stairs. It may be only a few minutes before they reach the roof and capture me, so my last words must mean something to the students; I have to say something to make them believe, to hopefully incite a revolt.

I cast about, saying the only thing that I think will help. "Think for yourself! Don't use the contrapulators tonight. Don't let the Society brainwash you any longer. Pledge allegiance to no one but yourselves. Revolt against the Society and save your lives!"

Mass confusion reigns below. Some students scream and some cover their ears as though they aren't programmed to hear this negativity. Others crumple to the ground, crying. Seeing them this way makes me think that I'm too late. They may be too far gone to think for themselves, but I want to hope that just a little bit of what I've said sticks with them.

The Society guards bang on the roof access door behind me. Their shouts filter through; my time has run out. I toss away the remote and peek over the edge, but jumping from heights to Wander is never easy for me since I have just as much chance of leaping to my death as I do leaping through time or space. The guards release their fury, and break through the door. Just as one rushes over and snarling, reaches out to grab my arm, I take a leap of faith. With the crown relic clutched in my hand, I pray that I'm able to open the door of time travel by falling six stories down from the bell tower, instead of running.

No
33
MONA'S HOUSE

AS I JUMP FROM THE BELL TOWER, THE HEM of my long dress flips over my head in a whoosh, blocking my eyes just as the wormhole opens up, allowing me to skip through time. When entered vertically, the tube becomes a slide.

I land in Mona's townhome in Chicago, just a few blocks from the Academy. The real Bishop and Sera pace the living area. When they see me, they rush forward and overwhelm me with hugs.

"You're brilliant, sending Hologram Turner to release us so we could sneak out of the Academy," Bishop says proudly.

"Wouldn't have been able to do it without him, and that's only because you took the time to have him made." I touch Bishop's arm to thank him again for giving us just this small piece of Turner, even if I'm unsure now if the real one exists.

"Are you okay?" I ask Bishop who looks unusually frazzled.

"They tortured me with electric shocks. That was my punishment for fighting against them." He looks down.

"Oh no." I throw my arms around him, pulling him into a quick hug. "I'm so sorry."

"I'm okay," he says before stepping back. "I mean, I'm better now that we're here."

"Where's Hologram Turner?" Sam asks.

"He's on his way in Animate form, but he's going to meet us elsewhere, in a more secure place."

"I don't much like being here without Mum," Bishop says, looking around.

"I know what you mean." Without Mona's warm voice and comforting personality filling the house as she tidied, attempted to cook, or worked on her colorful glass mosaic art projects, it seems hollow and cold. "The good news is that we have everything we need to go back and change the past and set all of Nocturna free. Your family will be saved soon. I promise."

"Everything but the Oaths tomorrow. How will you sneak into the Grand Lodge without the Grand Master knowing? You won't be able to complete the prophecy without the transition and getting anointed," Sam reminds me.

"I hadn't thought that far ahead, I just knew we needed to rescue you. Do you have any idea what the Grand Master had planned for me if I brought him the crown?" This is the loose thread that nags at me; I still have no idea what it is that makes him live so long, what he needed from me that no one else can do.

"I have no clue," Sam says with regret. She approaches and takes the crown from my hand. Instantly her eyes spark with admiration for the powerful relic. I'm familiar with the look because I've been drawn to it as well, in much the same hypnotic way. She traces a finger over the shapes of the gems, scorpions, wings, and eyes with an intent smile. With her Seeing abilities, like mine, she can't help but feel the influence of the powerful relic, or control the almost desperate need to view its life path. "The pieces are coming together. It's almost done."

I nod, feeling a little bereft after handing over the crown. "I'm going to go find some clothes to wear and change out of this dress. If there's anything you guys think you need, I would load up with supplies. We're going undercover for possibly the next several days."

Everyone agrees, and we go our separate ways. I run upstairs, heading for Mona's bedroom. Once inside her doorway, I shiver a little; it feels weird to be here without her. Uncharacteristically, the sheets on her bed are rumpled and unmade. I drift to her bedside table and pick up a cup of cold tea. Some liquid has evaporated, and a dark brown ring is left behind.

It's as though Mona received a phone call in the middle of the night, perhaps from Bishop's dad, warning her that Charlotte had shown signs of becoming a Wanderer. In a state of panic, Mona jumped out of bed, quickly packed a bag, dressed, and fled Chicago for London to pick up Charlotte and hide her away from the Society.

Without realizing, I zone out, staring across the room, seeing the events in my mind, all from holding the teacup in my hand. I had actually *seen* the life path of the teacup and what transpired the night Mona left town and ultimately ended up in Nocturna.

I can't exactly say that I blame her for wanting to leave, for wanting Charlotte to have a different kind of life. Especially knowing what she does about how the Society functions. She wouldn't want that for her own children, and it appears that she didn't have a choice in the matter with Turner and Bishop. She lost control of them to the Society a long time ago.

"Did you find what you needed?" Sam pops her head in the room.

"Yeah." I give myself a little shake, refocusing on why we're here. She leaves without a word and I head for Mona's closet, pulling out a pair of long jeans and the smallest shirt and jacket I can find.

When I finish, I head back down the stairs in a robe, jeans in hand. I find my team in the kitchen. Bishop's loading a backpack with supplies while Sam ties off a Popsicle stick splint for her fingers.

I catch her eye and frown at her, guilt slamming into me at seeing her injuries again. "We should go to the hospital. A doctor should really set those for you."

"The Society will only look for us there. Besides," she adds with a wry smile, "Dr. Bishop helped pull them straight and tape them."

"Yes, you missed the fun." He grimaces, and I can only imagine the feeling of the broken bones between his fingers, and Sam's agonized reaction when he realigned them.

"I've read a few medical and first aid books." He taps his head. "At least our perfect memory is good for something."

Walking past, I nudge him with my shoulder. "You're such a Boy Scout. Thank goodness you're around." I zero in on the kitchen junk drawer, and paw through it until I find a pair of shears.

"So, where do we go now?" Sam asks.

"I know a place," I say as I scrunch up my nose. "It won't be great, but we'll have shelter, and then we can regroup and plan for tomorrow. We'll need three Wandering compasses to travel to Gibeon. Do you think Mona has any here?"

"I'm sure she does with the size of her relic collection. I'll go check." Bishop exits the kitchen, leaving Sam and me alone.

I wait until he's out of earshot. "I wanted to ask you something, Sam." I look down at the jeans, grasp the scissors in my hand, and begin cutting off some of the length of the legs. "Do you think there's any way that Turner's still alive?"

"Why would you ask that?" She shifts uneasily and crosses her arms.

"I ran into Drake and some members of the Underground when I traveled to find the crown. In passing, he mentioned that Turner and Cece are still alive."

"In passing?" She laughs. "You make it sound like you ran into him at the supermarket."

"Just answer the question. I'm serious." I look at her, meeting her gaze, and see a stirring of interest in her eyes, mingled with a touch of hope. The same questions are probably rolling around her head like they have mine since I first heard. Could he still be alive? Is it possible?

"I don't think so. No," she says.

The breath I'd been holding squeaked out on a disappointed sigh. "You're right. He can't be." He's really, truly gone. There's no way he's alive. How can I be so stupid to hope for the impossible? I can't keep letting my heart do this, so I let go of my thoughts, locking them away in a deep compartment in my mind.

"You think he's alive?" Bishop asks from behind us.

My heart skips a beat as we turn to see him standing in the kitchen doorway, black fabric draped in his arms.

"N-no," I stutter. "I mean, I'm just being stupid. Drake was totally trying to trick me when I Wandered back to find the crown. He probably wanted the relic or something." After all, the leader of the Underground gang has never given me any reason to trust him.

"Oh," Bishop says as his posture deflates. "That makes more sense."

"What do you have there?" I point to his arms, wanting—no, *needing*—to change the subject.

"Found exactly what we need. Several Wandering compasses so we can sneak into Gibeon for the Oaths. But I also found a few black cloaks and Society uniforms. These must have been Mum's when she was younger. They're not exactly the same as ours now, but they're close enough that no one will notice the difference," Bishop explains as he places everything on the counter.

Pinching the shoulders, I pick up the Society uniform, a military-style fitted gray jacket with black piping, leather shoulder pads, and a metal emblem on the upper arm, with matching gray slacks.

"These will definitely work," I say.

Bishop grunts with relief. "Great, let's pack and get out of here."

№ 34

THE MARK

I T'S DARK BY THE TIME I BREAK INTO XAVIER'S
garage. I've only been here once, the night I came with
Macey to watch his band play last semester. Those carefree
days seem like a lifetime ago now.

"Stay here for a sec," I ask of Sam and Bishop as I stumble
across the room, climb over several boxes to reach a window,
and close the heavy curtains. When I peek around them, lights
in the main house across the yard pop on. Silhouettes are
shadowed in the illumination of an upstairs room—Xavier's
parents. They can't know that we're here. They may be Wanderers themselves and loyal to the Society. I have no idea, but

we'll have to be careful either way.

Letting the curtain fall closed, completely darkening the room, I navigate back to the door and flip on the light. White fluorescent tubes buzz, hanging between the open rafters.

"Come in," I say, waving them inside.

"Lovely." Sam walks in and drops a bag of supplies on the floor, causing a circular plume of dust to explode. She scrunches her nose and sneezes.

"It's not pretty, but it has everything we need to survive the night. Couches, refrigerator, and bathroom." I point around the room.

"And camping equipment," Bishop says, removing two sleeping bags hanging from a nail on a wooden stud.

"Oh my God! What was that?" Sam screams as a mouse zigzags across her feet. She covers her mouth and jumps on top of the couch.

"Shh! Sam, no one can know we're here, so you're going to have to suck it up." I wave angrily at her, urging her to be quiet.

"There's another one!" she screeches, flapping her arms wildly.

"No, it's not." I bend down and scoop up my pet. "It's just the Animate." I stand and place him on top of a stack of old paint buckets.

When the scorpion is oriented, a beam of light shoots from his crystal face across the room. Hologram Turner appears in a haze of particles and steps forward.

Sam steps down from the couch and pulls him into an embrace. "Thank you. You saved our lives."

Bishop extends his arm and he and Hologram Turner shake hands, but then fall into a manly guy embrace that involves some heavy-handed pats on the back. "Thank you, brother. I'm in your debt."

"I'm glad you're all safe," Hologram Turner says and turns to look at me.

"It took you forever," I say with a frown. "I was starting to worry."

"I had some things to take care of before leaving."

"You want to elaborate?"

"Let's just say that your lovely speech inspired me." He quirks his lip into a half smile, and I know he's up to something. "So now what?" He looks around the room.

"We should try to make ourselves at home here, strategize, and get a good night's sleep. We have a big day ahead of us," I say.

"Agreed," Bishop adds.

I set my bag down and shoo Sam out of the way. She moves and perches on a single high stool sitting next to a stack of dusty boxes, and rests her head on the palm of her uninjured hand. I feel bad that I can't do more, that I hadn't done a better job of protecting her from the Grand Master, but I'll do everything I can to make it up to her, to make everything better.

With Bishop and Turner's help, we unfold the couch,

which converts into a bed.

"Can you hand me those sleeping bags?"

Bishop tosses them to me, and I drop them on the mattress. I grab one and unroll it while Hologram Turner works on the other. "If we zip both of them together, we can make one huge sleeping bag. We'll huddle in them together," I suggest.

"Yes, I'm afraid we're going to have to, considering the draft." Bishop nods toward the curtain, which moves slightly even though the window is closed.

My body instantly shivers, and when I look around, I realize that this probably isn't the best place for us all to recoup. I wish I could have done better on that too.

"Sam, why don't you go to bed. You look exhausted," I say after the sleeping bags are zipped together.

Without a word, she kicks off her shoes and crawls inside, then curls up into a ball, shifting to and fro as she tries to make herself comfortable. "It's just like home, except for the metal pole of the bed frame sticking in my back." She looks at me with a weak smile.

"Only the best for you," I joke, patting her on the leg, but she's already closed her eyes. She should be asleep in minutes.

Bishop cuts the overhead lights and flicks on the switch of a camping lantern. He walks forward, settling the lamp on an end table, and falls into a chair with a sigh. "I ripped a map of Gibeon out of one of Mum's books. It's in my bag." He places a hand over his eyes and leans on his elbow.

I retrieve it and settle on a low stool at the coffee table, smooth the map down, and move the light closer so I can see.

Hologram Turner nudges a drowsy Bishop with his foot. "Wake up, brother."

"Leave him alone, he's tired," I scold.

"Yes, some of us have to sleep." Bishop rolls over and tucks his hands under his cheek.

Hologram Turner sits down and leans in to inspect the map.

"The students will be meeting here, in this area." Turner circles a plaza on the south side of the city with his finger. "Then they'll march in the parade and move down Tanis Street, across the Mermaid's Bridge, and into the Grand Lodge for the Oaths and anointing."

"How do you know that?"

"Let's just say that being in this form"—he jerks his chin at the scorpion on my shoulder—"allows me entrance to restricted places where I can hear some top-secret things."

"I've wondered where you go when you're not with me." I smile. "Figures that you'd use it to snoop. I would have thought you'd sneak into the bath while I shower."

"Who says I haven't?"

"You didn't!" I say too loudly, and Sam and Bishop shush me.

Hologram Turner nudges my arm. "Of course not. Give me some credit."

"Stop flirting and get serious." I turn my attention back to the map.

He leans in and whispers, "You started it." He blows on

my ear, and I smack him in the shoulder.

"Okay, I think that if I sneak into the plaza while students line up for the parade, I'll have the best chance of fitting in. No one will really be able to see me within the hood of the cape. I'll pull it low and—"

Sharp pains shoot down my spine, sending my body into an eruption of spasms.

"Sera?" Hologram Turner lunges forward.

I can't respond because I fall headfirst into the dusty shag carpet, screaming for dear life. My various body parts jolt in uncontrollable fits, and I hit my head on the table, the chair, and anything else nearby. Though my eyes burn with irritation, I can still make out three figures sitting me upright. They're talking, maybe asking me questions, but I can't focus on their words through the agony. Bolts of electricity shoot through my body, crawling over my skin, reaching into every cell, extracting the life from me, forcing that focused energy down my spine. Muscles contract until they're rigid; arms, legs, digits, and neck crank into painfully awkward positions, and then the shivering begins.

I have the sensation of being lifted from the ground and carried, and after several moments, there's finally relief. Cold water rushes over my body, and I grab at the nearest thing, which I suspect is Bishop. Droplets run over my eyes, and I blink the grogginess away until I clearly see Hologram Turner and Sam across from me, crammed into the small bathroom of the garage. They look worried and scared.

Bishop clutches me when I shudder again. "What happened?" I mumble as my teeth chatter.

He ignores me and rests the back of his free hand on my cheek as he speaks over his shoulder. "Her color's returned and her temperature is falling. The cool shower worked. Good thinking, Sam."

He reaches past me, turning off the faucet, but I'm still shuddering in pain. "Here." Hologram Turner hands Bishop a camping blanket. He wraps me like a burrito and leads me out of the shower stall, back into the garage. They gently settle me on the chair and gather around.

"Sera, can you hear us?" I give them a strange look because I thought I asked them a question, but they never answered. Maybe I just imagined that I'd spoken.

"Sera?" Hologram Turner asks. He places his hand on my soaked arm but the electricity from him sends a shock through my body, and I scream again.

"What happened?" I mumble and pull the blanket tighter. I shift in the chair and tilt my head from side to side, trying to relax my aching muscles.

"I think you were going through some kind of transition," Sam says, sitting on the coffee table, facing me. "How do you feel now? Are you still burning?"

"Burning?" I ask numbly.

"You kept saying it burns, over and over. That's why we took you into the cool shower. Your skin was burning up."

"You were delirious," Hologram Turner explains.

"I don't remember." I squirm, feeling uncomfortable, thinking of a similar feeling on the day Dr. Shockey tortured me, which leads me to my next thought. "It's the mark, I've been marked!" Still shivering, I jump from my seat and run back to the bathroom, dripping water all over the floor. I don't have to think about where the mark is because I know from the pain; it radiates from my spinal column. I lift my wet shirt over my head, exposing my bra, and turn around, trying to see my back in the reflection of the full-length mirror behind the bathroom door. I catch a glimpse, just a shimmer of color in the dim light.

"It's me, let me in." Sam pushes on the door.

"It's there. It's really happening. It's all true." The true weight of what I'll be doing settles on my shoulders. Up until this moment, I hadn't known for sure if the prophecy could truly be real.

"Turn around. Let me see."

I turn around and she adjusts me in the low light, and I understand what she's doing. The light must hit the mark a certain way in order to be seen. It's iridescent, like mother of pearl, varnished over my skin in the form of a tattoo.

"It's here." She runs a finger down the length of my spine. "It starts on your neck at your hairline and runs down the center of your back."

"But what is it? What is the mark?" I look over my shoulder, trying to catch another glimpse in the mirror.

Sam leans toward my back, mumbling as she inspects it

more closely. "It's writing, looks ancient. Resembles Egyptian but it's not. It's more sophisticated in style. Different."

"What do you think it says?"

"I have no clue."

"Sera." Bishop knocks on the door. "Are you okay in there?"

"Fine, hold on." I drape the soggy shirt over my front, covering my chest, open the door, and walk out. Sam follows.

"Well?" Hologram Turner asks.

I turn around and the group steps closer. Sam rushes to the table and grabs the lantern. She returns and lifts it, illuminating my back, which warms my skin.

"Do you have any idea what it says?" Sam asks Bishop.

"Give me a second." Bishop pauses. "Sam, stand over there with the lantern so that it hits the mark the correct way."

She shuffles around slowly, moving the lantern. My shadow casts darkly on the floor, wavering with each new position she takes.

"Stop, right there. Now, don't move." Bishop stands directly behind me and pushes my hair over my shoulder. He's standing so close I can feel his breath on my bare skin. He touches a fingertip to the mark and begins to read.

№ 35

THE GRAND LODGE

BISHOP DRAGS A FINGER ALONG THE MARK, translating the ancient words running the length of my spine. "'Only purity of soul will bring about the return of paradise.'"

The room quiets. I tense, clutching my damp shirt to my chest.

"That's it?" Sam asks.

"But what does that mean?" I shimmy into my shirt and face them.

"Hmm, perhaps it's speaking of Gibeon before we were made Wanderers?"

"I wish we could ask Mr. Tash."

"If we had more time, we could research it," Sam adds.

"You know, I'm not sure it matters." I cross my arms over my stomach, holding back the shivers. "I'm set on my course. I know what I need to do now, and we have our relic. By this time tomorrow, you'll be back with your family, and we'll all be free." I touch Bishop's arm. "I hope after I'm anointed everything will become clear."

"You're right. We can't do anything more than we already have. Maybe we should just turn in for the night," Bishop suggests.

There's nothing more to say that hasn't already been said. And clearly there's nothing more we can do until after the Oaths ceremony. I cross the room and dig into my backpack for dry clothes. Behind a pile of tall boxes I change, slipping into thick wool socks, a flannel shirt and yoga pants, just enough to keep the chill away tonight. I wring my hair, allowing the water to drip onto the cement floor in the corner, and pull it back into a braid. When I'm done, I crawl into the chair, burrowing myself back in the blanket. Bishop and Sam crawl into bed, and Hologram Turner spirals, rebounding back into the scorpion Animate.

Finally, when everyone else is asleep, I'm alone with my thoughts. I hope that tomorrow I have the courage to be who I'm meant to be. The thought is so strangely calming that it scares me. I'm thankful when pure exhaustion finds me and releases me from consciousness.

Very early in the morning we prepare to leave. We're all looking rather tired, but we've been tested and abused these last few days, so it's understandable. Sam and I dress in Society uniforms, covering ourselves with cloaks borrowed from Mona's home. The scorpion Animate sits inside my pocket, and the crown hangs in a drawstring cloth bag from my belt. Bishop dresses from another time period, a World War II uniform we found in one of the old boxes in the garage.

"Is everyone ready?" Bishop pulls an officer's cap over his head, and the bill blocks his eyes somewhat. The outfit makes him look older, more regal, and I think in Gibeon, where time travelers converge from many time periods, he'll easily blend in.

With all the furniture moved to the edge of the room, there's a large open space in the middle. We stand equidistant, each with a Wandering compass in our hands. These magical tools will allow us to travel as a group to Gibeon.

The leather strap of the Wandering compass hooks around my wrist like a bracelet. On one end, a chain links to a glass sphere, a compass sits suspended in the middle. Etched into the face are the names of the twelve cities of time. At the north marker sits Gibeon.

Thinking about it, I'm sad that I've never seen the other cities, but only by advancing through the levels of the Society are you granted entrance. With the capital city of Gibeon as amazing as it is, I can only imagine the grandeur of the others.

I stand tall with one hand cupped in front of me, the

sphere resting in my palm.

"Ready?" Sam asks.

We nod. With synchronized precision, we flick our wrists and the spheres roll out of our hands, dropping toward the floor—the chains release like a yo-yo. Slowly, gently, we rock forward and backward and our sphere sways with the movement. With another sharper flick of the wrist, the sphere hanging from the chain rotates three hundred and sixty degrees and continues circling, its pace quickening when each wide circle traces the air, causing a resonant buzzing noise.

The hum communicates with my body, asking it to move from this spot to another. Xavier's garage and all its contents blur, disconnecting with true time, sending my team and me to Gibeon.

Initially a cloudy vision, the city of Gibeon solidifies into a new reality. The skyline stretches for miles in every direction. We've entered via one of the elevated landing pads, where Wanderers from many time periods arrive and exit.

Our landing pad descends from the luminous sky, and when the structure touches bottom, a staircase rotates, locking into one side. We step down into the masses of Wanderers walking around.

The city is a crazy quilt of mismatched architecture from every time period. Every culture is represented, and just for today it's accessorized with brightly-colored banners, hovering oversized balloons, festive streamers, and twinkling lights. Spectators already settle on the main road, Tanis Street, finding prime spots along the parade route to cheer on the new members when they walk past on their way to the Grand Lodge to be anointed.

The day of the Oaths is a special one for all Wanderers, which is why all attend in their true time, every single one. Even the Underground members lurk in the shadows, watching from afar. Something in our DNA binds us to this city on this special day, and no one knows why.

"We have to sneak into the square," I say.

Bishop nods. "I'll make my way to the Grand Lodge and wait for you there. I'll slip inside in case you need me."

I reach to hug him, something in me needing the connection, needing to let him know that I still care. What we are about to do is dangerous, and as I hold him tight, it's not lost on me that this could be the last time I see him. He pauses, rigid for a moment, but squeezes me back. He leans away to look at me and kisses my forehead, just like he used to. "Be safe. Okay, love?"

"Always. You too."

Sam grabs my arm and tugs. "We have to go, other students are arriving." We run, winding our way through the stream of Wanderers, dressed in the attire of their time period.

"There's Gabe."

We follow him but lag far behind. The hoods of our cloaks hang low, dipping over our faces. No one will identify us if we're careful. We turn the corner and walk into a large plaza lined with buildings with beautiful facades. Students from our class gather in the center, and Gabe makes his way to them.

"Look, students from other schools," Sam says.

"Sometimes I forget that there are others outside our Academy."

Students from at least twelve other Wandering schools mill around the square. Each school has their own special color uniform, but all have the same dark cloak.

A series of loud bongs reverberate off the walls, apparently coming from the roof of a nearby building. A bronze bell, positioned at the top and center, jerks back and forth.

Ding dong, ding dong. At the sound, the students scurry to their proper positions.

There should be some sort of chaos in the moment of so many moving bodies, but it's as though everyone's choreographed, knowing precisely where to go and where to stand. Swept up in the herd, Sam and I stealthily merge into the back of our school's group.

Rows and rows of students, perhaps a thousand altogether, align to perfection. Too perfectly. Every single body stands tall and poised, feet together, and looking suspiciously very much like zombies.

I turn to Sam and she raises an eyebrow. This must strike her as strange too.

When the bell stops tolling, everyone in the formation takes one precise step forward and then the next. I try very hard to mimic their movements, so that I won't stand out in this robotic crowd. Stepping with a stride too long or too short could instantly give us away. And with this thought, I realize something. They've all been programmed for this moment as part of the brainwashing. Every student listened to their contrapulator last night, which took away their dreams and replaced them with the instructions of exactly how to walk in the parade, and probably explained the events of the Oaths. Obviously they didn't heed my warning from my grand speech in Olde Town, or maybe, sadly, I was just to late to affect them or to help them help themselves. I lift my chin and think of the prophecy. I can't let them down again. I will not.

We march out of the plaza and turn the corner onto the main street. Thousands upon thousands of visitors cheer. People hang from trees, rooftops, and windows, just to see us. There's not one Wanderer in this town that's not watching excitedly.

The scorpion Animate turns in my pocket, and I know he's dying to have a look because he's been in there a long time already, but we're still at least a mile from the Grand Lodge.

Sphinx-like Animates with the sinewy body of a lion, the head of a woman, and enormous wings fly around the opalescent sky. When we reach the mermaid bridge, named for the mermaid Animates whose fish tails wind the columns where the bridge meets the water, the Animates break out into song, play water instruments, pump their tridents in the air, and splash water with their mechanical fins.

Finally we reach the end of the avenue, marching into the square that faces the Grand Lodge. The building is a ziggurat, a stair-stepped pyramid that shelves steeply into the sky. Animates of every form, animal, and deity wrap the levels like oversized dolls on display.

The entrance of the lodge looms before us, and its impossibly tall double doors slowly open with great ceremony as we approach and walk through.

Nº 36

THE ANOINTMENT

I'VE NEVER STEPPED FOOT IN THE GRAND LODGE, nor have I ever even seen photos of the inside because the interior is sacred and shrouded in mystery. Of course the anointed have, but seeing the zombie-like empty stares of my friends marching next to me, I have to wonder if anyone really remembers this day after it's over. I suspect they don't. Somehow the Society must make them forget that too.

Two men rush to shut the doors behind us, severing us from the sounds of the cheering crowds and also from the sunlight. Inside, there's only darkness, so I grab for Sam's hand as we march forward in the same pattern we have for the last several miles. I wonder how Bishop snuck inside. My gut says he hasn't.

A series of locks click, trapping us inside, and Sam grips my hand tighter. I want to say to her that it will be okay, but the truth is that I really can't promise that anymore. I honestly don't know if I ever really could.

There's a murmur coming from the students around us. They're chanting in a language I've never heard. And there's another sound too; aside from the rhythm of our boots tapping over the hard floor, the sound of running water can be heard.

We round a corner to see a sparkle of light in the distance. A sheet of water appears to be falling from the ceiling in a thin veil. Students walk through the liquid curtain, but they don't react to the wetness or deviate in any way as they move through, so when it's my turn I do exactly the same.

Water rushes over my hood, pours over my shoulders, and rolls down my body, dripping onto the floor. I curb my instinct to tilt my head away to protect my eyes, opting to move in sync with the group.

But what's on the other side of the waterfall is the most amazing. The room is a mirror reflection of the exterior, only reversed. Step formations reach to the ceiling, which is open to the sky at the apex. Gold Animates line narrow shelves here too, but everything's gold, and with the large roaring fire centered on a raised platform, every surface reflects the warm and buttery tones.

Each school's group breaks apart into neat square formations. I follow ours until we're positioned at the walls, facing the center of the enormous rectangular-shaped room. The fire is contained within a pit that opens at the center of a long platform that runs the length of the building. A reflection pool circles the platform like a moat, and at the edge of the moat, stairs surround it, leading into the liquid. Students at the front of the groups stand in a row at the water's edge.

Now that we're in position, the chanting becomes more intense, echoing off the hollow interior, and finally crescendos into a high pitch right before the strange tongues suddenly halt to complete silence.

Keeping my head as still as possible, I scan the area to see if I can spot Bishop, but I can't because several tall pillars block my view. Society guards clutching ceremonial poleaxes stand at attention behind our area. I don't dare speak. No one else moves a muscle because they've been programmed for silence and compliance.

In front of us, a commanding figure ceremoniously strides across the platform. With the high-reaching headdress that sits upon his shoulders, he appears very tall. The shape of the mask resembles the Egyptian god Anubis, half human, half jackal, except there is a single horn from his head. But as I take in the sight of the figure, I realize this is a replication of the Time Reaper, the one that almost killed me in the church courtyard in Gibeon. Has it really only been a few days since that happened?

When the imitation Reaper reaches the center of the stage, standing in front of the fire pit, he raises his arms to the heavens and speaks. I can't make out the words; they're in another language, the same one that the students chanted. The sounds are hard consonants, long vowels with tongues clucking and hitting the roof of the mouth in strange repetitions.

His words cause a reaction in our group, and everyone around us quickly drops to the floor, palms flat, bodies curled, resting on their knees. The motion happens so fast that Sam and I are left standing, sticking out from the crowd.

Before we can react, the Reaper's already seen us. He speaks again, this time directly to us but in English. "I'm glad you made it, Seraphina. But where is your fine gentleman?" The Grand Master's voice echoes from within the mask.

I'm not sure if we should take off and run or stay. I don't even know if I've been technically anointed because I feel no different from this morning.

"Bring him." The Grand Master waves.

Two guards appear at the water's edge, Bishop held tightly between them. He thrashes, desperately trying to free himself.

Grand Master Levi removes his mask, lifting it above his head, and hands it to Rex. Then he descends the stairs and wades through the water to meet them. Instantly, I rush through the bodies curled on the floor.

"Stop!" I scream.

"No, Sera! It's a trap," Bishop yells.

Before I reach the water's edge, the Grand Master plunges Bishop's head beneath the water, holding him there for longer than any human can withstand. He's going to kill him!

"Stop!" I launch myself into the water, but when I do, I realize that it's not water; it's oil…clear, golden, and thick like olive oil.

"But I'm only anointing our friend here." The Grand Master lifts Bishop's head, and he takes several large gasps of air, choking. "And now that you've stepped into the anointment pool, you'll have to as well. Those who leave without submitting die." The Grand Master smiles.

He pushes Bishop in my direction. The weight of him crashes into Sam and me. Sam slings Bishop's arms over her shoulder and struggles to move him safely to the pool's edge.

"I'll still need that item we discussed. And you'll need to be anointed to acquire it for me," the Grand Master says.

"I'll take that trip, but not for you."

The Grand Master throws his head back, laughing. "I highly doubt that. Besides, I've taken out some insurance." He waves to the edge of the room and two more people appear in the care of Society soldiers.

My jaw drops as I see my dad, Ray, standing at the pool's edge, blindfolded and trembling. As a human, his presence here among the Wanderers in my world is insane. And then Macey, still robotic and brainwashed, walks forward without complaint, doing everything they ask of her. I know that if she were herself, she'd kick their butts.

"How did you bring him here! He's a Normal!" I cry out.

"I have my ways, child. Do you think you know everything there is to know of this life? You know nothing." Grand Master Levi ascends the stairs to the fire pit to meet them.

I straighten at the statement because it's so true. "I only know that this shouldn't be happening. That you abuse our gifts and that shouldn't be allowed. I also know that all these innocent Wanderers are dragged into this without any choice, or freedom, or knowledge of what they do!" I scream at him. In the back of my mind, I think of Bishop's family, stuck and rapidly aging in Nocturna. Everything has gone so wrong so fast, and all I have to do is finish the prophecy to change things, to save everyone and make things better.

"Like I said, you know nothing," he says, drawing out the last word.

Grand Master Levi takes Macey's hand and guides her to the fire pit. "Now, what were you saying about not helping me out?" He looks down at me.

"You won't do anything in front of everyone. You wouldn't want them to think any less of you."

"They're practically catatonic." He laughs. "Haven't you been paying attention?" He waves a hand in front of Macey's face. She doesn't blink, doesn't move a single muscle.

"She's going to make her own self-sacrifice today because she tried to warn the other students that they'd be sent to Nocturna if they didn't take the Oaths. There always has to be at least one."

My heart sinks at this. Bishop and I sent her on this mission, knowing she would reach everyone, and now she's in this mess because of me.

The Grand Master moves to Ray. "And he'll pay if you don't give me what I want. I don't think you want either of them hurt, but that's just a hunch."

"Sera, is that you?" Ray reaches out blindly, unable to see because of the blindfold, and my heart aches to see him here. Though we've chatted on the phone a little, we still haven't made up since our big blowout with each other a few weeks ago, right after the attacks on the Academy when he tried to take me home. I was so stupid back then. I should have listened, but what good would it have done? They'd only exile me to Nocturna for leaving.

"It's me, Dad." I swallow hard. "You're going to be okay."

"Where am I?" His voice cracks; even though he's trying to be strong, he must be scared out of his mind.

"Don't worry about that, just try to stay calm. Everything's gonna be fine," I say in the most soothing voice I can muster.

He nods his head and bites his lip.

"Just tell me what you want me to do," I say to the Grand Master. Maybe there's some way to trick him into letting everyone go, into letting him think that I'll do what he wishes.

"Now, that's much better," he coos. Two guards step up next to me and grab my arms. Grand Master Levi descends the stairs again and when he plunges into the thick liquid, it sloshes around, reaching his waist. He extends an arm as we come face-to-face and lodges one hand firmly on the back of my neck and squeezes, with the other hand he grips my shoulder. He steps to the side and with a quick snap, submerges my head into the oil before I have a chance to hold my breath. I'm not beneath the surface long before I feel the uncontrollable urge to gasp. I want to resist and desperately punch them to release me, but the guards hold me tightly at the wrists and elbows. I'm completely restrained and drowning.

When I can't take another second, my body finally does what I can't make it stop doing, and I breathe. Warm oil rushes into my system, flooding my lungs, and the Grand Master quickly brings me to the surface.

"That's right, you only need to surrender to the oil of the Masters to be anointed," he says as I choke and retch, searching for the air that will save me. But even as I hack with deep coughs, I can feel the warmth of the oil spreading through my insides, coating every organ, every vein, and every blood cell. It takes over, releasing chambers upon chambers of information into my system, as though all of it had always been there, the story of our beginning, our reasons for this Wandering life. Light floods my eyes and a peaceful calm overcomes me.

"I see light," I whisper.

He hugs me in a loving way that makes me want to run away, but I can't.

"It's done. The transition's finalizing. It won't be long now," he says to soothe me.

My body weakens, my muscles turn to jelly, and my brain is practically unusable. I'm transforming into a Chosen. A million needles full of otherworldly information inject into every pore of my body, and I'm unable to move. The Society guards drag me from the oil, up the stairs to the platform, and toss me onto the ground. I can't see anything just yet, only feel that the Oaths continue to take place around me. I lay my head on the concrete and in the back of my mind, behind everything else, I hear Sam scream as she, too, is anointed.

The chanting begins again, and as the students' cloaks rustle, drums beat wildly and rhythmically in the background. Somehow in my mind I see everything in my head, as though the information of what's happening has been given to me. This must be a gift of a Chosen.

Each row of students steps into the oil and plunges into the water. With no help they practically drown themselves to the point of suffocation. As the first breath of oil rushes into their bodies, they simply stand, compose themselves, and move away for the next row to do the same. But they're so robotic, they have no clue what they've done, that they've almost died. They don't even know that they submitted themselves to the Oaths. They know nothing.

Someone comes to me, pulls at my clothes, removing the heaviness of them, and then dresses me in something new of lighter-weight material. They take off my shoes and replace them with sandals, and then they secure a rope around my waist, tying me up like a present.

I moan and roll from side to side, trying to lift myself out of this fog, needing to wake up to do something to save everyone.

Finally the sheen of oil clears from my eyes, and the information I've downloaded settles into my soul like something I've known all along. Through newborn eyes, I sit up and look around, though I realize that I don't need my eyes anymore. I can see everything in my mind in a bird's-eye view, the way I do when I "see."

My old clothes lie far away in a pile and I peer at them groggily, thinking that the Scorpion Animate must be stuck beneath them. When I shift my perspective, I find four priestesses wrapping Bishop and Sam in fabric. They have removed their uniforms and are swaddling them in long sheets of flowing golden silk. My mind reels when it occurs to me that the priestesses are going through the steps to turn them into mummies. Somehow they've sedated my team, or maybe it's the effect of the oil. And to my horror, there's no sign of Ray or Macey.

Even though I'm still sluggish, I attempt to stand to help them, but the Grand Master kicks my chest, sending me back to the floor. "First, we must sacrifice."

"No, no, no!" I press a hand in the air in their direction.

Several elder members in robes lift first Bishop and then Sam into one wide wooden casket, laying them flat. Another member arrives with a lid, which is placed on top and nailed in place. A long chain lowers from the ceiling with a large hook at the end that is secured to the top of the box. Grand Master lifts both arms in the air, a signal to pull the box upward to the ceiling. A cranking noise echoes throughout the building as they are pulled hundreds of feet to the ceiling.

Once they've reached the apex of the temple, the box halts for a moment, hovering high above the center of the room and swinging gently to and fro, the absence of the cranking noise leaving the room eerily silent. I hold my breath as my heart beats wildly, and startle when drums begin beating and the chanting begins anew. The box slowly descends with each drumbeat, keeping time with the chanting. In a few moments, the box will plummet into the fire pit at the center of the room, and Bishop and Sam will burn to death.

I scream with anger, with heartbreak, with helplessness. There's nothing I can do; I'm too exhausted to fight, and he knew I would be. Jerking my head in the Grand Master's direction, I narrow my eyes and scream at him as I tremble with fury, "Why are you doing this?"

He leans down, leveling his eyes with mine. "Why even worry? Now that they're anointed and ready for the Masters, we can sacrifice them. You don't need them anymore. All your connections have been severed. Don't you see? Don't you feel the difference? You've taken a majority of their gifts from them, sucked them right from their bodies over this past year. They've made you what you are and you've made them weak, while they've given you the power of three, making you a Chosen. They've already made their sacrifices—to you. Now they must make them to me."

"What?" I say the word automatically, but in my heart I know what he's saying is true. I can see the truth of it for myself in my own mind. The Wandering connection has been broken. I don't sense my team the way I had before, or need them the way I used to. Sam was right; I'm finally free, but in the worst possible way.

I look away and gasp a sob. They're almost completely defenseless and it's my fault.

"Tsk, tsk. Don't cry, sweet child. You're meant for something greater than the use of a mere team. You'll embody the spirit of the Masters now." He stands above me, crossing his large arms over his bare chest. "And now it's time for you to go back and retrieve what I need."

"You haven't even told me what that is!" Slowly it seems, he's pinching my freedom so tightly that I have no choice but to comply with every request, and the thought sickens me. I glare at him and demand, "And how do you know that I won't betray you and fulfill the prophecy instead?"

"For one, I told you I've taken out insurance," he says with a self-satisfied sneer. "Macey and your father stand at the edge of the pit of Nocturna, and if you don't return with what I need, I'll send them there too. They can keep Mona and sweet little Charlotte company in their final living days. And two, you won't fulfill the prophecy because that possibility requires you to kill someone, and I know once you're there, you won't have the will to follow through."

"I'd kill *you*," I spit out, in that moment believing every word.

"No, you'll do exactly what I ask to save your former team members." He gestures to the box above the fire and turns to me, his lips twitching with amusement. "And by the look of things, you'd better hurry."

No matter how much I don't want to give him the satisfaction, I can't help but glance at the box lowering slowly toward the fiery pit. It's closer now, much too close, and the warmth of the flames has already begun to darken the bottom. The fire briefly surges a little higher, and a few flames actually singe the edge, causing my heart to beat faster. My hands clench so tightly into fists that my fingernails pierce my skin, and I can feel the warmth of blood dripping from my palms.

I swivel my head slowly toward the Grand Master and glare at him. "Just tell me what you want."

Nº 37

EGYPT

GRAND MASTER LEVI PACES BEFORE THE PIT. "What I want is for you to travel back to our beginning with Unika's crown and retrieve a canteen of the aqua vitae—the water that gives life."

"Water," I repeat flatly.

"That's all. And if you succeed, all of this will be over." He gestures around the Grand Lodge.

"Everyone's safe, my friends and family. And what about Bishop's family and the people of Nocturna?"

His lips quirk to one side. "Bishop's family and the others of Nocturna sealed their fates the moment they violated the laws of the Society. 'Tis a pity, I had such high expectations for Charlotte. Lovely little thing." He turns back to me. "Save who you can, Sera. It's some or none at all."

With a nod that is clearly meant to end the debate, he says, "Rex has prepared you for your trip." He gestures to my body, and I look down. I'm dressed in a linen tunic with a rope belt tied at the waist, a leather canteen hangs from my shoulder, and woven straw and reed sandals protect my feet. And I realize I saw this in my mind too, but my brain was just too cloudy to compute the information.

The Grand Master hands me the crown of Unika; he must have taken it from my drawstring bag. I wipe the blood from my hands on the hem of my tunic before I accept it. "Hold the crown in your hand as you run to Wander. As a Chosen, your body will know where to take you. You are the only one who can Wander from Gibeon without a Wandering compass."

"But where am I to find this special water?"

"In the palace there is a fountain with an obelisk. From it runs the aqua vitae."

Like the fountain in the drawing in my mom's journal? I think of the room with the stars on the ceiling in the sketches. She's drawn each room of the palace, the entire layout of the city, but where she found information so ancient, I still have no idea.

"Ticktock, Sera. Your friends and family need you to save them."

I push myself to my feet and look around. All the students

still stand zombie-like, but now they're anointed and dripping with oil. Each glistens with the golden hue that is reflected from the walls by the flames of the fire pit. Somehow they've become part of the interior, just another tool for the Society to abuse.

"I'll be waiting for you, Sera," the Grand Master reminds me.

Now more than ever I must end this misery. I grasp the crown in my hand and look inward for the place I should Wander. In my new mind's eye I see it clearly, though I've already seen it several times before: in dreams, in the hot air balloon ride, and in painted murals in the Academy's atrium. It's the desert.

Feeling my energy coming back, I sprint over the raised pedestal, down its long length. There's just enough running room, like an airport runway, and at the end, I leap into the air over the anointment pool and catapult into the blinding light of a glittering wormhole. The world doesn't turn over for me like it has in the past, but I'm not the same as I was before. I'm not sure if I ever will be again.

Wandering through time, I land in a field of wheat and fall to the ground. I rest for a moment, feeling the wind brush the long willowy strands against my bare arms and legs. I look up, not at the bright blue sky, but at the golden obelisk that stands pointing toward the heavens, just like in the story about King Unika.

The strong sunlight beating down from directly overhead

reflects the surface, creating a blind spot, and I cover my eyes as I stumble to stand. Trying to get my bearings, I desperately come to terms with the fact that I've traveled through time back to ancient Egypt. After all I've been through I should believe anything by now, but the strength of my new gifts will never cease to surprise me.

Shielding my eyes, I scramble to my feet and pivot, surprising myself by walking directly into the bare chest of a guard. Before I can react, he grabs my arms, speaking angrily in what sounds like an ancient language. A second guard, somewhat younger, stands behind him and points a spear at my chest, poised menacingly just inches from my heart.

It would have been helpful to know the language before coming here, but since no Wanderers travel here, only the Chosen such as myself, I'm not that lucky. Even in our world of Wanderers, some things are still a mystery.

He screams at me again.

"I don't know what you're saying," I plead with outstretched hands.

His eye widen at the unfamiliar sounds; of course they've never heard English before. Though I think I'm dressed properly for the time, he looks me over, his lip curled with what can only be disgust. His eyes widen when his gaze reaches my hand, and he rips the crown of Unika from me. Being caught in any era with the jewels of their king can't possibly be good, so I cringe and await his reaction.

Understandably he freaks out, gesturing wildly at me as

he barks louder in his strange language. The younger guard
with the spear takes the relic from him, and the older guard
drags me around the obelisk to a donkey. The younger packs
the relic into a pouch that hangs from the animal, and then he
mounts the donkey and straddles it. He throws a rope to the
elder and says something.

The guard nods in response and jerks me to face him while
he binds both my wrists with rope made of woven reeds. My
mind spins…I have a decision to make: I can either let them
take to me who knows where, or I can fight them. I'm not
sure that my strength has completely returned or what it's
even turned into, but I decide to take my chances.

Retracting bound fists, I bash him squarely on the nose.
His head jolts backward as his nose erupts with an instant
nosebleed. The reeds around my wrist loosen, releasing my
hands, and I punch him in the face again, then launch away
from him, running along the path through the fields.

The younger guard yells at me as he takes chase on the
donkey, the animal galloping faster than I expect. I'm running
as hard as I can, pumping my arms as the breeze pushes at my
face, my hair flying in the wind. If I can outrun the Reaper's
horse in Nocturna, I can certainly outrun a donkey. I push
harder at the thought, but my toe catches under a large rock,
tripping me, and I fall face first into the dirt. Before I have
a chance to scramble to my feet, the young guard leaps off
his moving animal and lands, pinning me to the ground. We
struggle in the dusty dirt of the field—arms twisting, knees

kicking, hair pulling—and I lean in and savagely bite his ear. He's stronger than I expect, and though I draw blood, he continues to fight, restraining me until the second guard arrives.

On my belly with my face shoved into the dirt, it's impossible to resist anymore. They tie my arms again, this time so tightly, the wrapping of the reeds draws blood like a thousand paper cuts. The restraints wind their way from my wrists to my elbows—probably five times stronger than anything they'd do to a Normal.

Then they tie me to the end of a long leash that stretches across the back end of the donkey. The young guard mounts the animal again and kicks its ribs. The donkey takes off in a gallop, forcing me to keep pace with them or I'll fall and be dragged behind, which is probably what they're hoping for.

We travel for several miles, and even though I run the entire time, this is not so bad; the worry is much, much worse. Where are we going and what will they do to me? This isn't a school field trip Wandering back in time. There's no Gabe to guide me, no notes to peek at with instructions.

We enter a city alive with retail and trade, and when we pass through the market, everyone stops to stare, but they are the least of my worries. The donkey stops at the gates of a palace, and the young guard dismounts, shouting out several commands. More guards pour out from the main gates and I'm handed over to them, who then cut me loose from the horse and use the tether to pull me inside like an animal.

Up the stairs, through the columns, they force me inside,

pushing me through several chambers and hallways. It's not until we reach the grandest room that they knock my legs out from under me, and I collapse to the floor on my hands and knees. A guard presses his foot on my back. He yells and I stay put, using the time to catch my breath and rest.

Someone approaches. Through my new mind's eye, I view the room from above. The room is full of people, but I only focus on the woman in front of me. Cascades of dark hair flow beneath a petite crown. Though I can't see her face, I understand that she's their queen.

"Who are you?" a woman's voice asks in English.

Automatically I look up in confusion, only to glimpse a pair of ornate sandals.

"I said, who are you?" She kicks my side until I flip over on my back. At the sight of her face, I instantly curl away in shock, because this face is one that's haunted me for years.

№ 38

A QUEEN

THE WOMAN STEPS FORWARD; HER SHAPELY BODY shifts gracefully beneath her cream gown. In her hand she holds the crown of Unika, the relic I used to Wander here from the future.

"Mom?" The word slips from my lips as my brow furrows. Confusion roils inside me, stealing my breath and clutching my heart in a vice grip.

She's taken aback by my words but looks at me as if she doesn't know me. I leap to my feet and reach forward to hug her, but the guards stop and restrain me and the courtiers gasp at my action. Clearly it's not acceptable to charge a queen, because this is what she is in this time.

"I thought you were dead!" I grit out as I struggle against the guards.

The queen inspects me closely, her eyes narrowing as she allows her gaze to travel from my head to my feet and back again. When she meets my eyes again, she tilts her head slightly to the side. "I have no idea who you are, but I can guess why you're here. You've come to fulfill the prophecy."

"I'm your daughter," I state defiantly. "That's who I am."

She steps close, so close that she's inspecting my features, looking at every detail, no doubt trying to find some piece of herself within me. We look exactly alike and I realize that she's very young, too young to have a grown daughter. This meeting is taking place before she's ever given birth to me.

"My own daughter would not come here to kill me."

To fulfill the prophecy I must kill the queen and king or stop them from ever meeting. I guess I'm too late for the latter option. Grand Master Levi said I wouldn't have it in me to kill them, and he was correct. Somehow he knew that my mother was at the beginning of time, responsible for the setting off the prophecy of the Masters.

Of course I would never hurt her; I've spent most of my Wandering life trying to find her and, finally, here she is standing before me. How will I set everyone free now? How will I save Bishop's family?

While I'm piecing the information together, she utters several words in the direction of the guards in the ancient language. They respond by dragging me away.

"Stop! You're making a mistake," I cry out. "I'm your daughter. I'm Seraphina!" My screams echo off the interior walls of the space, but she doesn't respond. To my dismay, she allows them to carry me away, and as I'm screaming for her to listen to me, someone smashes the back of my head and the world spirals, soaking my vision in black.

I awake in a dark pit, lying on a floor of dirt. The walls are high, at least twelve feet. Sitting upright doesn't make anything any better. Pain shoots from the back of my skull to my forehead as I stand and wobble to the wall, placing my hand against its coolness to steady myself. From here I catch a glimpse of the moon. Its low position in the sky tells me it's been at least twelve hours since I arrived.

Several figures appear up above, and a guard throws down one end of a rope. It bangs against the wall, falling to the floor at my feet. For a moment, I consider whether I should take it, but I have a better chance of survival if I'm out of here.

I coil the rope around my arms and hold tight, allowing the guards to drag me up the side. When I reach the top, they pull me to my feet, yanking me by my tunic.

My mom, the queen, stands before me. Carefully, she looks me over but gives no indication of whether she believes me.

"Follow me," she finally says.

The guards stay behind. At least this is a positive sign.

I follow silently behind her as she walks across the courtyard, taking in my surroundings along the way. The darkness is dotted with fireflies, just like the fireflies that I dreamed about the night Mona told me I was a Wanderer.

Beneath the moonlight, I catch a glimpse of her mark, stretched along her spine but mostly hidden beneath her long locks. The ancient hieroglyphs glisten at this angle. She's a Chosen too, just like Terease explained.

She guides me into the palace and down a hall with grand columns, just like one of the rooms I saw in her journal. Now I realize that my assumption that she researched the palace was incorrect. The drawings weren't sketched from descriptions from others; they were drawn from her own memories. She'd actually been here herself and sketched the drawings that represented her life.

The queen steps out onto a balcony and stops at a railing lined with torches to stare out at the twinkling stars. With no lights from the city of the modern world, they're the brightest I've ever seen. Despite their beauty, I lean against the balcony and stare at her instead. I can't believe that I've found her here, of all places.

"Do you believe me now?"

She sucks in a shuddering breath and lets it out softly in a sigh. "Yes."

"What changed your mind?"

"You told me your name." She turns to me. "It's the one

I hope to name my daughter, a name I haven't shared with anyone yet." She reaches for her belly and rubs it in a circular motion. From the fullness of her dress, the tiniest baby bump appears.

"That's me?" I point. "You're pregnant? But, but—"

"Yes, and with one child who's already died and the other hidden away, I've held on to hope that this child will be strong enough to survive." She turns to me. "I want to hope that you're telling me the truth, that you're my child. But if you are, and you're from the future, that means that I don't stay here. My time here is limited."

"I have siblings?" I shake my head, confused. I can't even begin to fathom the thought. "But don't you want to return to Ray?"

"Ray?" She laughs at this. "How do you know Ray?"

"What do you mean? He's my dad."

She reaches a hand to my shoulder. "No, he's not. The king was your father, and he was a great and noble man."

"Was?" My heart sinks at these words for so many reasons.

"He passed not long ago." Her eyes glisten in the moonlight; she lifts an elegant hand to brush away a tear before it can fall.

I want to cry too, for her heartbreak and for mine. Ray, the man who raised me, isn't my dad; at least, not in the technical sense. Maybe it's something I've known all along, something I've felt deep inside but never acknowledged. Haven't he and I always been at odds? Haven't I always felt disconnected from him? This information should not surprise me but I look away, trying to hold back the tears. Even though Ray and I never really connected, I still love him. He's the closest family I've ever had. The closest I've ever gotten to Normal, and it's another lie that makes me realize I never had any true blood family of my own. No Aunt Mona, no true father…just lies.

"I can see this makes you sad," she says. "But since I haven't lived that part of my life yet, I can't explain how it happened."

I nod, taking a deep breath. Before, I would have run away from this information, but now I can't. There's so much more I need to know, so I compartmentalize the facts, suck in the emotions, and change the subject, hoping it will give me some relief. I wipe a tear away. It's the only one I will allow for this. Later, I can grieve for my hurts, my losses. Now, I need to focus on my mission.

"I'm confused. How are you here? How am I here?" I gesture to her belly again.

"As you've surely guessed, I'm a Chosen too. After growing up and finding myself at the Academy and then at Wandering College, I became disillusioned with that world. I knew it was wrong, the manipulation that they used for time and the mind control of their people. I'd already taken the Oaths, but it took me some time to be marked with the tattoo and decide to fulfill the prophecy.

"I Wandered back to this time, but when I arrived, there was no queen, only the king. I thought that I'd gotten here before they meet. What a wonderful chance for me to curb the engagement as opposed to ending someone's life. I gained access to the palace by securing a job, helping in the kitchen, so I could watch the king. That's when I realized that he showed no signs of being a Wanderer as our mythologies suggested. The inaccuracy perplexed me."

She pauses for moment, her eyes unfocused as she looks back into her memories, then continues. "But one night as I served him dinner, he asked me to stay. Of course, this was absolutely unheard of, but you don't disobey a king, and I was curious, so I did as he requested. We talked. By this time I had learned the language quite well. Each night as I served him dinner, he asked me to join him. He was handsome, truly a gentleman, very romantic and powerful. We fell in love, and before I realized what happened, I was his wife." She speaks with the elegance that you would expect from a queen. "At that point I never wanted our love story to end. That's why meeting you here is quite bittersweet. Yes, I'll have a beautiful daughter," she says as she gently lifts my chin, "but I've also just lost the love of my life."

I pause, taking this in. "So who is Ray to you if he's not my father?"

"Ray was a very lovesick boy I dated when I was in high school. He loved me very much, and I cared for him too, just not in the same way Wanderers love. At that time I was still bound to a boy who should have been on my team—the twin brother of Joseph, my Protector, who is now Mona's husband.

But I was desperate to be free of loving this other boy; he was an awful person." Her eyes closely briefly as she shudders with distaste, then looks my way again. "Because of our Wandering DNA, I had no choice who I loved. So I tried dating a Normal, Ray, a boy from a nearby Normal school. I hoped I could force myself to fall in love with him, but as you know, it's impossible. Our Wandering ties are unbreakable—unless you become a Chosen. Only then are you free."

I jolt at this. Though the Grand Master said that I was free of my team, I hadn't even considered that I could choose to love freely now. I should be happy for at least this little thing because, finally, the face of one boy dances behind my eyes. I push his image away; this is neither the time nor the place because I need to focus. I look up to Mom, who continues to talk.

"Still, I wanted to be Normal despite all the chaos around me. My team was no help. Mona and Joe were inseparable after college, getting married, getting pregnant. And at that time I was already an anointed Chosen, but not marked. I wasn't even sure if I would ever be. The further I sank into the Society life, the more corruption I witnessed. I spent years debating and calculating the good against the bad. But when the mark appeared, finalizing my transition, I couldn't allow their evil to continue, so I decided to fulfill the prophecy. It just so happens that at the same time, the Grand Master beckoned me for a task of his own and at that time informed me that he had made me a Chosen, by allowing the twins on my team to live."

"Right." I look down now, recalling Mona telling me that Mom had disappeared after college.

"So, it seems that sometime in the near future, I leave Egypt to return to my true time, have a lovely little girl, name her Seraphina, and raise her with Ray?" She looks at me in question.

"Yes and no. You leave me with Ray and then you disappear."

"Why?"

"Well, from what Terease tells me, you worry for my safety. You leave me with Ray, fake your own death so that the Society and the Grand Master will leave me alone, and then you join the Underground."

"I see." She looks down. "But you're here to kill me, so none of that will happen."

"I obviously don't kill you since I'm standing here now." I smile. "But if I can't follow through with the prophecy, how will I set everyone free from Nocturna? And set the others free from Wandering?"

"There is a way," she says hesitantly.

"How?" My voice rises in excitement.

"I'll tell you, but we have to talk first."

My mind churns, wondering how I can still set everyone free, but then it migrates to the next thought. "And there's that small problem of taking back some aqua vitae from some fountain with the obelisk."

"For the Grand Master?"

"Yes."

"I'm sure he's still waiting for me in my true time, just where I left him in Gibeon." She laughs. "Though when I return, he won't know that I've been here for years."

"Years! But how? What about schalg?" In fact, I'm starting to feel the effects of it myself. Time travel jetlag makes you groggy after several hours of being in another time.

She smiles coyly and winks. "That's where the aqua vitae comes into play."

No

39

AQUA VITAE

"NOT ONLY DOES IT CURE SCHALG, BUT IT ALSO gives life."

"Life?"

"Let me show you." She waves for me to follow.

Mom leads me back through the palace, up and down several ramps leading to various chambers and levels. We walk quickly through all the beautiful spaces that I remember from the sketches in her journal, and I want to stop and gawk but she urges me on.

She stops in one room and walks to the corner, then does something very unexpected: she flips on a large light bulb.

I watch in amazement as she drifts across the room and lights another. The large glass bulbs illuminate the space, but their power is multiplied a million times over through the use of flat, mirror-like copper panels placed strategically around the room, which reflect the light. "How is that possible? You need electricity for a light bulb." I inspect the strange invention and shake my head in amazement.

"Isn't it funny? When you know the right things to combine to make a battery: a clay jar, vinegar, copper wire and a few other goodies—it's easy."

"You're responsible for this? You brought technology to them?"

Her shoulder lifts in an unconcerned shrug. "I needed some comforts from home. Anyway, this is what you're here for." She raises her hand, gesturing across the room. In the middle stands a tall obelisk, from which water trickles into a square basin.

"Where did this come from?"

"I've taken the water from Gibeon. Unfortunately, it's dried up in our true time. The settlement of the original Wanderers is just over the hills at the horizon." She points out an arched opening where the sun peeks over the Nile Valley desert, painting the landscape with pinks and oranges.

"*The* Gibeon? Do you mean before it started moving through time?"

"Yes, exactly." She turns bright red. "I guess you could say through my passing on of technology, I will eventually cause some problems. Do you know the story of why Gibeon moves through time?"

I think back to Mr. Tash and his explanation for this. "The city itself was a gift from our Makers as a place for our kind to colonize on earth," I say, practically reciting the information. "At that time, the city of Gibeon did not move. For a thousand years, the people happily lived there. But it's said that a young woman roamed past the limits of the city and befriended those of a nearby village of Normals. Although forbidden by our Makers, she taught the Normals our secrets: magic, weaponry, science, mathematics, farming, hunting, etc., giving them the keys to better themselves, and perhaps, become more evolved than was meant to be. She also fell in love with a Normal."

I stop and whip my head toward her. "That's you! You're the girl who fell in love with a Normal and gave away our secrets?"

"Well, they've mussed the information up some over time, I suppose, just like the King Unika myth. Yes, I'm the girl who came from Gibeon and fell in love with a Normal. The part they failed to pass on is that I came from the future Gibeon. But the thing is, the real Gibeon? I've been there, seen it for myself, and it's so different from the future Gibeon, so much more magical and much purer. The inhabitants there would never dream of straying from Gibeon's perfection to come here. They have no reason to because they have everything they need or would ever want within the city walls—happiness, contentment, compassion, patience, sensitivity, humility, loyalty, intelligence, and most importantly, unending love. It's a utopia. I spend time there, pretending to be one of them. Because of their complete trust in others, they never even question my presence."

She glances at me and continues. "But what I visit most is their fabulous hanging garden. Not only is it my favorite place on earth and in history, but it has these magical waters with special healing powers." She gestures to the fountain.

"And what about the other part of the story?" I remind her, beginning to recount the rest of our history. "This secretly continued for some time, until the nearby town, whose rulers had become corrupt, drunk on their new knowledge acquired from the girl, decided to attack Gibeon for its wealth of unlimited enlightenment." I stop and glance around. "I can see that hasn't happened yet."

"No, my kingdom hasn't attacked Gibeon. Maybe that takes place after I leave?" She looks sad. "But I have no idea who would do this."

"It doesn't matter who, it has to happen. We know for a fact that is does, or I wouldn't be standing here."

"Yes, of course, you're right." She takes my hand and smiles sadly, and then pulls me forward until we reach the fountain. We sit on the ledge facing each other, our knees nearly touching. She leans to the center, removes a copper cup from a hook at the base of the obelisk, dips it into the water, and then she takes a long sip. After, she immerses it again and offers it to me.

"Drink, you must be thirsty."

I hesitate for a moment but I am very thirsty, so I place the cup to my lips and take a long drink. Never have I tasted anything so refreshing or delicious. She refills the cup and I drink again. Then I fill the Grand Master's canteen. When I'm done, I loop it back around my shoulder.

"So, Grand Master Levi still rules in your true time, just as he was in mine, and just as he was in 1894?"

I nod.

"He's sent several Chosen back to retrieve this water for him from time to time so that he lives on to rule the Society. And each time, no matter what true time they come from, they've come back here and found me."

She gives me a wary look, then continues. "The first arrived when your older brother, Bomani, was only a year old. That first Chosen came back not only to retrieve water for the Grand Master, but also to try to fulfill the prophecy. He took the water, and then he tried to kill me. Because I drank the aqua vitae he did not succeed, but he did murder your brother." Her voice wavers and she clears her throat. "I guess he thought that this would break the chain of events and set everyone free."

I place my hand over hers and squeeze it gently. "I'm sorry."

"It didn't work. Then everything played out in a similar way with your sister, Saqqara. That's how your father—"

Her voice catches in a silence that explains his death, and she shoves her knuckles against her mouth as she gasps a sob.

"I'm sorry that I never had the opportunity to meet him." My voice cracks on the words and when her sad eyes meet mine, I lean forward to hug her.

She rubs the tears away. "The king protected your sister against the Chosen, just long enough for me to hide her away. The Chosen didn't fulfill the prophecy, obviously, but did manage to help the Grand Master by stealing aqua vitae."

My head is spinning with all I'm learning, to the point a headache starts to form at the base of my skull. So I lift my hand to rub my neck, and ask, "I'm confused. What does all this mean?"

"It means that since I've been drinking this water—and if I continue to drink it—I cannot die. Several have tried, but have failed."

I think of how she died in my true time, but she must have stopped drinking the water, leaving herself vulnerable. "You should know that in the future—"

"No, please don't tell me any more." She holds up her palm. "I know what you're going to tell me, and I don't wish to hear of my death. I recall our words from yesterday."

I told her I thought she was dead, so she knows. I look down at my hands, my fingers entwined so tightly that my knuckles are white. She knows that it happens, that it's in her future. I can only hope that makes her take all the necessary precautions. "But how were they able to hurt my brother and the king? Didn't you let them drink from the fountain?"

"Of course I did." She stiffens and frowns at me. "I bathed the children in it, let them play in it, and it was the only source of water for the king and me, the only water I allowed."

"Then how?"

"I didn't realize it at the time, but apparently the children were not protected until they matured and received their Wandering gifts. Nor did I know that the king was immune since he was a Normal." She grabs my hands. "But what I discovered is that it's not I or the king who needs to die to fulfill the prophecy. It's the selfless act of their Wandering child that will set everyone free."

Someone pure of heart, just like the tattoo says. Miss Swift and the Society scholars were wrong. Mom's explanation makes perfect sense.

"Like me?" I sit up straight, placing a hand over my chest. My heart beats rapidly at the thought that I'm at the root of the reason we're so wrong, so impure and imperfect, unlike the original people of Gibeon. I'm unsure if I'll ever be pure enough or selfless enough to set us free, to prove to the Masters that we're worthy. I've been everything but worthy my entire life.

"It's okay, now that you're here. You're safe." She runs a hand over my cheek and her fingers caress my hair. "You can stay here in this time to have access to the water and no one will ever harm you, like they did your brother and father."

I jump to my feet. "But what about everyone else? Ray,

Macey, Bishop, Sam, Mona, and Charlotte! I need to save them, I need to change things." My skin begins to heat with the fear and anger that is growing inside me. I suck in a deep breath, and another, then the next comes too quickly and before another second passes, I'm nearly hyperventilating.

"Seraphina." She stands up and rubs my shoulder, trying to soothe me, then grasps my chin and locks her gaze with mine. "You're my child, and I can't allow anyone to hurt you." She grabs a bag. From it, she pulls out the king's crown and places it on my head. "I wanted to break this crown apart, dispersing all the pieces after your father's death, keeping a part for you. But now that you're here, I want you to have it for yourself. You, like this crown, belong here. You're the princess of this kingdom and you'll stay here. Your kingdom will protect you and your sister when I leave."

"No." I remove the crown and throw it to the ground.

She rushes to pick it up and hands it back. "Please don't argue." Her eyes plead.

"I love you, Mom." Tears prick at my eyes, blurring my vision. "But I can't let my friends, my family, or my team die. I just can't."

Because I have nothing else to say, and I don't want to argue, I take off running down the long hall. She comes after me, but I've already activated the relic in my hand, asking the crown to send me back to my true time. When I've gained enough speed, the wormhole opens in a blast of light, and I jump through.

№ 40
AN ARTIST

I'M IN THE WORMHOLE, HOPING TO MAKE IT back to my true time, but a spasm explodes through my body, causing me to lose the keyword from my concentration. The pain rushes from my fingertips and toes, leading to the core of my body, settling in my back.

The wormhole loses solidity; it flexes and tears, crumbling like dirt. Still fighting the pain, I struggle and reach for the walls but they disintegrate, sifting through my fingers like sand. The crown drops from my hand, and I slide out, falling into limbo. With the wormhole broken in the transition, my body convulses and I crash-land into mud, spread-eagle on my stomach, my location and my time unknown.

Rain pours over me in a deluge that should pound away the painful prickling that runs over my Chosen mark, but it doesn't. That, along with the deep rumbling boom of thunder and the crack of lightning striking nearby, confuses me even further.

I shriek and wail from the misery, stretching my arms out from my sides, grabbing for anyone that can help. Unexpectedly, my fingers graze the crown. Somehow through my agony I can see it's broken. The green gem hangs barely affixed to the golden setting. Yes, the relic pulled through with me, but somehow in its fragmented state it must have collapsed the wormhole, hurting me in the process. Or maybe this is part of being a Chosen? Maybe it's from the special water I drank? Whatever it is, I wish the torture would stop.

Rolling from side to side on my stomach, I try to turn onto my hip so I can curl into a ball, thinking that if I could change position, this all-encompassing burning would lessen. But this doesn't happen, because I have the sensation that I'm spitting in half, right down the middle of my back, cracking open like the shell of an egg.

No amount of tears will make it stop. No amount of screaming will make the pain go away because it's alive, somehow birthed from my soul, ripping though my body. Long fingers of agony crawl inside, pulling, dragging, scraping, and knocking on my bones. The pain rips through my skin and tears my tunic, seeming to extricate itself from me. This sensation brings a release, but just for a fleeting moment. The intensity builds again, erupting twice more, allowing an excruciating pain to roll over me, smashing what little life I have left.

I sense that someone's found me, or perhaps it is they who are harming me, ripping my clothes away and slicing open my back. Dark figures move around me, their silhouettes fleeting in the flash of the lightning. Their forms cause a flickering strobe of brightness and dark. Then their dog growls. He sniffs at my face, pressing his muzzle to my cheek, and I stiffen in fear. The animal's pointed teeth snap at me and it snarls. If the pain in my body doesn't kill me, surely this wild beast will.

I close my eyes and pray that they'll leave me, stop this torture, and allow me to die. At the moment that I think the words, the figures miraculously move away.

Exhausted and completely confused about what's happened, I let my eyes slowly close. No person, Normal or Wanderer, could withstand being ripped to shreds in this way without dying.

And at this point, I think dying might be okay.

·

Sometime later, something wriggles through my consciousness, jerking me awake. Through low-lidded eyes, I see a person cautiously approach. They pick up a nearby stick and poke me, and I moan at the sharp pain, but have no energy for words. If they want to hurt me, I'm done. I have no idea who I'm dealing with or what time in history I've fallen into.

It could be a hostile war territory, the jungle, or the mountains of Peru. The only fact I know for sure is that I'm somewhere between my true time and our Wandering beginnings in Egypt.

The person does not turn me on my back; instead, they grasp my shoulders and haul me onto a blanket. I scream from the movement, still wailing as the person wraps me carefully. Slowly, one foot at a time, the person drags me across thick mud.

Swinging in and out of consciousness as I'm being so crudely transported, I finally relax when I hear a door creak open, and soon I find myself inside a dry structure. The sounds of the rain and storm are muffled now and the blanket falls away, allowing me to see across the floor. A fire warms the room, and the person who moves around me speaks in what sounds like Italian. It's different, much older than the modern language Bishop and I heard spoken in Venice, but it's familiar nonetheless. Then I make out a few words that worry me: blood, much blood.

•

I awake on my side, lying in a bed. The mattress is lumpy, perhaps filled with hay. The feather pillow beneath my head smells of body odor, so I lift myself in order to mumble, "Save them." Though my limbs are stiff, I attempt to sit up. When I do, someone rushes to my side and rubs my head. "Sleep," the voice urges in Italian.

Still in pain, I'm in no position to argue. I close my eyes.

Water drips over my parted lips and I choke until I open my eyes. Light floods my eyes, and I blink several times to clear my groggy vision. An older man stands above me, drizzling water into my mouth with a wet rag. His faded eyes are enclosed within wrinkled folds above a long curtain of salt and pepper facial hair.

"Drink," he says in Italian. Reaching behind me, he lifts my head to a bowl. The taste of the water makes me realize how dehydrated I am.

"*Grazie*," I manage through cracked, dry lips. He gently settles my head back on the pillow.

Though I know some Italian, he talks as if he assumes I speak the language well. When I glance around, I see that I'm in a studio. Paintings stand on easels, rest in stacks on the floor, or lean against the walls. Miniature flying contraptions hang on rough cords from the ceiling, and papers and books teeter high in unsteady stacks on a wooden desk. From my history studies, I place myself in early sixteenth century Italy, and in the company of a very important man—Leonardo da Vinci.

Remembering that I should be on my way back to my true time to save everyone, I quickly push myself up on my elbows and swing my legs over the edge until I'm sitting upright. Sharp pains shoot up my back and through my head, and I grab my temples.

The pain that afflicted me in the broken wormhole still exists, but now it's a dull emptiness that consumes me. There's a void, and I don't feel like myself. My only answer is that it must be the aftereffects of becoming the Chosen.

I shift my body slightly, working the kinks out of my limbs. Strangely, the skin on my back feels too tight across the ridge of my spine. I reach a hand to my back, allowing my fingertips to follow a short way along the long line of woven stitches over rippled skin, which, from what I can feel, extends from my tailbone to my neck.

My stomach rolls with nausea and I look up to my host to ask bleakly, "What happened?"

He's been watching me, so even though he may not understand my words, he'll hopefully understand my shock by reading my reaction.

"You had quite a large gash in your skin that needed a proper stitch," he says slowly, enunciating each syllable with care.

"You speak English, but they said you only spoke Italian."

His bushy gray eyebrows rise an inch. "Whom says these things?"

"Um," I start, then I look around. History, I want to say, but after I think about it, it's the Normals' history that says this.

"What happened to my back?" As soon as I say the words, the memories rush back: fingernails scratching and ripping through my skin, the burning pain of being cracked open, and the growling beast that could have killed me. "Did you see the people that attacked me?"

He waves his hand as if to pluck the correct word from the air. "Because of your broken relic. A fragmentation." He gestures to the table, where the crown sits. The emerald's fallen off, just like I remember.

His explanation for the wound on my back doesn't make sense, but whatever the reason, I can't dwell on this. I can't take the time to figure out what he means; I have to return to my true time. So I test my legs and stand. The old man watches, worry creasing his brow as I take a tentative step. I seem steady enough, so I walk away from the bed. A draft brushes against my bare legs, and I look down to see that he's dressed me in a new tunic. This one looks like something a young boy would wear rather than a woman, but in the whole scheme of things, what I'm wearing is the least of my worries.

"I have to leave," I say grimly, and stumble to the window to confirm my location. Renaissance Florence sits in the distance, just as I expected. I remember my teacher, Mr. Matchimus, telling us that Da Vinci had a studio outside of Florence in his later years.

When I face Da Vinci, he's standing behind an easel, painting and watching me with the keen eye of an artist. Curious, I shuffle over. You'd think that meeting him is crazy enough, but to see the drawing on his canvas, what he's working on at this moment, causes me to take a few steps away to compose myself.

"How? I mean—" For once I have no words because the painting he's working on right now is of the Seraphina Angel.

This is the exact painting that hangs on the wall in the main atrium at the Academy of Wanderers in my true time. The one that Bishop always told me looks exactly like me. The one that I realize only bears my name because it actually is me.

"The Seraphina," I mumble.

Just like me, the painted angel has flowing dark hair, but she has three sets of wings. With one set she flies, with one set she hoods her face, and one covers her feet. Black words scroll across each set of wings, along with simple symbols. Each set of wings symbolizes one of the Master-given gifts— Wanderer, Seer, and Protector. But in this painting, the angel has all three gifts, just like me, just like the Chosen.

I step closer to admire the heavy-handed sketch on the canvas. He's just begun filling in the loose shapes with long washes of sepia colors.

"Why did you paint me like this?" I ask. Only another Wanderer would understand the marks on my back, and it would take a high-ranking Wanderer to know what they actually mean.

"You are the Chosen, no?" He looks at me, raising a very bushy eyebrow.

"Yes." I nod. There's no point in denying it anymore.

"So then, you're a Wanderer too?" He laughs at my expression, sets his brush down, and hobbles to the nearby desk. He picks up a large piece of paper, scribbled over with doodles of aircraft inventions. "Many think me brilliant, but it's easy to invent when you've seen the future through your Wandering family. No?" He looks at me with a twinkle in his eye.

"You are brilliant, with or without help."

The old man gives me a wink. "I knew I saved you for a reason." He places a gnarled hand on my shoulder as he passes by and totters to a cabinet, pulling out a piece of fruit and a crust of bread. He turns and places them on the table.

"About that, thank you for helping me."

He shakes his head. "It is I who am honored to be in the Chosen's presence."

As I flip through his drawings I find one of Unika's crown— a simple charcoal study that he's sketched. But in his drawing, the emerald is where it should be, mounted between the wings of the golden scarab.

I trace a finger over the loose lines, remembering a sketch just like this one, drawn by Stu a year ago. Stu explained that he found a book with the sketch of the crown. It must have been Da Vinci's. I could never imagine every detail of my life folding around and meeting me again for a second time. Every instance in life, every path has a purpose, and this meeting is more proof of that.

Picking up the green gem, I study it thoughtfully as it rests in my palm. "I have a favor to ask before I go. Can you set this gem into a bracelet and mail it through Gibeon to an address I give you?"

"Sì." He looks up in question.

Good. I needed to verify that we could still send mail through to any time period via Gibeon, just like Turner sent

Bishop's photo to me on that day that now seems like a lifetime ago.

It's imperative that the green gem makes it back through time to my sixteen-year-old self. I'm the only one who can reset my path, and send it on the proper course. So I remove the quill from the inkwell, lean over the desk, and quickly jot down instructions of when the item should arrive in the future, and to whom it should travel to.

Fit this gem within a sundial bracelet and send it through Gibeon mail to the future:

Mona Bishop
3838 Schiller Street
Chicago, IL 60611

Instructions:
Mona, please give this to Seraphina on her 16th birthday. A gift from her mother.

This is all I can do for now. I have no idea of the details of how this relic will travel to my sixteenth birthday in the future, what problems it will cause, or how it will be broken apart. What I do know is I've now ensured its life path will collide with my own, and all of history will play out as it should.

I look to Da Vinci and manage a smile. "Thank you." As I hand him the note, I ask, "Now, can you tell me where my things are? I have to leave."

N₀ 41

ROME

"THERE." DA VINCI POINTS TO A PILE OF CLOTH-ing in the corner.

I rush across the room to riffle through it. "My canteen, it's gone. Do you have it?" I turn to him.

He shakes his head. "This is everything." He lifts his shoulders into a shrug.

"The others, the ones who hurt me, they must have taken it." I go through each piece, inspecting them to decide if I can use them as relics to return to my true time. The tunic is ripped down the back, soaked with blood, and is as useless as the fragmented crown relic. But my sandals, though they are mud-coated, are still usable. When I pick them up, a garnet ring lodged within their straps falls to the floor, and I lean down to pick it up.

"What's this?" I hold it up for him to see.

"It was in the mud near you. I thought it was part of the crown, but no."

I glance closely, looking the gold setting over, and the memory of exactly where I've seen the garnet ring before floods back. In vivid detail, I see the image of Cece in my mind. She was wearing this ring the very first time I met her in Rome, last semester. That is the only place in time that I know for sure where I can find her. And I have a feeling that my canteen of aqua vitae will be there with her. It's a start and for now, it's all I have.

Quickly, I slip my feet into my sandals. My body aches, pain burning all over my body, but I ignore it. The sooner I can return, the sooner I can retrieve the water and find a way to set all Wanderers and Nocturna free.

I scurry over to Da Vinci to give him a kiss on the cheek. "Thank you, sweet friend. If I make it through this life alive, I will look at this painting every day and remember your kindness. I promise."

He chases after me through the door, concern pinching his features as he waves his arms in protest. "But your wounds are not healed."

With no time to waste, I wave off his concerns and throw him a smile. As soon as I hit open air and find a clear patch long enough for running, I ignore the discomfort and sprint across the field with the garnet ring tucked tightly within my palm, until a blast of light sucks me into a wormhole.

With the powers of a Chosen, there's a new connection between myself and relics. I can feel it within every pore of my body. This garnet ring relic will take me wherever I wish; I only need ask it to return to the last place I laid eyes on this ring. So I focus on Rome, where I know it will deliver me straight to Cece.

This time the wormhole holds together, only flexing and bending to shoot me in new directions, and it spits me out at my new place in time.

My feet stumble to a halt atop cobblestones in Rome, Italy, more than half a year before my true time, and a day before I arrived to find my mom with the sundial bracelet.

A double sense of déjà vu comes over me as I take in the scene before me; I never thought I'd return to this place, never dreamed I'd face my past in this way. I march across the Piazza Del Popolo. The soaring obelisk at the center of the plaza casts a pointed shadow in the direction of the Church of Santa Maria dei Miracoli. As before, tourists move around snapping photos of the beautiful Italian architecture, unaware of what lies beneath this space—the hideout of the Underground.

I race up the church's marble stairs and burst through the carved doors. There's no choir singing today like before. Instead, a mass is taking place beneath the ornate oil paintings that adorn the domed ceiling. My entrance is so loud that everyone in the extravagantly designed church turns to glare at me, including the priest, who stops in the middle of his homily. Ignoring them, I head for the entrance to the catacombs. The dark opening, flanked by small obelisks, leads beneath the church's structure.

This time, instead of stumbling through the darkness, I grab a torch and light it. With the light raised, I make my way past dark catacombs and into the room of lined skulls, careful to watch for snakes and avert my eyes from the mummified monks hanging from the walls and the heinous bone chandelier.

Unlike before, Underground members sleep in piles of trash along the walls, ignoring me. The stench of garbage tweaks my nose as I travel around and around the circular hallways. They spiral in wide rotations until I find the opening that leads out to the balcony, which hangs over the enormous open pit.

It's the one I fell into last semester, the same one I watched Francis die in. I don't have the luxury of worrying about such things anymore, so I race across the natural bridge, paying no heed to the fact that I am crossing over a pit.

Once I reach the other side, I step behind the dark stone obelisk that rises from the center of the floor, piercing through the ceiling and emerging into the plaza above.

"Cece!" I roar her name as I rush though the corridors searching for her. She laughs somewhere off in the maze of hallways, and her voice ricochets off the walls as it did the first time we met. Somewhere she's waiting for me, mocking me.

Finally I find her in a room made of stone, seated on a crumbling throne. Cerberus, her Protector beast dog, growls at her side and snaps ferociously when I enter. Exeter, her Seer, stands at her flank, hands folded in prayer.

Drake, the gang leader, lounges in the corner with other Underground members including Francis, the bum who tricked me into meeting Cece in the first place. But in my past, that meeting doesn't take place until tomorrow. They stand as I enter and he's the first to approach, but Cece quickly waves them away.

"This is not the young Sera we seek," she says, somehow knowing. "This Sera is of the future." The dog growls at her side and she hushes him with a wave of her hand.

"How can you tell?" Drake asks and crosses his arms.

She smiles. "She's glowing from the mark of the Chosen."

"I'm here for the canteen you stole." I throw her garnet ring across the room to the floor. She ignores it, but Francis scurries to pick it up.

"Pity we won't be giving it to you." She pushes her long, sweeping red hair over her shoulder.

"I disagree."

"Child, how do you think we've lived this long? The water is almost gone."

"Lived this long?" I'm not sure what she means. I stop to think about it. She attacked me in Italy, sometime in the 1600s. I thought that maybe she had Wandered there, but if

she's saying she's lived all this time with the special water…
"You've lived since the time of Da Vinci?"

"For a Chosen, you're a stupid one," she says.

Everyone in the room laughs.

"Shall I kill her now?" Drake asks with a yawn.

Cece seems to consider this for a moment, looking me over with a narrow gaze. "We thought maybe if we let the boys erase you in your true time, we'd live even longer, but now that you're here, we have another idea."

"What do I have to do with you living longer?" I rest my hands on my hips.

She stands and descends the stairs of her throne and steps forward. Standing rigid, I don't fear her like I did when we first met. I'm a better fighter now, and she has something that I desperately need.

"You have everything to do with us living longer." She smirks.

Now that she's in front of me and I have a moment to really look at her without the overwhelming fear I'd experienced during all our other meetings, I sense something in her I didn't notice before—I see all the bad, all the evil that good people suppress. Hers is born from the smallest seed of hate, nursed until it is exaggerated and overgrown out of proportion. In essence, I see myself. The idea of it scares me so badly that I step away in disgust. It's something I can't fathom, can't even bear to think about.

I shake my head, trying to dislodge the abhorrent thought.

"No, no!" Da Vinci's explanation of what happened to me, why my wormhole fell apart, floods my senses. He called it a "fragmentation" because of my broken relic, but I was so busy trying to leave and follow through on my task that I hadn't given myself enough time to understand what the word fragmented meant for a Wanderer, but I do now. I understand completely.

It was not just the relic that was fragmented, it was *me*. I became fragmented, literally breaking into several pieces, or in this case people. Cece, Cerberus, and Exeter were all born from me, exiting through my Chosen mark, all extracted from my body, from deep within my soul. The stitches that run over my spine throb as the memories become clear, and my face twists in horror.

Even Elijah Vanderpool mentioned that this could happen when I saw him at the exposition. And in Nocturna, Stu said that the Time Reapers were fragmentations, all born of each other. So it is possible that I'm not the only one this has happened to.

"Yes, we think you've caught on now, haven't you? The three of us," she gestures back to her team, "are from your blood, fragmented from your body, birthed from you in the rain in Italy through your Chosen mark. But instead of killing you like we originally planned, we think we'll use you." She steps closer, so close that we are only a foot apart.

I step backward, bumping into a wall of Underground guards. Instead of cringing in fear or even trying to fight, I face her.

She grabs my chin, clenching my jaw between her long black fingernails. With their points, she draws blood, and then lightly touches her blood-covered nail to her tongue. As she samples, she jolts in shock at the taste.

"Mmm. You—taste—like—life." She draws out the words with a hiss. "You'll be better than the aqua vitae." She snaps her fingers at this and her army descends.

One man approaches before I can react and jabs a syringe into my arm. The plunger depresses, releasing a black liquid that pulses beneath my skin. When I look down, I can actually see the ink traveling through my veins, and helplessly watch it spread whatever poison it carries throughout my body like a tree rooting in the soil. It branches to my fingertips, turning them black, and then reaches across my chest, up my neck and to my face until it consumes the whites of my eyes, bleeding into my corneas and blocking my sight.

Desperately, I grasp at the air, thinking someone may help me but there's no one here. I'm as alone as I've always felt, and I drop to my knees as the vile concoction weakens me and I pass out.

Several jolts of electricity awaken me, and my hand falls to the side, clutching the arm of a chair. The commotion around me urges me to open my eyes. I tell my eyes to open but they protest, taking all the energy I have just to open a sliver, but it's enough to see.

Three figures float across my vision. Cece, the farthest

away, struts back and forth wearing a long red cape. Her dog-beast falls in line behind her, growling with his hair raised on his back, and then nearest to me, Exeter. They move in a peculiar way, like vertebrae, one piece connected to another; the image reminds me of a snake slithering back and forth in an undulating wave. When I saw them for the very first time when I was here before, they seemed to be connected to a person in a wheelchair, the person who I assumed was my mother, but who I now realize is me. *I'm the person in the wheelchair.* We're all connected, and I remember through my haze that they're a fragmentation of me.

During the first meeting in Rome with Cece, I believed the woman in the wheelchair draped in a green cape was my mother. We looked exactly alike, but I can see now that it was always me. Back then, I needed my mom so badly that I only saw what I wanted to see.

This horrifying revelation makes me want to scream out loud, but I have no energy to do so. The life that beats weakly through my body somehow surges out of me and directly into Cece and the others. Because of the black liquid, they're able to suck the life from me, extending their own. They're connected to me in a way that I never could have understood until now.

A strange understanding pours over me as I watch Cece strut around, and I realize that I've been fighting myself all this time. She—they—are me, a part of me. This entire time I've been fighting against the evil part of myself. I've literally been my own worst enemy. I'd laugh at the irony if it weren't so heartbreaking.

Each time Cece and I met, she said that she knew me better

than I knew myself. Being a part of me she must have my memories, as well as my secrets, hopes, and dreams. That's why my blood heals her and her team, and why she always speaks in the third person for her team members who are all deeply connected.

"What shall we do with her?" Cece asks a crowd of Underground members, whose heads poke through several levels of archways around the pit. They cheer loudly, arms waving.

She walks dramatically in a circle and I see myself—my past self—lying on the ground, trembling with fear in front of her. I'm watching a replay of our first meeting, reliving it from the other side. Somehow I've been under the influence of the black poison since yesterday and now my true timeline is colliding with my past self.

Even though I can't see him from my position, I know Past Bishop is somewhere in the background, fighting off the Underground guards, probably too far out of the field of my foggy vision.

Everything is falling into place, every little detail explained. This is why Cece seemed to know my every move and know everything about me every time we fought, both here and at the theater in Gibeon. We practically share the same brain; we *are* the same.

"Or shall we send her into the pit?" Cece stops and stares down at Past Sera.

"Never," Past Sera says vehemently.

Cece rushes to her, lowering her gaze to the girl. "We

tricked you into reconstructing the relic," she says in a playfully sinister tone. She holds up the sundial bracelet, dangling it in the air like a cat's toy.

Past Sera sets her jaw and her face turns determined. In one precise movement she smacks the bracelet from Cece's hand and it flies across the room, landing ten feet away.

Sera dives for it, sliding across the floor to snatch it in her hand, and then she flips over to defend herself. Cerberus descends, foaming at the mouth, anticipating a fight.

Cece approaches, hushes the dog, stroking the lines of his head. "Relax, Cerberus. There's plenty of time for that. He's such a good Protector, isn't he?"

At this, Past Sera inches away from them, toward the edge of the pit, and several loose rocks fall away. The top half of her body hangs over the edge, the endless black pit below.

"Wait!" she yells and extends an arm in the air, allowing the bracelet to hang over the pit. "I'll drop it," she screams.

Cece laughs out loud at this, so completely taken by the action that she cries tears of joy. And now, from this new perspective, I understand why. To destroy the gem and the bracelet would destroy the life path of the relic, which might lead to Cece and her team's beginnings—where she was born of me in the rain in Italy. She might be vulnerable there, laid out in the mud and probably weak from new life. She doesn't want anyone to know where she came from, doesn't want anyone to trace her beginnings or know her weakness.

"Drop it!" Cece yells out, egging her on.

Past Sera looks confused, and I remember feeling the same way.

"See," she says, "you're already doing what we want, and you don't even realize it!" She laughs, delighted with herself. The team rumbles with laughter again and the energy it takes to do so causes me to convulse with electricity. My green velvet hood falls away, revealing more of my face.

Past Sera stiffens with shock, looking at me wistfully and with hope because she thinks I'm her mother. My heart aches to have that hope back—to feel it again, instead of feeling everything falling apart around me. I wish I could speak to tell her the truth, to save her in some way. But this is my life and even the awful, horrid things have happened for a reason, sending me on a path I was destined to follow. I have to believe that there's a reason for all of this.

"Kill him!" Cece yells out to the guards. Her wicked words pull me back to the moment.

A guard who has been fighting with Past Bishop has moved within my blurry range of vision, and strikes him down. He falls to the floor of the bridge and the tattooed man kicks him in his rib cage. Each kick causes Bishop to scream out, unleashing his misery.

The crowd cheers, and I'm horrified as much if not more than I was the first time I witnessed the brutality.

"Join us! You'll only know your true strength here, with us. The Academy will keep you weak, revealing only their truths. There's so much more you can learn with us." Cece reaches out to Past Sera.

She was right, there was so much I didn't know, so much

I could have never imagined, and Past Sera looks at me again. She's trying to choose between saving Bishop or saving me. She thinks I'm sleeping serenely, but if she came close she would see tears in my barely open eyes.

Go, I want to tell her. It's okay. You're not meant to stay here with me. I'm not your mother.

Bishop is unconscious, lying on the bridge. The tattooed man steps forward onto his arm, breaking it under his weight with a sickening crack. It flops limply, dangling over the edge.

Past Sera shudders with horror.

Another guard squats down and shoves Past Bishop's lifeless body over the edge of the bridge and into the bottomless black pit. Without hesitation, Past Sera rolls her body over the edge of the platform and falls away to save him.

I'm relieved when she lets me go because I know that she and Past Bishop are safe. In a few moments, they'll return to the Academy through Wandering and move forward with their lives.

Cece screams like a crazed woman, stomping from one side of the room to the other. Cerberus follows, howling.

She turns and locks her gaze on me, rushing forward. "You little witch, you should have listened to me!"

With her full strength, she smacks my face so hard that the wheelchair teeters, falling to the side, and I smash my head on the ground. Still weakened by the black liquid, I can barely move; I only lie here as she sucks life from me to propel her rant.

After her anger recedes Cece stomps away, followed by her team. And now that there's nothing more to see, the crowd disperses from the archways of the Underground. When the cavern quiets, someone approaches and bends down.

"Dearest. What has she done to you?" The woman lifts me from the floor and slings my arm over her shoulders, dragging me into a corridor. When we're alone, she positions me on a rock that protrudes from the wall.

With little energy remaining, my head falls back and I open my eyes to see her. She's my mom, older now, and as beautiful as I remember her on the day of her death in Gibeon. She'd joined the Underground, and I should have remembered that she'd be here, somewhere, even if it wasn't in the wheelchair.

"How are you a part of this?" I mumble so low that she has to move close to my face to hear my words.

"I'm only here for you. You told me I joined the Underground when I returned from Egypt to my true time, and everything played out exactly like you said. I left you with Ray as a baby, faked my death, and came here. And finally, after all these years, I understand why. I'm here to save you from Cece. The poison is wearing off and your color's returning. I'll help you return to your true time with this. She holds up a vial. "This is all that's left of the aqua vitae. Take it back to the Grand Master and save your friends and family." She tucks it into my pocket.

"It's not enough. I need to save the others in Nocturna."

"It's a start," she says. "You'll find a way to fulfill the prophecy. You're pure of heart, I have faith in you. I have since the day you were born and I first held you in my arms." She strokes my hair. "I love you and am so proud of you." She kisses my head.

"But I can't run, I have no energy, nor a relic."

Mom holds up my sandals and bends down, securing one to my foot. The other she ties to my hand. "These are not for running today, but for flying, like Hermes." She smiles with her eyes.

She hoists me to her side and drags me back to the pit. "I'll toss you over. Do you have enough energy to activate the wormhole?"

"Yes." I frown because leaving her is never easy.

She presses her warm cheek to mine, hugging me tightly before she lets go. When I fall away from her outstretched arms, my heart breaks because now I'm certain that this is the last time we'll meet.

I force the keyword into my mind, asking to return to my true time, and a blast of light explodes, opening the wormhole and sucking me in. I fall through the slides of time, landing back in Gibeon, right next to the fire pit within the Grand Lodge where the Oath ceremonies are still taking place.

No

42

PURE OF HEART

A S EXPECTED, EVERYTHING IS AS IT WAS WHEN
I left. Students stand around the Grand Lodge, glistening
in oil as they chant like zombies. The casket box holding Bishop and Sam swings above, hovering over the enormous fire
pit. With each beat of the drums, they're lowered closer to
their deaths. The wall of flames dances beneath, teasing their
fate.

When I land, the Grand Master joins me and bends down.
"Strange, I don't remember putting you in these clothes. Why
does it look as though you've taken a detour?"

I push myself to a sitting position. "I have your stupid water—somewhere else," I lie. "But first I need my team, Ray, and Macey back. I need to know that they're safe."

"You don't have it with you?" he hisses.

"I have to make sure you give me what I want. You certainly haven't given me any reason to trust you."

"Very well." Grand Master Levi stands and snaps his fingers. At his bidding, many Society guards take off.

I stand, taking my time, hiding the fact that it pains me to do so. Between a back lined with stitches and having the life sucked from me, it's hard to appear as strong as I was when I left, but I must. I shrug out of the green cape and let it fall to the floor. Beneath I'm wearing the tunic that Da Vinci dressed me in.

The Animate scorpion appears from underneath a pile of clothes that I was wearing before I left, scampers across the floor, climbs over my toes, and settles on the rise of my foot.

When I look up at the commotion across the room, I expect to see Macey and Ray on their way back from the pit of Nocturna, but instead, I see Cece—very alive in my true time, just as Drake suggested. Her team follows her into the Grand Lodge. And since she drank the aqua vitae, she could live for as long as she has access to it. But most importantly, she's part of me, so she could Wander from Gibeon like a Chosen and survive the fall into the pit, which would have killed any other Wanderer who had not used a Wandering compass.

Cece ascends the stairs, stepping onto the pedestal and reaches both hands out to the Grand Master. He joins her, takes her hands into his own, and kisses each of her knuckles.

This meeting between the two is unexpected, and I can only imagine what they're up to, but then the worst part happens. They lean into each other and kiss—an open-mouthed kiss with tongues tangling and gentle arms caressing, and I choke a little as I feel my gorge rising in my throat.

Still embracing, they turn to me.

"She returned with the water, my love," Grand Master Levi says, then kisses her on the cheek.

"You always know how to please me." She traces his ear with her fingernail.

The group moves toward me, and as they do the Animate crawls off my foot and activates, shooting a beam of light from his face, revealing Hologram Turner. He solidifies and crouches, taking a defensive position.

The slight wobble in Cece's demeanor suggests she's taken aback by this. "What do we have here?" she asks.

"Just a hologram of a boy," Grand Master Levi says in dismissal.

Cerberus, the overgrown beast, barks at him.

"Sera." She waves her hand, fluttering it about. "Be a doll and bring me what's left of the water."

I cross my arms over my chest. "Why don't *you* be a doll and bring me my friends."

"You may have fooled my young prodigy here, but you don't fool me. I can see that you've just come from Rome. I recognize your clothes, and I know that you're in no state to fight. I sucked the life out of you when you were there, leaving practically nothing." She leaves the Grand Master's side and circles the fire pit to approach me. Her Protector and Seer follow because they're always connected, even without me.

"And when your body dies," she continues, "I'll drain the blood from you and drink every last drop, and then I'll boil your pieces to consume them. I'll squeeze every last ounce of life from you, and if you hadn't stolen the crystal dreamdrives from me, I'd be living off your dreams too." She pauses and looks around. "Or I'd control you with it, just like I did with the Underground, just like I do with the Society now, and just like I have for hundreds of years."

"You won't touch her!" Hologram Turner yells.

"And you think this thing," she gestures at him, "is a replacement for the real thing?" She laughs. "He's not nearly as handsome or as strong."

Hologram Turner steps closer. "Don't listen to her, Sera." He then turns and roars at the crowd, "No one should listen to her or the Grand Master! You must wake up, my friends!" He pumps his arms fiercely above his head like a war cry. "Awaken!"

Something in his last word seems to trigger the brainwashed students to life. They lose their stiffness and begin to shift in their places, looking around with a new awareness. With a stunning leap of understanding, they suddenly rush forward, each challenging the closest Society guard and overpowering them. With numbers on our side, we may be able to win this fight.

"Did you do this?" I rush my words with excitement.

"Your speech inspired me!" he screams over the commotion.

"Did you do this with the contrapulators?"

He nods and continues screaming the special word until it affects everyone in the room.

Quickly, I piece together how this might be possible. Somehow he altered their programming on their contrapulators to release them from the Society's mind control at the sound of the trigger word. He's given them enough understanding to riot against the Society. This must have been what he did after he freed Bishop and Sam from the Grand Master, when he explained he was inspired by my speech. Working as the professor's assistant gave him inside knowledge, allowing him to manipulate the contrapulators.

"You're a genius!" I glance around in absolute awe. I never should have doubted him.

Turner's trigger word continues as a battle cry as the students begin to chant "awaken" over and over, becoming louder until the golden walls nearly tremble with the roar of their anger. And with that, the battle begins. Oil-covered students and Society guards collide in chaos just as Hologram Turner dives at Cece, pulling her to the ground.

As a guard escorts Macey and Ray into the Grand Lodge, the chanting of the word "awaken" has the same effect on Macey and her blind eyes become alert. She shakes her head, taking in her surroundings, and I can nearly see the gears turn in her head as she quickly puts the pieces together. With one kick she takes out the guard that brought them here and then she turns to Ray, removes his blindfold, and ushers him to safety.

Other students who have no guards to fight have made their way through the oil moat and up onto the pedestal to take on Cerberus and Exeter.

Hologram Turner and Cece still fight, and the entire scene is an eerie reminder of how the real Turner died a few weeks ago. I can't allow him to fight for me anymore, so when he pulls away from her for a moment, I take the opening and attack her myself.

At my back, Hologram Turner engages the Grand Master and the two clash in a life-or-death struggle.

Anger wells within me, pulling up a power I didn't know I possessed. For the short time that I've been a Chosen, this is the first time I can feel more strength, and it leads me to believe that I'm doing the right thing, finally following the correct path. I'm certain that my new powers will guide me to some way to set us all free once and for all.

Cece and I circle each other and I kick, swiping at her head, the movement causing the stitches in my back to pull and rip open. Each time I kick, another stitch loosens and the skin on my back feels like it's peeling away, opening further.

Cece lunges forward, landing a jab to my stomach followed quickly by an uppercut to my jaw. When her knuckles make painful contact, I use my elbow to shove her away, then bring my other elbow down in a pile-driver move to knock her to the floor.

I step onto an ornate ceremonial carpet and too quickly for me to react, Cece reaches forward and tugs on it, making me lose my footing, and I collapse to my butt with a thump. I scream out in new pain because something's lodged into my back, poking into the raw, exposed wound.

She takes advantage and lunges at me, but I kick her in the face, sending her flying backward. Her head slams into the edge of the flaming pit, allowing me a few moments to gain my bearings.

The pain in my back is so severe that nausea rises in my stomach, threatening to make an appearance. When I roll over to heave, I see what it is I've landed on. It's the Animate scorpion, crushed into a thousand tiny pieces, and all that remains intact is the crystal dreamdrive. I grab it from the floor, clutching it within my palm, and turn to see Hologram Turner sizzling with electricity and fading away to nothing. He's leaving me again for a second time, and the sheer devastation of it causes me to drop to my knees gasping for air.

"Make your last wish, love," he says with a smile as he shimmers into nothing more than a hazy outline.

"For you to be alive!" I scream, my heart breaking in two as tears stream down my face.

Through my watery eyes I see someone walk up behind the hologram, stepping within the disappearing shape and filling it perfectly. Filling it the way it should be.

Turner.

The real Turner.

Alive.

My heart pounds in my chest, and if I don't spring to my feet to attack him, my heart surely will.

"Turner!" I race to him. He catches my eye and leaps toward me with open arms. We come together desperately, devouring each other with our mouths, our eyes, our touch. Tingles dance over my skin in a parade of delight, and I want to worship every inch of him with my love. "My wish came true," I mumble repeatedly through my tears, and throw my arms around his body, holding him tightly. "I can't believe it. How is this possible?" I press my lips to his again and again.

"I thought I lost you," he whispers in my ear, his voice ragged with emotion. In this moment I know I love him, even without the binds of Wandering. It was always meant to be; I understand that and feel it now. Real love. Normal love. Being here with him makes me so happy that I want to explode with joy from the inside out.

Wrapped in his embrace, I look over his shoulder, remembering that this might not be the best time for a reunion. "Duck!" I pull him to the ground and he falls on top of me, just as a small flaming chandelier flies past. Though we're consumed with each other, we're still in the fight of our lives.

Cece and the Grand Master are back in action and descend on us. Behind them, the casket is so close to the pit that flames lick and burn its bottom.

"I'll take care of these two. I need you to free Sam and Bishop."

"Where are they?" He looks around.

I point to the box hanging above the flames.

"Be safe, love." Turner squeezes my hand and takes off running, dodging several Society guards along the way.

The students around us are holding their own, so I call out for several closest to me to run and bar the main doors shut so that we can keep all the people of Gibeon out. To win this war, we'll need to start here at the top.

I pick up the chain attached to the flaming chandelier and swing the fixture at the end around my head. It makes several wide rotations before I release it and it flies across the room, its heavy chain wrapping around the Grand Master's neck several times. With wide eyes and an open mouth, he gasps and falls to the ground, clutching at the links that are strangling him to death.

Unaffected, Cece looks down at him.

"Don't you want to help your lover boy?" I ask as I move forward for the kill.

She lifts a shoulder and gives an unconcerned sniff. "He was merely a means to an end, someone to keep me supplied with Chosens who could obtain aqua vitae. But most importantly, I needed him to make sure you became who you are, an insider, allowing a Chosen to be born, so I could eventually be born of you through your fragmentation."

Her eyes meet mine. "I made him who he was, helped him to a leadership position, and rationed him aqua vitae, extending his life. But now that you've matured into a Chosen, I can finally stop this charade." She wipes her lips of him. "Now I can take control of the Society, and merge it with the Underground. Everyone will do my bidding, and I will control all of time."

She kicks the Grand Master and he teeters forward, hitting the ground. Slowly suffocating, his body convulses as he claws at his neck, trying to set himself free.

"You forgot one thing." I step forward, pivoting on one foot before landing a kick to her gut.

"What's that?" She lets out a small *oomph*. Recovering quickly she rotates, connecting a foot to my side.

I leap backward, minimizing the power of her blow, and grit out, "I'm going to fulfill the prophecy."

A ceremonial guard has fallen dead on the ground near me, and I take up his weapon, a poleax, and swing it in her direction. She leans away from the curved blade each time I slice the air, so I adjust and jab the end at her, hoping the piercing spike mounted at the end will stab her through.

Now that I have the upper hand, I have just a moment to see that Turner—thank God, the real Turner—sits on top of the casket, trying to open it from above. Muffled screams can barely be heard from inside the box as flames catch the wood bottom on fire, sending fiery fingers racing across its surface to lick their way up the side.

"Swing!" I yell to Turner.

He must hear me because he plants his feet on either side of the box, grabs the chain, and shifts his weight until the box swings back and forth. Cerberus and Exeter join Cece's side, so now it's three against one. I can't hold them off much longer so I do the last thing I can to distract them—I take out the vial of aqua vitae and hold it up.

As the three stiffen in surprise and stare, I toss it to the ground at their feet. In an utter frenzy, they dive for it.

"Release it now!" I yell.

Turner releases the chain from the hook and the enormous wooden box flies through the air, landing directly on Cece and her team. To avoid its path, I dive into the pool of anointment oil and pop up to see that the box has crushed Cece and her team. A mess of bloody arms and legs bend in awkward positions beneath the pile of flaming splintered wood.

Desperate to check on my teammates, I rush through the oil and back onto the platform. Sam and Bishop lie on top, partially unwrapped from their bindings. Grasping Sam's shoulders, I haul her to safely, and then return to pull out Bishop. As I'm struggling with Bishop's weight, Macey appears beside me and nudges my shoulder, grinning at me as she grabs one of his arms to help.

With Sam and Bishop pulled away to safety, I scramble back to the platform and frantically dig through the debris, searching. Beneath several flaming wooden boards, I find Turner. The real Turner. He's moving; he's still alive. With all my strength, I lift and drag him from the wreckage, and then collapse with him in my arms. I sit up and pull his back against my chest, hugging him to me as I look over his shoulder at the mess, hardly capable of believing that this is over.

"You're okay, I know you're okay," I whisper urgently in his ear. Part prayer, part mantra, whatever it is, I have to believe it.

He groans.

"You can't go anywhere now, you know. I wished for this." Pulling away, I look at his face, bruised and bloody.

Turner grimaces a little and then shifts around to face me as he smiles at me. "I wished for this too."

"But where have you been all this time? I thought you were dead."

"Long story. Let's just say that Cece took a liking to me, and I played along until I could make it back to you."

"Ick," I say with a sincere shudder.

He laughs, deep and heavy. "The red hair was very sexy."

"I hate you."

"Your kisses say otherwise." A smile plays across his dirty but handsome face as he reaches out a finger to trace the curve of my cheek.

"I love you." Looking into his steel-gray eyes, I'm certain that this is real love, urged only by my beating heart, not my DNA. I lean forward to kiss him playfully, happily, and hug him close, wrapping my arms tightly around him, glancing over his shoulder at the scene playing out around us.

A movement catches my attention. An undead, yet severely injured Cece races forward with the poleax, ready to spear Turner through the back. Instinctively I shove him out of the way just in time, but the knife at the tip penetrates my chest, puncturing my body. I gasp and look down as liquid warmth drains from me. Despite the blood seeping through the fabric of my clothes, I feel dizzy but strangely feel no pain.

Above me there's instant chaos, but I ignore it, focusing on the light that rushes my soul and finally, the real love that consumes my heart.

No 43

SPIRIT EYES

MY SOUL FLOATS FROM MY BODY AND HOVERS above it. At least, I think it's my soul, I'm not sure, but through it I can see everything as it's happening below. My viewpoint is from the ceiling, an aerial view like that of a soaring bird, just like I could see when I became Chosen.

The fighting has stopped, and everyone has laid down his or her weapons. Ray, Macey, Bishop, Sam, and Turner—all those that I love—are safe. Cece's body lies in an unmoving heap on the ground right next to mine. She probably used her dying breath to kill me. I suppose it's only fitting that we die together since we're the same, made from the same skin and blood. The world is better off without us.

I float a little higher, gliding right out of the top of the Grand Lodge until I have a full view of Gibeon. The city is quiet; streamers and balloons have fallen, decorating the city like confetti.

Effortlessly, I move in a new direction to hover directly above the pit of Nocturna. I hover here until the suns sinks into evening, settling on the horizon in watercolor splashes of pinks until the sky turns to velvet indigo. It's not the twinkling stars that make me happy and hold me here, but other tiny dots. With my new eagle eyes, or maybe spirit eyes, I see these little dots move toward the surface, ascending the stairs of the pit of Nocturna. With my death, by making the ultimate sacrifice for love, I've set the inhabitants of Nocturna free, just as the prophecy called for. Maybe my heart is pure after all.

I watch my people climb toward the surface for what seems like hours, waiting until I see them all emerge over the pit's edge. One by one they appear; with each step their wrinkles and age spots begin to fade, and they stand a little straighter, making their way purposefully to Gibeon.

Charlotte steps into view, a child once again, and Mona and her husband, Joe, crawl over the rim just behind her—alive, and their true age. Terease and her crew appear, and then Stu climbs out and turns to help Perpetua. Thousands follow, one by one, and gather just outside the city limits, consoling each other and crying with happiness.

Despite the fact I no longer have a body, the sight makes me want to cry tears of joy. God, I've cried so much and hurt so much. I never realized I could change so much, that I truly had it in me to stand up, to make a difference, and to fight back. I did this amazing thing, I actually fulfilled the prophecy, and by doing so set not only the inhabitants of Nocturna free, I set *all* Wanderers free. My heart swells with happiness.

A child born unto a Wanderer and Normal died, but not just any death. I died protecting the one I truly loved with a pure heart. For the first time in a long time, I could feel the emotions of a Normal, and know what was real and what was not. That's all I ever wanted, to be free to make my own decisions and to control my own destiny.

Though I long to bask in my contentment, I feel a tugging and know it's time to move on. I'm ready now; I accept it. I've done everything I came to do and this fills me with love and contentment, so when the light comes for me, I welcome the love that floods my eyes.

The pull becomes more defined and I follow it, like I'm tethered to a string, and I glide with it. It guides me along and I'm so content that I close my eyes, allowing the gentle tug to deliver me wherever I'm meant to go.

Maybe I'll fade into nothing, or perhaps I'll fade into the sparkling stars. I think I might like it there.

Or maybe...maybe I'll become one of the fireflies.

№
44

HEAVEN

I'M SWIRLING, BEING FORCED INTO A FUNNEL,
and I rock back and forth with the centrifugal force.
Though I don't mind the feel of it, it's as though I'm returning to a fullness that I haven't felt in a while.

There's a cranking noise. Suddenly I'm aware of a body
being rocked back and forth under a dull rumble.

My body. A real one. A live one. I tentatively lift a fingertip, surprised that it actually works, and then wiggle my bare
toes. Fabric shifts over my body.

A cacophony fills my ears, overwhelming me, and eventually I discern it's the sound of cheering and clapping. And

there are smells, oddly enough; I inhale and detect the scents of violets and sweet oranges.

Suddenly I cough, inhaling smoke, and at this strangeness, I open my eyes to find I'm lying in a clear glass box, looking at puffy clouds floating in the sky above me. Flying Animate beasts circle above, flapping their widespread wings. I allow my head to fall to the side. There, on the other side of the glass, many people stand crowded around, watching me. Some are smiling, clapping, or even crying. Separating himself from the crowd, one person steps forward. The one that matters most. Turner.

When he looks at me the way he is now, I think that maybe this is heaven.

As he reaches me, he opens the door to the glass box, and all the smoke roiling within rushes out, allowing the fresh air in. Turner steps to my side and smiles. "And I thought the last time I saw you was the happiest day of my life. Little did I know." He reaches in, offering me his hand.

Even though I'm dazed, I gently slide my hand into his warm grasp. I'm still not sure if he's real, if I'm real, or even if this is a dream, but whatever this is, as long as I'm with him I'm happy. As I sit up, the flowers and orange slices that had adorned my body fall away. I look over my shoulder, glancing back into the box. A red cloak sits piled in the corner, along with a monk's robe and a dog collar. I know what those items signify, but I'm still unclear what's going on.

"I'm—" My voice is hoarse, so I clear my throat. "I'm confused." I look around, a little shy with so many people staring. I lean toward Turner and whisper, "What's happened?" I hesitate on my next words. "I remember dying." With alarm, I look down at my chest. There's no blood, no hole from a poleax, and every part of me feels refreshed. I reach for my back but there are no stitches, and I've been cleaned and dressed in a white eyelet dress, just like the one I dreamed I was wearing the night Mona told me I was a Wanderer so long ago.

I look up to Turner with wide eyes, seeking an explanation.

"Well, technically, I guess you were. Or you really couldn't have been since we believe you drank the aqua vitae. But then there's that bit about you fulfilling the prophecy and setting all the Wanderers and the people of Nocturna free. You've been very busy since I was gone."

He smiles with an impish grin that I want to kiss, then leans in and whispers, "I barely breathed until you were whole again." He squeezes my hand, lifts it to his lips, and presses a kiss to the palm of my hand. His touch awakens me from the inside, electrifying my heart.

I swing my legs out over the ledge, letting them dangle. Turner lifts me from the box and gently places me on the ground. Still unsure about what's happening, I keep my arms around him. He seems to sense my unease and hugs me back.

Peeking over my shoulder, back inside, I quickly realize that this is not just any glass box, but a contraption. The unfragmentation machine. The one invented by Elijah Vanderpool, designed to put relics back together, but also, as I recall in my most recent conversation with him—for unfragmenting Wanderers.

"The items in there—the red cloak, the dog collar, the monk's robes..." I point. They're all pieces of Cece, Exeter, and Cerberus.

"All very strangely a part of you, returned to your lovely vessel." Turner taps a finger to my nose.

"Well, that's going to take some time to absorb." I smile, thrilled to be rid of them, finally free for good.

"For me as well. Although," he teases, "there was something insanely sexy about that red hair."

"You mentioned that already." I smack his arm.

We're not left to ourselves for long as everyone who had been watching steps forward, surrounding us. There are smiles on every face I see. Some faces I recognize and many I don't. Turner squeezes my hand and with that reassurance, I step forward.

Little Charlotte, Bishop and Turner's younger sister, rushes forward. "Sera, these are for you. I picked them myself in the hanging gardens." She lifts a bouquet and I take it.

"They're lovely. Thank you so much." Charlotte smiles with her eyes much like her brothers. Mona and her husband, Joe, step forward and hug me too. "I'm so happy you're all safe," I say as I choke out a sob, looking from one to the other. "I was heartbroken to leave you in Nocturna."

"I never worried, not once, darling," Mona says, gently resting a palm on my cheek.

Leaning into her hand, I sniff back my tears and manage a smile. "Now I understand why you kept so many secrets. I could have never understood until I experienced everything for myself."

"I'm sorry, sweetheart," she says. "Your mother made me promise to keep you on a certain path. She said you wanted it to be so. She believed you would be our best defense against Cece and that you would be the one to set us free. She always believed in you and was proud of you. She told me you would correct her wrongs and she was right. Everything worked out the way it was supposed to." Her hand falls away and she wraps it around Charlotte's back and squeezes the child to her side. "Thank you for saving my family."

I nod and look to the ground, a little embarrassed at the attention. My time with each person is not long as I'm pushed forward through the crowd. Many hands pat my shoulder, or drift over my arm as congratulations are offered.

That's when Gabe appears at our side. "Moon pie!" he screeches with excitement. He places his hands on my shoulders and offers me a kiss on each cheek, European style, with the kind of excitement that only Gabe can supply. "Are you ready? Everyone's waiting."

"Ready for what?" I glance between him and Turner.

"For your special day." Gabe's face splits into a huge smile as he bounces on his toes and claps his hands together excitedly.

Before I have time to respond to this or even consider what he means, they urge me forward. That's when I realize we're standing on a plateau, at the very top of a mountainous set of stairs. As I step to the edge, I can see the city of Gibeon and all its inhabitants who are waiting below as they erupt in a deafening roar of cheers. I clutch the flowers tighter to my chest, overwhelmed by the moment.

I squeeze Turner's hand. "What's going on?"

"They're all here for you, to thank you for setting them free and returning them to paradise." He has to speak loudly in my ear for me to hear him.

Overcome by emotion, I gasp out a joyous sob. Turner slides his hand around my back and tugs me close, and I drop my head on his shoulder, looking out over the city of people who are here to thank me for what I've done.

Gabe leans in from the other side and steals my empty hand and raises it above our heads, shaking it about as though we've won a gold metal at the Olympics. At this, the thunderous sound of the crowd explodes. As if on cue, sparkling confetti falls from the sky, fluttering over us, tickling my face and sticking in my hair.

"It's time to go." Gabe urges us to walk down the stairs.

Turner and I descend them together. He encourages me to wave to the crowd, even though it feels weird to do so. I surely never expected this because I don't think I even thought I would survive. At the foot of the steps, a horse-drawn carriage awaits. Animate horses adorned with long curling feathers, draped velvet, and jewels stand at attention as Gabe hops up onto the coachman's seat and grabs the reins. Turner opens the door, helping me inside, but I'm surprised when he shuts it behind me.

"Aren't you coming?" I turn and lean out the window.

"I'll meet you on the other side." I raise an eyebrow at this. I don't want to be away from him for another second. "I promise." He laughs with a deep rumble that leaves my heart aching. "There's a surprise waiting for you." He slaps the side of the carriage twice and it lurches forward with creaking wheels.

"Okay," I say with reluctance and wave.

When I settle back and place my bouquet on the seat, I'm surprised to see Bishop sitting across from me in the far corner. His face is unreadable as his gaze glides over my features, but finally he smiles and leans forward for a hug. "I can't believe the machine worked. Thank the Masters you're okay."

"You're not mad at me?" I stiffen at the thought.

He leans away with his hands holding my upper arms. "Of course not. I've never been so happy in my life."

I relax in relief.

Bishop's gaze connects with mine. "Thank you, Sera. I always knew you'd give me my family back. And since you've set us free, I understand everything now. You and Turner make sense," he says with passion. "We were never meant to be more than friends." He squeezes my hands. "I think, in my heart, I knew it from the beginning."

"You did?" Though I've felt our connection slipping with each minute we closed in on the Oaths ceremony, I was unsure if he experienced the same thing. Since I was siphoning away his Protecting abilities to become a Chosen, our binding ties were apparently being slowly severed.

He nods and looks away to focus on a distant point. "Remember when I told you that I thought you would never choose me over Turner? That's why I went to watch you from afar at the train station the day you arrived in Chicago. I never meant to steal you away from him." He looks out the window and bites the inside of his cheek. "And as strange as I feel saying the words, I have to admit that I'm relieved that we're both free to choose love for ourselves." His gaze finds mine again with a simple smile. "I'm already starting to forget exactly what it felt like, but I remember it was agonizing not to have you for myself."

Nodding, I squeeze his hands. "And you have no idea what it was like for me, to know that I was hurting you and couldn't control my actions. I'm so sorry for everything. I hope you'll forgive me."

"There's nothing to forgive," he reassures me. "When I see the two of you together, it just feels right."

I look deeply into his eyes, finding only friendship and affection there, not romantic love and hurt. To know that Bishop is truly free of me eases my mind. He kisses my forehead and relaxes back into his seat with a grin.

"Thank you. That means so much to me."

At our confessions and the comfortable silence that follows, the activities around us creep back into the moment.

"You should wave to your fans." He laughs and gestures out the window. The carriage moves slowly but no matter how far we travel, the amount of people standing and cheering has not thinned. Together we lean to the window and I wave until my hand hurts, feeling strangely like a royal princess. When we finally reach a bridge with no sign of people, I lean back inside and we laugh at the craziness of where we were the other morning, freezing in Xavier's garage, and where we are now.

Finally the carriage halts and when I peek out the window again, I'm shocked to see where we are.

No
45

FOREVER

T HE ACADEMY OF WANDERERS NOW IMPOSSIBLY
stands in front of me in Gibeon.

"How in the world?" I glance up at the tall, regal facade as I exit behind Bishop. I hop to the ground and turn in my spot as the carriage rolls away, only to see the soaring obelisk of the courtyard behind us.

"Well," Bishop says as he grabs my arms and pulls me toward it, "now that you've set the inhabitants of Nocturna and all of the Wanderers free from the Society, you've also reverted Gibeon to its original state of paradise." He waves his hand through the air as we step to the edge of what I think is a cliff, but it's not.

"Whoa!" I hop back a step after accidentally kicking a few rocks from the rim. But the piece of land we're standing on doesn't seem to connect with the ground. Somehow the entire Academy floats on its own little island, drifting several hundred feet above the city below, only connected by a series of bridges. When I glance around, I can see floating islands covered with buildings filling the sky like a multitude of hot air balloons, in every size imaginable.

"What are all those? What's happened to Gibeon?"

"A lot of things happened when you fulfilled the prophecy. You've stopped the sporadic movement of Gibeon and also collapsed time, merging the twelve cities of time into one enormous world. I believe that there wasn't enough space for them to reside here on level ground so some pieces seem to drift about on their own island of land."

Still overwhelmed, I watch as wild Animates fly by, playfully weaving their way around the hovering land masses. Then I squint, trying to find the horizon. When I zero in on it, buildings still sprawl at its borders.

"But the Academy." I turn to it. "How is this here?"

"It seems that you've erased every trace of us in the Normal world. Every single item and everything we owned now resides here."

"But can't they see us?" I ask, my eyes wide. "The Normals, I mean. Can't they see these islands floating above them?"

Bishop chuckles. "There's no way to know for sure, but I

believe that we're on a different astral plane. That is, if we're even on the same planet. If we are, as far as I can tell, they can't see us, and we can't see them."

I look away, rolling these revelations around in my head and thinking hard about the ramifications. "What about the Academy buildings that are missing? Don't the Normals notice that entire buildings are gone?"

"Another unknown since we're now completely disconnected, but I hope that all memories of us are erased as well. Any more questions, or can I continue?"

"Nope, I'm good. Go on." I smirk, trying to guess what he will say next.

"The Wanderers who were here from other times have vanished, returning to their true times, and since every current Wanderer was locked here on the day of the Oaths, you've trapped all of us in Gibeon. We've been cut off from the Normal world."

As we stroll back toward the Academy steps, Bishop glances at me, probably expecting me to rattle off more questions, but I'm uncharacteristically silent while I try to wrap my mind around all that's happened. That's when Macey and Sam appear with smiles on their faces, launching themselves at us so that we converge in a group hug.

"I need to have a word with you," Macey says as she steps back, locks her hand on her hip, and glares at me. "Really? This is what you've been up to the entire time?" She waves her arms wildly. "You should have told me! You could've been killed! You were killed! Sera, if something had happened to you, I would have killed you myself."

"Sorry, Mace." My mouth twitches as I attempt to hold back a grin at her twisted logic. "I just wanted to try to keep you and everyone else safe." The truth is that I'm apologizing because she scares me—in a best friend kind of way. But I would do it all again in exactly the same way, and she probably knows that.

"I know you did," she admits with a frown. She smiles and reaches out a finger to tuck a lock of my hair behind my ear. "But next time…" Then she waves that finger at me with attitude and a bit of a warning.

We giggle.

"Let's hope there's no next time," Bishop says as he urges us forward.

"I'm just glad to have my sister back," Sam says and wraps her arm around me, pulling me up the stairs.

"And I'm glad to have a sister. Thank you for being there for me, Sam."

The conversation reminds me of what my mom told me about our real family history, and for a moment, my thoughts drift back my real sister, Saqqara, that my mom had hidden away to keep safe in ancient Egypt. I'm sad that we were never able to meet, then I realize that without her, there would be no bloodline of Wanderers to continue on and populate our race. I smile inside at the thought, and remind myself that everything happens for a reason.

As a group, we walk back through the main doors of the Academy, through the atrium, up the stairs, and around the catwalk.

"Wait, you guys." I leave them to take a moment to stand in front of the Seraphina Angel painting, the one that Leonardo da Vinci really painted of me. I step up close and lean in to examine the brushstrokes, remembering what it looked like as he started. I run my hand over the canvas and whisper, "Thank you, sweet friend."

"Are you sure you're okay?" Sam steps to my side. "You're whispering to paintings now? Maybe they should put you back in the glass box to make sure we've thoroughly fixed you," she jokes.

"Maybe I should put *you* in the glass box." I nudge her with my shoulder as we move away and walk down the corridor to our apartment.

"So, what's the big surprise Turner told me about?" I open our apartment door and step in, then I stop in my tracks when I see him. How have I forgotten?

"Dad?" My eyes widen and I rush to him, throwing myself into his open arms. "I'm so glad you're okay!"

Ray crushes me with a hug and his glasses slip down his nose, then fall onto the floor with a clank.

"I'm fine, kiddo. Thank goodness you're okay! I was so worried about you." He pulls me into a tight hug and pats my back awkwardly.

"I'm great now that you're here," I assure him. Then, in a

move that shocks me, he lifts me off my feet and swings me from side·to side with happiness, making me want to giggle at the absurdity of the moment.

I lean away. "But how are you here?"

"Turns out that since I was here when time collapsed, I'm stuck too."

"I'm sorry you were pulled into all this."

"Are you kidding!" He throws his arms open wide with excitement. "Your mom told me everything about Wandering and the cities of time. And believe me, when she did I thought she was crazy"—he rotates a single finger at the side of his head—"but I never thought I'd have the opportunity to see it for myself. This place is amazing! Did you see those animation things?" He speaks quickly, winding himself up as he speaks until he stops and shakes his head. "Sera, honey, I'm happy to be here. I'd much rather be here with you than anywhere else." He looks over at Terease, who I now see is standing across the room, and winks at her but quickly turns his attention back to me.

"So you've known all along?" I step back, looking at him in amazement.

Ray composes himself and reaches out to clasp my hands within both of his. "When your mom left you with me as a child, she warned me it wouldn't be easy, but I had no idea. She only told me to keep moving you around until the Harvester came for you." He jerks his head toward Terease. "And then she'd keep you safe within the Society. But when she finally came for you, I didn't want to let you go." His eyes glaze over and his nose turns a little pink. "Even though I know you know the truth now, I may not be your blood father, but I love you like my own daughter. I always have." A tear rolls down his cheek and he smiles. "I hope you know that."

Ray's words wash over me, filling a hole in my heart that has hurt for as long as I can remember. I've wanted so badly to be loved by my dad, to feel important to him and cherished by him, and instead he's always been awkward around me, never getting too close, and constantly moving us from place to place, keeping me feeling rootless my whole life. The emotional distance that he's always kept between us makes so much more sense now, and I forgive him for it in the space of a heartbeat. He's sacrificed more for me than any dad could ever be expected to, real or otherwise. The loving family that I've always wanted is finally standing here right in front of me, and it fills my heart to overflowing.

"I love you too, Dad," I choke out. "And I know you do."

He plants a kiss on my forehead and pats my shoulder, smiling proudly at me with tears in his eyes.

"Sorry to cut the reunions short, my lovelies." Gabe appears in the living room with a massive garment bag in his hand. "But we've got to get you ready."

"There's more?"

"Crumpet." Gabe pauses and sighs dramatically. "You've just set the Wandering world free and you think that's it. That we're just going to hang out here, eat pizza, talk about boys, do each other's hair, and paint each other's toenails now?"

"We can't? Because, I kinda feel like I've earned a girl's night, complete with ice cream. Please tell me we have ice cream here."

"You can chill with ice cream tomorrow," he says firmly. "Tonight, we party."

"Of course we do," I say flatly and cross my arms in protest.

It turns out that I have no say in the matter. Within moments I find myself shuffled into my room, sitting in a chair, having my hair sculpted into ringlets and woven with ribbon and sparkles. Macey and Sam hang out and we do in fact, do our makeup, and our hair, and dress for the "biggest party of the millennium," according to Gabe.

When he's done dressing me, I step in front of a mirror to admire his handiwork. The top of the dress is strapless with transparent ruching in shiny copper fabric. Matching sparkles cascade the length of the dark teal ball gown, making it look magical. When I rock back and forth, the bell-shaped layers of tulle swish around my legs, reminding me of the special dance that Hologram Turner and I shared in the training room.

"Gabe." I turn to him and press a kiss on his cheek. "Thank you."

"Anything for you, snickerdoodle."

"That reminds me, there's something I need to ask you—"

Gabe quickly presses a single finger to my lips. "Not another word."

"But—" He shushes me and leaves the room, blowing kisses as he exits. I let the question go, not really sure if it's important anymore.

When we leave, Dad, Bishop, Sam, and Macey load into a carriage, but I'm ushered into my own exquisite vehicle. I'm promised that I will meet Turner and my friends at the party. And as the guest of honor at my own ball, I'm told that I need to arrive separately, but when the carriage takes a different route from my friends' carriage, I begin to worry.

Minutes later, the carriage halts and the door opens. A hand reaches inside for mine and at the moment I take it and the skin touches my palm, I know exactly who it is. Heat radiates from Turner and surges into me. There's no need for a hologram now. Electricity follows us wherever we are.

"I hate being away from you." Turner appears at the door, dressed in a tux with his hair loosely pulled back into a low ponytail. A few wavy strands dangle around his face. His hands slide to my waist and he lifts me out of the carriage and places me on the ground, pressed against his body.

"Then please stop leaving me."

"Never again." He kisses my cheek. "You look absolutely stunning, Miss Parrish."

"I can't really take credit. Gabe practically painted me into a fairy princess."

Turner leans in and whispers in my ear, "Only because you are the perfect muse."

My body rushes with heat and I twist in my dress, looking down at my satin shoes. He lifts my chin so my gaze meets his sparkling gray eyes and he places a teasing kiss on the corner of my mouth and pulls away.

"Where are we?" I look around only to see a high stone wall.

"I wanted to bring you someplace very special before the party." Turner wraps my hand around his strong arm and guides me under a stone archway covered with moss. Once inside the open structure, I immediately understand what this place is when I see the obelisk fountain with aqua vitae surging from the rocky aqueducts and into the basin. This is the same fountain from my mother's palace in Egypt.

"How did you know?" I look to Turner.

"Know what?" We walk through the gardens, thick with lush greenery and the most beautiful flowers I have ever seen, and sit at the fountain's edge, facing each other.

"That this was my mom's favorite place." I reach down and glide my fingers along the aqua vitae, thinking of her.

"I only knew that I had to bring you here after I saw it for myself because I thought it was the perfect place to give you this." From his jacket, he removes a flat box. "Happy birthday."

"Birthday?" I take it from him and stare at the present. I'd been so busy trying to save the world, I totally forgot. I can't believe it's been an entire year since I first saw Terease. Since I first began this crazy journey. I remove the bow and open the top and inside, beneath polka-dotted tissue paper, sits the framed photo of my mother and me when I was a baby. The same one Gabe removed from my luggage in the Member Archives. The one I wanted to ask him about just before we parted at the Academy. I'd wrongly assumed he meant to use it in a hurtful way. I should have known better, and I shake my head at myself for doubting him.

"You told me once about all the things you lost on the day you moved to Chicago," Turner says. "I stumbled across the Member Archives some time ago while working with the professor and figured this was there. Before I left Gibeon, I talked Gabe into retrieving it for me. After everyone thought that I died, he decided to give it to you on his own, as an Oaths gift. Lucky for me that never happened, so I could give it to you myself."

I run my hand over the glass, touching the photo. In it Mom is young and beautiful, just like when I met her in Egypt when she was a queen. Though she's gone in my true time, I'll never forget the little time we shared.

"Thank you. This means so much." I press it to my chest. "She'll be with me always. You'll be with me always." I look up at him from under my lashes.

"That reminds me," I continue. "Where were you all this time? Why would you let me suffer without telling me you were alive, without giving me any hint you were okay? I've never cried so much in my life." I look at him, needing answers.

"Love, I'm so sorry to put you through that, but I truly only stayed away to protect you." He takes the picture from me, places it in the box, sets it aside, and moves closer. "It took some time for me to piece together how I survived. But when I did, I understood that you and Cece were essentially the same person, that she was born of you through fragmentation, and that I could time travel with you and her interchangeably, like she was my Wanderer too."

"I know." I nod and look away. "I mean, I knew about our connection, but I never imagined that you were still alive, that you could Wander with her. It makes sense now that you say it. But why didn't you come back?" I glance up and he places a palm on my cheek.

"I tried to send you a message through Drake, but really, I did it for your own good. I stayed with her to keep an eye on her activities. After a short time it was easy to see the enormous threat she posed to you, so I stayed close to her to protect you. Besides, Hologram Turner looked over you and so did Bishop."

I press my cheek into his palm and close my eyes, so relieved that we're even having this conversation. I grab his wrist and turn his palm to my mouth and kiss it tenderly. When I gaze up at him, he's staring at me with such love and intensity that I can't help but feel blessed for this second chance. That's when I notice a strange buzz around us.

Animate fireflies flash bright green as they dance in the gardens in the waning daylight. "It's like they're here *for* us." I reach out my hands toward them.

"They are." Turner pulls me to stand, pulling our bodies together. That's when the fireflies begin to fly around us in a choreographed dance as though Turner's asked them to do it.

"What do you mean?"

"We've lost our Wandering abilities but are slowly starting to regain our old gifts. The ones the Masters took away long ago, when they stripped us of our wings. Every magical thing we will be able to do is even better than time travel."

"If I succeeded, I guess I always thought we would become humans, not super-beings." I look away.

"But we aren't human, Sera. We never have been. I mean, there may have been a small part of us that became human, over time, but we're not meant to be. This is who we're meant to be. Don't you feel different? Complete? Content? Happy?" He grasps both my hands in his. "And Gibeon is a new place—a better one. There's new magic, the people are better, more caring, and the Society and Underground are dissolved. Everything is as it should be. Paradise has returned."

Turner's words soothe me, and we're swaying now, like we are dancing.

"I guess being superhuman in Paradise isn't so bad." I shrug, trying to wrap my brain around all the information.

"We've gained free will and in the most amazing place. It's better than the world of Normals. It's perfect here and even better, I'm here with you."

When he gives me that mischievous smile that's so unique-ly him. "Maybe one day I'll tell you everything that happened while I was gone, but for now, I just want to be near you." Turner drops a kiss on my cheek and stays close, allowing his lips to move over my skin when he speaks his next hushed words. "I thought when I rolled over the edge of that pit that I'd never see you again. And even though I survived, I wasn't alive until I touched you again." His words reach into my soul and swirl around my heart, stirring it in a way I've never felt before, and I look up at him in awe.

He slips his hand behind my neck, beneath the fall of my hair. There's no hesitation as he kisses my cheek again, drag-ging his velvet-soft lips over my skin, leaving a trail of heat behind them. I tingle with joy and scrunch my shoulders to my ears, unable to fight each fluttering breath that tickles my skin, and I giggle with happiness. When his lips finally find mine, they're warm and full and he kisses me deeply with intensity, but slowly. We have all the time in the world to lin-ger, to explore, to finally enjoy the moment. I slide my hands up his strong chest and lock my fingers around his neck to anchor myself to him forever. Though in this moment, feel-ing the real love we share, untouched by the Society, not ma-nipulated by the Masters, the way love is meant to be, I know we will never be apart again. Not ever. I have so much raw emotion and it's all for Turner. And for the first time in a long time, I'm happy, content, and fulfilled.

When I open my eyes, still wrapped in his loving embrace, I see that the two of us are floating several feet above the ground, hovering midair within the gardens that seem to bloom around us, for us, just for us. Perhaps we're flying with invisible wings, or even possibly held up by the magic of our love, and I never want to come down from this high.

Anything can happen in Gibeon. It must be true because as the energy that we share surges around us, in my mind, I ask the flickering green fireflies to transform into a swarm of sparkling white butterflies. They do in that instant and flutter away as we kiss again.

Somehow I managed to accomplish everything I set out to do. The Normal world is rid of Wanderers, and free of their control. Wanderers have returned to purity and to the original Gibeon, where we're meant to reside alongside the former inhabitants of Nocturna, who are now safe and free.

I look deeply into Turner's eyes and see love reflected back at me. Smiling softly, I lift a finger to trace his bottom lip and whisper, "All my wishes came true."

The End

If you enjoyed this story, please take a moment to write a review on Amazon, Barnes & Noble, or Goodreads. By sharing your feelings in a review, on your blog, on Twitter, or with a friend about the book, you support this independent author.

Please join my mailing list to learn about new releases and more!
Use your QR code scanner to open the link and join.

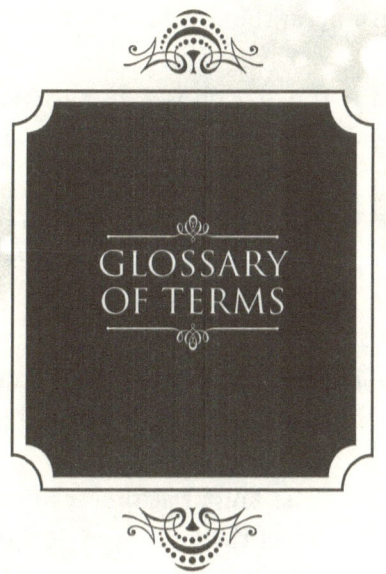

GLOSSARY
OF TERMS

ANIMATE: Mechanical, living and breathing, animated animals.

ANIMATE ANATOMY: Class taught at the Academy of Wanderers focusing on the mechanics and care of Animates.

CHOSEN: A time traveler chosen by the Masters to evoke all three abilities of a team: Wanderer, Protector, and Seer.

CITIES OF TIME: There are twelve hidden cities of time. Wanderers only gain access to each by ascending the ranks of the Society of Wanderers.

CONTRAPULATOR: Machine that traps and steals dreams while sleeping, trading them with recorded information.

DEFENSE ARTS: Class taught at the Academy of Wanderers for the instruction of the art of physical defense.

DREAMDRIVE: Crystal hard drive that inserts into a contrapulator to record and save all your dreams.

ELIJAH VANDERPOOL: *(b. 1849, d. 1894) Often called the Father of Wandering.* A Watcher who constructed both Olde Town and the Washington Square Academy of Wanderers in Chicago, Illinois. He and his father, Macon, also invented several important contraptions used by Wanderers: the Contrapulator, the Unfragmentation machine, and the Relicutionist.

E.Y.E.S.: *Acronym for Elusive Youth Electronic Surveillance*. The video surveillance system used at the Washington Square Academy of Wanderers to not only protect its students but also to watch them.

FRAGMENTATION: 1) The process of breaking apart a relic, rendering it unsuitable and dangerous for time traveling. 2) The process of breaking apart a Wanderer into two or more separate beings, usually occurring when attempting to Wander with a fragmented relic.

GIBEON: One of the cities of time. The capital city of Wanderers, which randomly moves through time to protect its location from the Normals.

GRAND MASTER: The high leader of the Society of Wanderers.

GRAND LODGE: The capitol building in the city of Gibeon, where the Oaths to the Society and other secret rituals are performed.

HARVESTER: A Wanderer possessing a special gift who travels the world, searching the minds of the descendants of Wanderers, seeking out those who carry the gift of Wandering, Protecting, or Seeing, for the purpose of recruiting them for the Society of Wanderers.

HOLOGRAM: A beam of light and energy that produces a realistic three-dimensional form.

KING UNIKA: Mythological Wanderer. Believed to be the first Wanderer of Egypt.

KING UNIKA'S CROWN: A royal headpiece originally belonging to the mythological first Wanderer of Egypt, King Unika. The ultimate relic that allows any Wanderer to travel to wherever their heart desires.

LIBRARY ARCHIVES: The library of ancient books in Olde Town.

LIFE PATH: The history of a relic and all the places it has traveled, visualized by the special gift of a Seer.

MASTERS: The makers or gods of Wanderers.

MEMBER ARCHIVES: An extensive storage facility for all Wanderers' past possessions.

NORMAL: A human.

OATHS TO THE SOCIETY: An anointment ceremony held in the Wandering capital of Gibeon at the Grand Lodge, where junior year Wanderers, Protectors, and Seers will dedicate their lives to the Society.

OBELISK: Four-sided pillar with a pyramid at the apex, similar to the Washington Monument in Washington, DC. Symbol of the Wandering people.

OLDE TOWN: The secret city beneath the Washington

Square Academy of Wanderers, constructed from the leftover remnants from the Great Chicago Fire of 1871. Although underground, the city gives the impression of being outdoors with the use of atmosphere machines, which control weather and light.

PHYSICS OF WANDERING: Class taught at the Academy of Wanderers focusing on physics as it pertains to time travel.

PROTECTOR: One of three in a Wandering team that travels time. The Protector is the middle link in the team's chain. He or she is connected mentally to the Seer through all senses and accompanies and protects a Wanderer during time travels. A Protector can traverse time only when in physical contact with his or her Wanderer. Protectors become experts in defense, history, linguistics, cultures, and the overall ability to blend seamlessly into any period of time. The symbol of a Protector is a scorpion.

RELIC: Any inanimate object.

RELIC ARCHIVES: The extensive library of relics that sits beneath the city of Olde Town. Available to all Wanderers for their time travel needs.

RELICUTIONIST: A machine that shows the life path of a relic by playing back a visualized image, like a TV.

SEER: One of three in a Wandering team. The Seer remains in true time and experiences time travels through the Protector's eyes and senses. Seers can view the life path of a relic, reading them like a road map, learning where a relic can lead throughout various periods of time. Seers become experts in history, linguistics, and cultures. The symbol of a Seer is an Egyptian hieroglyphic eye.

SCHALG: Time travel jet lag. Wanderers and Protectors become debilitated by schalg when jumping through time for extended periods, much like a human traveler becomes affected by jet leg when flying for extended periods.

SKIPPING: The instantaneous movement in true time from one physical location to another.

SOCIETY OF WANDERERS: A secret nation of time travelers.

SUNDIAL BRACELET: A bracelet containing a powerful emerald from King Unika's crown.

TEAM TACTICS: Class taught at the Academy of Wanderers promoting team strength and trust.

TRUE TIME: The current time.

UNDERGROUND BROTHERHOOD OF THE SNAKE: More commonly known as the Underground. An illegal group of Wanderers who seek to control time and take down the Society of Wanderers.

UNFRAGMENTATION MACHINE: Machine designed by Elijah Vanderpool to return fragmented relics or Wanderers to their original state.

WANDERER: One of three in a Wandering team that travels time. The Wanderer is the most important of the group. They, with use of a relic and keyword, open the gates of time. A Wanderer relies on their Seer and Protector to supply a smooth and accurate journey. Wanderers become experts in history, linguistics, cultures, and the overall ability to blend seamlessly into any period of time. The symbol for a Wanderer is wings.

WANDERING COMPASS: A small handheld contraption that allows Wanderers to travel as a team to one of the twelve cities of time, including Gibeon.

WANDERING TEAM: A group of three (Wanderer, Protector, and Seer) who depend upon one another to travel through time.

WASHINGTON SQUARE ACADEMY OF WANDERERS: *Often called The Academy of Wanderers.* A secret boarding school established to teach newly matured Wanderers the laws of the Society, while honing their time-traveling abilities.

WATCHER: A time traveler that evokes a combination of two of the three time-traveling abilities: Wanderer, Protector, or Seer.

Four years ago, I never would have imagined that I would write one book, let alone three. The journey of creating this sci-fantasy Wandering world has been an amazing and unexpected gift that has changed my life. So many family members, old friends, new friends, book bloggers, and readers encouraged me along the way, giving invaluable support, knowledge, and brutally honest feedback. Thank you, sweet friends, for everything. I'm a stronger writer and person because of all of you.

SPECIAL THANKS TO:
Tabitha Preast, Jenn Sterling, Christa Howell, Nikki Shah, Amy Bettwy, Michelle Mankin, Lisa Anthony, Jen Lowe, Deena Graves, and Pam Berehulke. These books would have been a hot mess without you!

Thanks to Jenn Sterling for her beautiful cover photos and for supplying the talented and gorgeous cover models. In my mind, Jordyn will always be Seraphina, and Andrew will always be Bishop.

*And finally to my hubby, Warren:
All my wishes came true. I love you.*

The Seraphina Parrish Trilogy

SEEING LIGHT

Find more info online at:

WanderDustTrilogy.com

'Like' Me On Facebook:
HTTP://WWW.FACEBOOK.COM/MICHELLEWARRENAUTHOR

Join my mailing list:
HTTPS://DOCS.GOOGLE.COM/FORMS/D/1XGTHR23BF-A0R5-
QXKUZNTV43IQOJK6801RB4JPYGCY/VIEWFORM

Michelle Warren